ABOUT THE AUTHOR

Elizabeth O'Roark spent many years as a medical writer before publishing her first novel in 2013. She holds two bachelor's degrees from the University of Texas, and a master's degree from Notre Dame. She lives in Washington, D.C. with her three children. Join her book group, Elizabeth O'Roark Books, on Facebook for updates, book talk and lots of complaints about her children.

ALSO BY ELIZABETH O'ROARK

THE SUMMER YOU FOUND ME

ELIZABETH O'ROARK

PIATKUS

PIATKUS

First published in Great Britain in 2024 by Piatkus

1 3 5 7 9 10 8 6 4 2

A CIP catalogue record for this book
is available from the British Library.

ISBN: 978-0-349-44077-4

Printed and bound in Great Britain by Clays Ltd, Elcograf S.p.A.

Papers used by Piatkus are from well-managed forests
and other responsible sources.

Piatkus
An imprint of
Little, Brown Book Group
Carmelite House
50 Victoria Embankment
London EC4Y 0DZ

An Hachette UK Company
www.hachette.co.uk

www.littlebrown.co.uk

For Lyden Elizabeth,
who will always be my favorite girl

THE SUMMER YOU
FOUND ME

1

KATE

The home my husband has bought in my absence is a mid-century dump, as far from our ultra-modern townhouse as it could possibly be. I hate it on sight.

It overlooks a lake—another thing I hate. Still, brackish water and the squelch of mud underfoot is something to be suffered through on a survival show, not enjoyed, but given that I had to get Caleb's new address from the divorce papers he had me served with, I'm not in a position to quibble.

I pick my way over the splintery dock in his backyard until I've reached its end. I've got no desire to be sitting here, but I could use some sun and I'm guessing I won't need to wait long. Caleb is heading to Maui today to announce his company's merger, and even if I had to learn about *that* from the press, I know my husband—there's no way he's showing up on a tropical island in a suit and tie. He'll come home to change first.

I stretch out on the deck, pulling back my long red hair while trying to ignore the stink of mud and sewage coming off the lake. Why the hell he'd have chosen this place with the Pacific a few miles away is beyond me. We'll figure it out—if he takes me back.

If, if, if. God, I can't wait to have this all behind me.

"He'll forgive you," I say aloud, not because I entirely believe it, but simply because I don't know what I'll do if that's not the case.

Yes, he hasn't heard from me since I cleaned out his checking account and skipped town a year ago, but I'm better now, and it was his photo I clutched in my hand all those long nights I spent in rehab, barely holding on. It was the hope of coming back to him that kept me sober at my lowest points. Surely, if I want to fix our marriage this badly, he must too? He'll be wary at first, but once he hears how long I've been clean, once he sees how committed I am, once I've reached for his belt and he's unable to say no...he'll come around. I know he will.

I close my eyes, relishing the sun on my face—the only place you could sit outside at the halfway house was always occupied by the chain smokers—but no sooner have I begun to relax than the slam of a screen door jars me. I raise up on my forearms and sigh as I spy the girl next door stepping onto her back deck, already staring in my direction.

Ugh. Another part of life at the lake I'm not interested in, above and beyond the gross lake itself: neighbors. Neighbors who want to host potlucks and "game night," neighbors who stop you every goddamn time you pull up to your house to talk about the weather or comment on how much you work.

I'll adjust. To the lake. To the fucking neighbors. I'm a shiny new version of Kate, one who's going to make Caleb happy. The last version mostly sucked at it. She sucked at a lot of things, actually.

The girl who slammed the door is heading my way. *Super.* She's younger than me, in her late teens or early twenties, and even from a distance she's striking—all glowing skin and curves and wide eyes. She's the sort of female who banks on her looks getting her anything she wants. I shouldn't fault her for this, since I am precisely that kind of female myself, but I'm not in the mood to be generous right now.

She walks down the dock, her perky ponytail swinging to and fro, and comes to a stop in front of me. "Hi. I'm Lucie. I, uh, live next door."

I force a smile, because I am the new Kate, the one who doesn't tell complete strangers to fuck off, especially ones I may be living beside for the foreseeable future. "I'm Kate. Caleb's wife."

She bites her lip and her face falls like a child's might, before stumbling away without a word. A silly little girl with a crush, and I can't even blame her: Caleb is delicious and smart and wears the hell out of a suit. He could have had anyone, but he chose me, and he'll choose me again.

He has to.

It's another thirty minutes before the moment of reckoning arrives. My breath hitches at the sight of my husband, broad-shouldered and lovely as ever, walking down the hill from his driveway. The cocky grin I remember is missing, but I ignore that, just like I'm ignoring those divorce papers he sent.

"Hi," I whisper, as I climb to my feet. Before he can even reply, I throw my arms around his neck and squeeze. *Ah, his size. His smell.* This is what I've missed, what I wanted all those nights in rehab. I breathe him in, trying to carry us both back to happier times, but his arms don't come around me the way they once did. He hugs me as if I'm a secretary who's retiring—one he never especially liked—then steps away.

"You should have told me you were coming," he says.

I stare up, drinking him in, unable to help myself. His eyes are a color I've only seen one other time in my life, hazel near the pupil, green at the perimeter. When I go to sleep at night, that's what I see. Those eyes of his.

I smile, still hoping to turn things around. "I was worried you'd run in the opposite direction."

He's supposed to laugh or deny it. He does neither.

"I guess you got the papers?" He glances at the house to the left before his gaze returns to mine.

I nod as my throat constricts. I've pictured this so many times. I've imagined his wariness giving way to a slow, uncertain smile once he sees how healthy I am. I've pictured him excited to have me home. But there's not a trace of a smile or excitement on his face. Persuading him might be harder than I'd thought.

"Yeah." I take a deep breath. "Can we talk?"

He glances over his shoulder again. "Sure. Of course. I've got a flight to catch, but—"

"I've been clean for three months, Caleb. I know I fucked up and I shouldn't have left rehab in the first place, but I went back. For you. For us. I want to start over."

He takes too long to reply, his brow furrowed with concern. "Kate, you were gone for a year. I had no idea where you were or if you were *alive* until a few weeks ago. I had to move on. I *did* move on. I'll help however I can, but anything between us is over."

I stiffen. *No.* I'm not sure what he means when he says he *moved on*, but no. He can't. He wouldn't.

"Look, I know I need to re-earn your trust," I begin. "I'd feel the same way if I were you. So, if you want me to, I'll take a urine test every hour on the hour. I'll—"

"Stop," he whispers, not quite able to meet my eye. "I'm with someone now. Lucie. I wasn't looking to move on, but we share the dock and it's just—"

My jaw falls. "*Her?* You're with *her*?"

I'd thought I might need to prove I was clean, that I might need to seduce him into giving me another chance, but I never pictured him replacing me...especially not with some little lip-biting twit.

"You saw her?" he croaks, tugging at his hair, finally showing some emotion.

This is what's upset him. Not all the shit going down at his company, which I've been following in the news, and not that his wife took off for a year without a word. But the pretty little teenager with the big eyes and palpable insecurity—*that* woke his ass right up. *What the fuck?*

"She came out here about twenty minutes ago and took off," I reply. "You can't be serious. What could you and that girl possibly have in common?"

"We have everything in common. Fucking everything that matters. What did you tell her?"

My shoulders go up—I'm the picture of innocence. Only an idiot would believe that *I'm* innocent, ever, but Caleb's clearly too distraught to think things through. "Nothing. I just told her who I was and she took off." I swallow hard and my voice is barely a whisper when it emerges. "Is it serious?"

His wince tells me this is going to hurt. "Yeah. As soon as this is done, I'm going to marry her."

My stomach drops and my lungs burn, but I remain very, very still, as if I've suffered a grave injury and it's safest not to move—I can no longer be the version of myself who reacts badly to unfortunate events.

Caleb doesn't want me back. Caleb thinks he's in love. With *Lucie*—rosy-cheeked and pocket-sized, all sweetness and light. She even has dimples, for Christ's sake. She is the anti-Kate. And I just laid there laughing at her, black-clad and indolent. Staying where I wasn't wanted, as always.

He glances back again at what is apparently *her* fucking house. His broad shoulders strain against his perfectly tailored suit jacket as he tugs at his hair. I've hungered for the sight of him for months, but right now, looking at him is painful. He's so worried, so desperate, and I don't recall him ever worrying like that about me.

"I'm so sorry, but I've got to go. I think we'll need to file the divorce paperwork differently now that you're back, but I'll give you a call?"

"Sure," I whisper, mute with shock. My hand goes to my neck, searching for the cold metal of a locket that is no longer there. How many damn years will it take before I stop searching for it? "I'll be around."

He turns and stalks up the hill toward his driveway, already on his cell. That's how fast I've been forgotten. Months and months of rehab to get back to him, to prove I've changed...and it's as if I never came home.

Recovery often feels like a ledge you've been clinging to for a little too long, and this is the worst kind of moment—the kind where your fingers begin to slip and you just want the relief of the landing, even if it kills you. It was only Caleb who got me through rehab, that fantasy I had about the two of us. Who am I without it? There is nothing to cling to, nothing to hope for.

I could be at my dealer's place in minutes, burying my face in a mountain of cocaine. I could feel fucking nothing at all for as long as I wanted to. But I still want Caleb more than I want to use, and there must be a way I can fix this. There *must*. Because it's the only outcome I can possibly survive.

There's a screech of tires as he peels out of the cul-de-sac. How incredibly insecure must this girl be for him to freak out the way he is? If I'd been in her shoes, I'd have called Caleb, put the phone on speaker, and demanded answers, but instead, she stumbled away from me, all sad eyes and despair.

And just like that, I have my answer. Something sick and sweet fills my chest.

No, today didn't go as planned...but they can't possibly be as solid as Caleb thinks if one tiny conversation with me could set her off. I've already created a fissure in their relationship without even trying, just by *existing*.

How much more damage could I do if I stayed?

A *lot*.

I won't even need to fight to get him back. Sweet little Lucie's going to do my work for me.

2

BECK

CALEB

Kate's back.

I stare at those words for too long. They could mean a whole lot of things, but for most of the people involved, none of those things are good.

Are you still going through with the divorce?

CALEB

Yeah, but I'll worry about it later. Lucie met Kate outside and misunderstood so I've got to deal with that first.

I grimace. I'm guessing Kate had plenty to do with that *misunderstanding*.

I'm behind the bar when Liam comes in later, meeting my eye and shaking his head as he takes a seat across from me. "What a fucking disaster."

I resent this a little, on Kate's behalf, but I get it. If life in Elliott Springs is like an elegant hotel at teatime, Kate's the gunslinger who walks in, flips a table, and starts shooting at the chandeliers. Personally, I sort of like agents of chaos—it takes balls to be a villain—but most of the people we know don't appreciate it much.

I pour him a beer and slide it in his direction. "I wonder if this will fuck up the divorce."

He pulls the mug closer and takes a sip. "Probably. Trust Kate to swoop in at the last second and cause trouble."

My jaw grinds. "She wasn't away at a fucking spa. She was in rehab."

"She was in rehab *some* of the time," he counters. "And God knows what she was doing the rest of it. Are you really going to defend her after she stole his money then disappeared entirely? I mean, how many trips to rehab has he paid for at this point?"

I pull out the inventory checklist and start scanning it, trying to get a grip on my irritation. "She's had a harder three years than I'd wish on my worst enemy. Cut her some slack."

He sighs. "Whatever. I should have known *you'd* be taking her side."

My head jerks up. "What the fuck does that mean?"

He catches my eye, telling me something he isn't going to say aloud. "Settle down. You had a bond with her the rest of us didn't. You were always going to see it from her side instead of his."

I could argue, but I don't bother. He could have accused me of worse.

"You think she'll stick around?" he asks.

I rub my eyes. "I don't know."

But if she does, then what Liam said earlier is absolutely true: it'll be a fucking disaster.

3

KATE

Beck's cabin is deep in the woods and straight out of every horror movie you've ever seen. You catch a glimpse of this house during any film—*Saving Private Ryan, High School Musical*—and you know someone is about to die. The seedy motel I stayed in last night is looking better and better.

He isn't home yet, which is hardly a surprise. Beck rarely sleeps in his own bed. I wait on his front steps, my legs stretched in front of me, pale in the morning light, and it's not long before a motorcycle roars in the distance.

As wheels rumble over the gravel lane leading to his house, my heart begins this weird, tripping rhythm—nerves, I suppose. I could take or leave most of Caleb's friends, but Beck is different. I've thought of him a lot this past year, his image often resting behind my eyes like the screensaver on a dormant computer—the dark brows that make him look like he's glowering any time he isn't smiling, the wavy hair falling to his shoulders. And his eyes, that strange light brown, glimmering as if backlit by a fire.

The bike purrs to a quiet halt in front of me. Even when he's seated, the sheer size of him is overwhelming. His arms, his chest—all the parts I've seen firsthand—are double that of a normal human's. I wonder, as always, about the parts I *haven't* seen.

He pulls off the helmet and raises a brow at me as he rises. My pulse speeds up in response. There's something dark and slightly predatory about him, like a housebroken tiger— maybe he plays along, but that thing inside him is always one step removed from violence. It appeals to me more than it should.

He's got a beard now. That appeals too.

He tucks the helmet under his arm. "I heard you'd come back."

God, I hate small towns. I should have known they'd all be gossiping. "I'm about to start my period. Were they talking about that too?"

Beck's smiles are rare and even then, barely noticeable, but his mouth moves slightly upward as he passes me to climb his front steps. It feels like a victory, that *almost* smile.

He unlocks the door and I follow him inside without waiting to be invited in. Nothing has changed in the year I've been gone. Aside from the bathroom and two bedrooms off to the right, it's just a small kitchen in the back and a tiny living area so empty you'd think he was in the process of moving out. There's a table with two old chairs and a shitty, ancient couch facing the TV—not a single vase, photo, or lamp.

"I love what you've done with the place," I say with a grin.

He acts as if I haven't spoken, tipping his chin toward the couch and sitting astride the nearest chair to face me. "Why are you here?"

I deflate a little at his tone. I knew I wouldn't be welcomed back by *everyone*, but I sort of thought it would be different with him. It used to be.

"Aren't we going to make friendly chitchat first?" I ask,

curling up on the couch. "You ask where I've been and I tell you what a good girl I am now?"

He raises a brow. "You? *Good?* Unlikely. Tell me why you're in Elliott Springs."

"My husband is here," I snap. "We aren't divorced yet. Nothing's been done that can't be undone." If he won't feign civility, why should I? I've never had to play nice with him anyway.

"I fucking knew it," he mutters, running a hand through his hair. "Kate, let it go. She works at TSG with him and she's a nice girl. They're happy."

I roll my eyes. "*Girl* is the key word. She looks like a Disney princess, just waiting for her magical first kiss."

There's a glimmer of amusement in his gaze. "And that makes you...what? The evil queen?"

He meant it as an insult, but I warm to the analogy. Caleb *wants* an evil queen, whether he admits it or not. When we were together, he appreciated my ruthlessness and he loved my filthy mouth, while Lucie's the kind of girl who couldn't resist a photo of kittens in a basket or utter the word *cock* if her life depended on it. Caleb will be bored any minute now.

"I'm the one he married," I begin. "I know I fucked up. But if he sees I've changed, he'll—"

"It won't matter." His voice is knife-sharp. "He loves her and she makes him happy."

I let my head fall to the back of the couch with an aggrieved sigh. "He *thinks* he loves her. There's a difference. And I made him happy once too." Though it's been a long while since I made Caleb happy, and it sure didn't last long. Beck is kind enough not to point this out.

"He blew off the entire merger to go find her yesterday, you know," Beck says, his voice gentle. "You want to think this is a fling, but I promise you, it's not."

He blew off the merger for her. That might really bother me, if I allowed it to. "Whatever."

Beck sighs heavily. "Great, we've now established that Caleb's moved on and that you don't give a shit, so why are you here at my *house*?"

My heart restarts its nervous, tripping pattern. I'm comfortable arguing. I'm comfortable demanding. But asking . . . *begging*? It's not my forte. "I was hoping I could stay with you."

"It's probably not the best idea," he says, prodding his cheek with his tongue.

My stomach sinks. I knew Beck would worry about Caleb's reaction, but he's always handled moral ambiguity well. I really thought he'd be the one person who wouldn't turn me away.

"Fine." I climb to my feet, shrugging with an insouciance I don't at all feel. "There are other people I can stay with."

This is largely untrue. There's only one person who'd welcome me right now, and he's the last person I should stay with. Beck knows it as well as I do.

"Stop," he says. "You can stay. Just until you're back on your feet. But there are conditions."

I fight the desire to smile. It's so cute, the way he thinks he's in charge.

"Condition one: no drugs." He waves a hand to silence my protest when I'd barely begun to open my mouth. "Yes, I know you said you're clean, but I've heard that from you about twenty times before."

My fists clench. This is what I'm in for here—a thousand reminders about how much I've messed up in the past. "You have no fucking idea how hard I worked to get to this point, so don't you dare act like I'm incapable of improvement."

His expression remains flat, *bored*. "I know you're capable of improvement . . . but that doesn't mean you're incapable of failure. None of us are. So no drugs."

None of us are incapable of failure, but you, Kate, are particularly susceptible to it. That's what I hear and the fact that he's right doesn't lessen my irritation. "Fine," I reply, blowing my hair off my face, trying to be Good Kate. I'm only a few hours in, and being Good Kate is already tedious as hell.

"Number two: you don't fuck with Caleb and Lucie."

Anger steamrolls over Good Kate in a second. "Why are you taking her side?" I demand. "You've known me for years. You've known her for what, a *month*? A *week*?"

"I'm not taking her side. I'm taking Caleb's." He rises slowly from the chair. "Do we have a deal or not?"

I click my tongue. "Whatever."

He appears to accept this as agreement, which it really was not—Lucie doesn't get to *keep* my husband just because I need a place to stay.

He gestures toward the spare bedroom and I cross the hall to peek in. I've never seen either of the bedrooms in Beck's house—it's oddly thrilling even if there's nothing in there but a bare mattress laying on the dusty floor and a light bulb suspended eerily by a cord from the ceiling. "This looks like the room you'd hold a captive in," I tell him.

His lips twitch. "I'll have to keep that in mind for the future."

I picture it before I can stop myself—Beck holding someone down on that mattress—and electricity surges through my blood. It's not the first time Beck has had that effect on me and I remind myself—as I have before—that it's probably the effect he has on everyone. I bet even innocent little Lucie fantasizes about Beck holding her down once in a while.

"I've gotta get in the shower," he says, rising from the chair. "I'm already running late."

A tiny echo of disappointment pings in my stomach. Even if Beck and I mostly argue, I sort of wanted him here. "You're already going back to work? You just got home."

He gets this dirty almost-smile on his face. "I wouldn't call what I was doing this morning *work*. I'll try to get back here tonight, but the bar doesn't close until two."

It's kind of him. There's this weird cavity in my chest anyway. Is it envy? Loneliness? I'm not sure. I fought my way back from the dead, but I still don't have a life. "Don't worry about it. I love staying alone in creepy, isolated houses straight out of a horror movie."

He tilts his head. "You're the evil queen, remember? This place is made for you."

"Nothing wrong with being the evil queen. Most men appreciate a little bad with their good."

I smile to myself. Caleb *definitely* appreciates a little bad with his good.

I just have to remind him.

AFTER BECK LEAVES, I drive to the grocery store, having discovered that his warning about there not being "much" in the fridge was the vastest of understatements. It's not as if ketchup and packets of soy sauce can be turned into a light but nutritious meal.

I climb from the car, doing my best to ignore the pale, jittery guy leaning against the building across the street. If he's not a dealer himself, he'd know where to get something, and my eyes close as I imagine that first hit. How it would wipe everything away, make anything seem possible. Just once more I want the sensation of floating above it all, of being set free. I want it so badly that my hands clutch the shopping cart handle, knuckles bleached white with tension as I walk into the store.

I go to the produce section, but everything I see looks like it was discarded already by a better store. Lucie probably shops at some fancy fucking place where all the food is organic and has cute handwritten placards. She's probably a good cook and will have a nice meal waiting for Caleb when he comes home, desperate to prove she'd make a better wife than I did.

It'll probably be fairly easy to prove.

I throw a few things in the cart and pay quickly before I hustle to my car because any moment now, my negative thoughts could stage a coup. I could find myself walking over to the druggie across the street before I've even thought it through. God knows it's happened before.

Caleb is the reason I won't. Because I earned this second chance. I suffered for it, and I'm not going to lose him to that stupid girl.

I get in the car and hit Ann's name on speed dial before I can give it any more thought, though.

"How's it going there?" Ann's heavy exhale reeks of concern. "Did you find a meeting?"

I close my eyes and let my head sink against the headrest. I'm really not up for a lecture right now about how meetings are necessary for recovery—a philosophy I've never bought into entirely. I don't need a meeting. I need Caleb back.

"Yeah. There's one at this church in town."

I went there, once upon a time. The setting was grim, the coffee was terrible, and I got hit on by two different men old enough to have fathered me.

"How was it?" she asks.

I should feel worse about lying to her but mostly it just makes me tired. "Not really my crowd," I reply. "What I don't get is why the coffee sucks at every AA and NA meeting. It's like someone's decided we haven't suffered enough."

She doesn't laugh, which means it's going to be one of *those* conversations—the kind where she calls me on my shit. "And did you talk to Caleb?"

I swallow. Saying it aloud will make it a little more real, a little harder to pretend it's not happening. "He's dating someone. He says it's serious."

She does not gasp in response. It's as if she always expected this turn of events. And why wouldn't she? Why the hell did I assume Caleb would wait nearly a year for me to return?

I suppose because I'd have waited a year for him.

"How are you doing with that?" she asks gently.

"Bad," I admit. My voice cracks. "I only got clean for him. If I can't have him, why am I bothering?"

"Because there are other things to want, honey. And you need to want it for yourself."

"I just want him," I whisper. "I don't give a shit about myself."

"That," she says, with a sigh, "has always been the problem. This isn't the time to be focusing on Caleb. You need to focus on yourself. I wish you'd give my friend Lynn a call. Go to San Francisco, stay with her, get yourself back on track."

I shake my head. She just doesn't fucking get it. Leaving here means losing Caleb, and if that happens, there was no point to any of this. None.

4

KATE

I wake with a start in an unfamiliar room. Pale morning light pours in through dirty windows, hitting the plain, exposed wood walls around me. I stare at the TV, the single hard-backed chair sitting a few feet from my face, and my breath holds as I try to remember how I got here. Waking up in a strange room with the night before a blank slate is an experience I've had a few too many times, and it never turns out well.

Beck's house. The breath I was holding in releases.

I guess he came home at some point, since the TV is off and I'm covered with a blanket that wasn't there when I fell asleep.

I go to the kitchen and start his ancient coffeemaker—this thing looks like it predates the *discovery* of coffee. All his appliances look like they predate the discovery of coffee, actually. I have no idea why he lives like this—that bar of his appears to be making money hand over fist, and if it's not, he ought to let me go over his financials.

I laugh to myself. No one familiar with my past is trusting their financial health to me.

I start frying bacon and eggs, hoping the smell lures him

from his room. It's selfish, but it's been nearly twenty-four hours since I spoke to another person. I'm desperate to hear a voice other than my own.

Just as I'm turning the bacon, he emerges, eyes barely open, clad in nothing but shorts. I stare, of course, because he's beautiful and comprised entirely of muscle, and how could anyone not stare? He's got a new tattoo on his chest—curves and pointed edges, like a portrait of waves as seen by Matisse, running lengthwise. I like it more than I should. Fortunately, he's too sleepy and perhaps surprised by the presence of food in his house to notice I've been looking at him like a woman who's gone without sex for the past year.

Which, actually, I pretty much am.

I pour him coffee, and he grunts something that sounds like *thanks*. Or maybe it was *why are you still here?*

I'm going to assume it was thanks.

"Didn't know you cooked," he says, his voice raspy with disuse.

I turn back to the stove, glancing at him over my shoulder. "Don't get all excited. One of us doesn't get fed at the bar."

He moves around the counter toward me, eyeing the bacon as I remove it from the pan. "That can't all be for you."

Joy tickles my chest as I shrug. "You think girls don't eat?"

"I think girls as skinny as you don't eat fifteen pieces of bacon and six eggs for breakfast, no."

Beck and I are like this. Playfully arguing, low-key insulting each other. It makes a friendship with him . . . safe. "Fine. I *guess* there's enough for you, but don't go expecting me to turn into your mom."

His eyes glide over me, from my chest to my legs, focusing on the point where my shirt ends just beneath my ass. "I'm pretty sure I won't be mistaking you for my mom anytime soon."

Our eyes lock, and a pulse flutters low in my belly for half a second. *Tick, tick, tick.* If this was an action movie, it'd be the first sign shit's about to explode. I've always felt like that around Beck, though, had this uncomfortable suspicion that I was safest not meeting his eye for long.

He returns to the other side of the counter. "So what's the plan for today?"

I pretend to be deep in thought. "Show up naked at Caleb's office, then perhaps a movie?"

His nostrils flare. "They went out of town for the weekend, but I was serious before. Leave them alone. No matter what you seem to think, she's suffered enough."

I laugh, the sound bitter and joyless. "How the fuck has *that* girl suffered? Did she not win Prom Queen last spring?"

"For starters, her ex is a cheating sociopath," he says, "and there's not a day that goes by without him threatening to take her kids from her."

My chest . . . caves. I recoil like someone's punched me as my breath lodges in my throat. Caleb left a few things out when we spoke. He very, very *intentionally* left a few things out. "She has kids?" I whisper. "She doesn't even look old enough."

Beck's eyes dart to mine. Beneath his tan, he's paled a little. He wouldn't have told me either if he'd thought about it. "Twins. She's about your age."

I flinch at the sting of tears, digging my nails into my palms to hold myself together. Lucie came home from the hospital with two children and I came home with none. And now she's got my husband too. "He likes them?"

Beck winces. "That's not why he's with her."

I look away, swallowing hard. Maybe he's right. Maybe Caleb isn't with her because of those kids. But the truth is that if I hadn't lost ours, Caleb would still be with me.

∾

THE DAY PASSES EVEN MORE SLOWLY than the one before it. I sit at Beck's small table, dust motes dancing in the air as my laptop slowly fires up. The only place hiring anywhere in Elliott Springs is TSG, Caleb's company, and I certainly can't imagine *that* working out. Even when I expand the search to Santa Cruz, I see no jobs I actually want, but I guess what I *want* is no longer relevant.

There was a time when it seemed I could do no wrong, when I was the girl who overcame unbelievable odds. Professors adored me. Employers vied for me. *That's* the woman Caleb loved—not the one I became here, the one who couldn't stay clean or remain employed—and he'll love me when I become her again. Even if I lost my last two jobs because of substance abuse, I am going to claw my way back to the top. And once I'm there, the shadow I cast will stretch so far that it covers Lucie completely. Caleb will forget she's even there.

I send out resumes and then watch hour upon hour of television, trying not to think about the fact that this is a holiday weekend, one I'm spending alone. Trying not to think about the fact that my husband whisked Lucie away on vacation when he and I never took a vacation together once.

I wake on the couch the next morning, covered by a blanket just as I was yesterday. I'm starting coffee when Beck emerges, his eyes barely open, greeting me with an unhappy grunt as he heads to the door. I don't seem to be interrupting his life all that much, but I get the distinct impression that he wishes I was not around.

From the window, I watch him moving through the backyard. He's created this crazy gym out there, where he pulls tires and pushes some big metal thing around, among other activities, because he believes exercise that mimics actual work is better for you. It sounds like nonsense to me, but the sight of him stripped down to his shorts would convince anyone he was right.

He showers and takes a seat at the counter just as I place a stack of four pancakes on his plate.

"So what did you do yesterday?" he asks, spearing several pieces of pancake on his fork, then popping them into his mouth at once.

There's something very *caveman* in the way he eats. *Fuck your salad forks and polite bites,* it says.

I sort of like it.

I shrug. "Sent out resumes and watched TV. Not a lot of other options until I get a job."

He swallows the bite down with a mouthful of coffee. "What kind of work are you looking for?"

"CFO. Like before."

I wait for him to challenge this, to point out the utter unlikelihood of anyone placing a company's financial health in the hands of a recovering addict, even one with an MBA from Wharton, but he does not.

"You always said that there was no job in Elliott Springs you even wanted, so why scrounge around here when you can live anywhere?"

I had my dream job in San Francisco, and I gave it up when I married Caleb. I don't regret it necessarily. I just wish I could have had both.

"Maybe it won't be exactly what I want," I say as I slide the pan into the sink. "But this is home for me now."

His nod is weak, his eyes flat. Fucking Beck and his built-in lie detector. Even times when Caleb bought my bullshit hook, line and sinker, Beck would sit there with that raised brow, waiting for me to confess.

"I can pay rent," I add. "I have some money set aside."

Beck frowns at his empty plate. I'm not much of a cook, but he's the most appreciative audience I've ever had. "I don't need your money. I just wondered if it wasn't a little lonely out here for you."

Loneliness isn't the kind of thing I'd ever admit to, and I've been alone nearly my entire life, so what difference does it make if I'm right back where I started? "I can't exactly go hang out at the bar with you, and the only friends I made here were the people I used to get high with. What other option do I have?"

He rises and carries his plate to the dishwasher. "The bar's going to be dead tonight. I'll come home early."

Tomorrow's the Fourth of July, so there's no way the bar's really going to be dead. I *should* tell him he doesn't need to come home, but for some reason I don't. I simply hitch a shoulder as if it makes no difference to me, the same way I always have.

Even though it's always made a difference.

IT's a little after nine at night when I hear a bike in the distance. I tell myself it can't possibly be him—not this early. By the time he walks in the door, I've got a smile on my face I can't quite hide.

He raises a brow. "I'm not used to seeing anyone here. I'm definitely not used to having someone happy to see me."

"Maybe you should take a captive when I leave." I pull the blanket around me and settle farther into the couch. "Make a girl go all day with no human interaction and she's happy to see anyone."

He pushes my legs out of his way and plops down beside me. "I was joking about you being evil, but the way you keep suggesting I hold someone captive is worrying."

I hand him the remote. "Fine. Don't take a captive. But you should know that based on the books I've read, it always leads to a ton of really kinky sex, followed by the development of a relationship based on deep, mutual respect."

He casts me a sideways glance and starts changing channels. "Do me a favor," he growls. "On a night when I'm not getting laid, try to avoid phrases like 'really kinky sex' and discussing your love of captivity porn, huh?"

There's a sharp pluck of desire in my stomach at the thought of Beck...*needy*. Though I doubt he's all that needy. Women have always been amply available to him, and he isn't one to turn down an offer.

He flips through channels, dismissing anything that might potentially have a plot. A hospital corridor flashes by on the screen as he presses the remote again, and I hit his arm. "Go back."

He frowns but complies. "*Grey's Anatomy*? This is like a million years old."

I curl up, sliding my toes under his thigh. "I never lived anywhere long enough to watch it consistently when I was younger. Growing up in foster care will do that."

"Maybe if you weren't talking about captives all the time, someone would have adopted you."

I choke out a surprised laugh. People have always tiptoed around my past. They tell me I'm *brave* when there's nothing fucking brave about enduring something because you've got no choice. Beck is the only one who's ever acted as if I'm not too fragile to tease. It feels like a sort of respect.

"I almost got adopted." I grin. "That's the best I've got. I *almost* got adopted."

He doesn't smile back. "What happened?"

I wish I hadn't brought it up, and I'm not sure why I did. "There was this woman, Mimi, who lived near my foster family when I was little. I used to go to her house after school. She said she was trying, but then she moved."

He turns to face me, his eyes hard and unhappy. "She said she was trying and then she just *moved*? Did she tell you why?"

I'd spent almost every afternoon and weekend with her for

nineteen months, and then one day she didn't answer the door. I sat outside until it was dark that afternoon, waiting for her. *Fucking pathetic.* "She sent me a card later, apologizing. She said she was too old to adopt a kid."

"That's...Jesus, that's shitty."

I shrug. It hurt at the time, but it's in the past. "She had good intentions—she pushed for all this academic testing and got me a scholarship at a private school. It could have been worse."

Beck looks weighed down by my story. His shoulders slump and he leans forward, elbows pressed to his knees. Being with me is a laugh a minute.

"It wasn't a big deal," I tell him. "And it was ages ago. I'd almost forgotten about it."

He frowns, his eyes flat. *Beck and his fucking bullshit detector.*

At least this is a lie he isn't holding against me.

5

BECK

I get told at least once a day that I'm living the dream, owning a successful bar. Maybe I'm living someone's dream. Not mine, though.

When my mother would bring me here as a kid and say, *"One day, all this will be yours,"* it felt like a threat—the hours were long, the staffing issues were constant and she was stuck indoors all day, all night. I had much more exciting plans—Caleb and I were going to become professional surfers or Navy SEALs, something that would allow me to be outdoors and moving around. Neither of us wound up with what we wanted, but Caleb owns a company worth millions and just texted pics of the mansion he and Lucie are renting for the weekend, so I only feel sorry for one of us.

Laura, the day manager, greets me at the door with twisting hands. "Fresher Foods called. Their truck broke down outside Salinas."

On the fucking Fourth of July.

Once upon a time, a situation like this would have made me panic. Now I just want to go back to bed. "Get one of the line cooks to run to the store and buy what we need." Paying regular prices for everything means we won't even make a profit off food today, but it just takes two assholes bitching on Yelp about how they couldn't get a burger here to ruin everything.

Laura falls into step beside me as I walk toward the office. "Mueller said you asked him to close last night because you had a guest," she says. "A *female* guest."

My shoulders sag. "I never told Mueller my guest was female."

She winks. "But you're not denying it, so...is she cute?"

I walk into my office, leaving her behind. "No."

It's not a lie. Kate is a hurricane in human form, and no one has ever called a hurricane *cute*—especially one who walks around my house in nothing but a fucking T-shirt. She clearly thinks being married to one of my closest friends will stop me from doing something I should not.

I'm somewhat less sure. One of many reasons I need her out of my home.

6

KATE

It's the Fourth of July.

Out in the world, people are hosting barbeques. Families are heading to the beach. On Main Street, there's a parade going on right about now—a group of veterans sweating in their uniforms, the town mayor waving from a car, all the little kids cycling along on their tiny bikes.

Tonight, they'll gather under the stars on picnic blankets and watch the city's lame fireworks display. Toddlers will fall asleep in their mother's laps with popsicle-stained mouths, the sticks still clutched in their grubby little fists.

Do those parents realize how goddamn lucky they are? Do they pull their children close and consider, really consider, all the ways fate could have stolen away everything they love? I'm sure they don't. I wouldn't, either, if it hadn't been stolen from me.

The box I keep in my suitcase calls to me, but I can't go there now. Not when I'm doing my best to pretend that darkness isn't still inside me.

I open my laptop instead and expand the job search to San Jose. The commute will suck but employment, in this case, isn't about happiness or quality of life. It's about reminding Caleb of who I was. Who I can be.

I email my creatively worded resume to several jobs I don't want and then the emptiness of my day hits me in the face.

I watched movies nonstop in rehab, but being in rehab was a lot like being stuck at the airport, waiting on a delayed flight —you did whatever you could to avoid losing your shit. I theoretically can do *anything* now. I never expected it to feel worse. I never expected to still have to fight this gnawing, craving thing inside me that wants something more.

To fill the time, I sweep, knock down cobwebs, scrub grout —and then I stalk Lucie. Beck didn't say I couldn't, after all, and it's a victimless crime.

Correction: at *present* it's a victimless crime.

There are loads of pictures of her online—mostly at events with her ex-husband, Jeremy, a smug bastard flashing a Rolex and a smirk in every photo. It's easy to see why she jumped at the chance to sleep with my husband rather than her own.

To my vast irritation, she's set all her social media profiles to private, but I'll get around that soon enough. I send her a follow request from the fake profile I've set up—BayLee652 #twinmom #organicbaby. BayLee's posts, thus far, are all about food (*"Yummers, homemade acai bowl for the win!"*)

It's possible I hate BayLee even more than I hate Lucie.

BayLee652 is in the process of posting a cute dog pic (*"Meet our first baby, Wilson . . . He thinks he's one of the twins, LOLz"*) when Caleb's name appears on my phone at last.

My heartbeat triples as I push away from the counter and swipe my index finger over the screen to answer. *Is his romantic trip already over? Was it so boring he came home early?*

"Hi, Caleb." It comes out as a purr and I mentally scold myself: *Be the new Kate—don't shit-talk Lucie, don't flirt unless he flirts first.* I clear my throat. "What's up?"

"Hi. How are you?" He is polite—nothing more.

When we first began dating, he'd say, *"I'm coming over. Get undressed,"* his voice all command and need. *That's* the Caleb I want back, not this merely *civil* one asking about my health as if he barely knows me.

"I'm—"

There's echoing noise from his side of the line, the chatter of people walking past. I suspect he isn't going to listen to my answer, that he doesn't actually care how I am, but if he's back in the office, his romantic trip is definitely over, so...silver lining. "You sound busy."

"Just stopped in the office to grab some stuff." He says something about quarterly reports that isn't directed at me. I'm beginning to think this conversation *won't* lead to nudity.

"Sorry," he says, returning to the call. "I just wanted to let you know that Harrison's drafting the separation agreement. It'll just need our signatures."

What? I stagger backward a little, closing my eyes, my hand gripping the counter. This is *crazy*—what's the damn rush? For God's sake, he barely knows that girl, so how the fuck can he really believe he wants to marry her? They haven't been together long enough for her to bore him. They haven't been together long enough yet for him to start picturing *me* when she's on top, but I guarantee it'll happen. He isn't the sort to like vanilla for long.

"Since we've already spent a year apart," Caleb continues, "Harrison thinks we can get a court date in a few months, maybe sooner."

I slump over the kitchen counter, my eyes squeezed tight. *God, it already sounds like a done deal.* "I didn't realize we'd be going to court."

"It's just a formality. I'm not going to fight you over anything. Just tell me what you want."

I swallow. It's too early to lay all my cards on the table. I wanted him to come to me willingly, but now it feels as if there isn't time. "I want another chance, Caleb," I whisper. "I know I don't deserve one, but I want one anyway."

A door shuts and his side of the line is quiet at last.

"Kate..." he says, and I can imagine him so clearly, the way he's pinching the bridge of his nose with his right hand, wanting to do this in a way that won't cause pain. He's good like that—the opposite of me. "We weren't happy together."

He's revising the past to justify moving in a new direction, nothing more, but it still hurts.

"Yes, we were. Until things went wrong, we were very, very happy." I'm desperate to convince him, and I want to weep at my inability to do so. "Don't you remember how it was when we first got married? It was perfect."

He hesitates. "I think that's how a lot of people feel at that time in their lives."

"And I guess your girlfriend is a proven commodity for the rest of it, right?" I ask with a bitter laugh. "She has twins. Doesn't get much better than that."

So much for the new, improved Kate.

"That has nothing to do with it." His voice is far gentler than I deserve. "You can't see it now, but someday, you'll look back and realize this was the right decision."

I force down the lump in my throat. I'm not giving up, but fighting with him won't get me anywhere. I tell him to let me know when the paperwork is ready, and then I sink into a chair at the kitchen table with my fingers pressed to my temples. I clearly cannot just sit around waiting for Lucie to fuck up.

I'm going to have to give her a little nudge.

A SUCCESSFUL PROJECT, of any kind, begins with research.

My forte is the ability to look at numbers and make predictions based on them. I won't have numbers, in this case, but I'm nothing if not adaptable. I'll gather the information I need and find the pattern, no matter what form it comes in.

Ideally, I'll find some dirt on Lucie, something I can leverage against her. But barring that, it might be enough to know what she wants and fears, then persuade her Caleb is a move in the wrong direction.

Beck, obviously, will tell me none of this, but Wyatt will.

Wyatt's a senior manager at Caleb's firm, one with the absurd overconfidence of a completely average man who doesn't realize he's average, and when Caleb and I were together, he had a crush on me that very nearly got his ass kicked at a holiday party. And he's apparently left Caleb's company, which might work to my favor.

I track him down on Instagram. When I message him about getting together, he immediately responds suggesting coffee on Friday down in Santa Cruz, *"so that we don't run into anyone from TSG,"* he says.

My guess is that it has more to do with not running into the girl all over his profile page. Whatever.

On Friday, I show up at the place he suggested, dying a little when I walk in and am faced with Wyatt's smarmy smile.

I'd forgotten just how much I loathed him. I'd also forgotten the way he'd hit on me the last time I saw him. I was out with my dealer and high as fuck, barely capable of remaining on my feet, and he kept trying to get me to go home with him. Even high, I found the idea repulsive. *"Let me go down on you under the table,"* he then suggested. *"You don't even have to reciprocate."*

How did I forget all that? I don't know. But I wish I could continue to.

"Damn, girl," he says, looking me over. "Only you could come out of rehab looking *better.*"

I manage not to gag as I ask how he's been. This leads to a solid five minutes of him describing the ever-so-exciting world of accountability software, interrupted only by the delivery of my latte, which is when he finally remembers conversations are supposed to be two-sided.

"I heard you and Caleb split up," he says at last.

I give a tiny little heartbroken sigh, my face that just-right combination of sad-but-not-too-sad. "He's in love, apparently."

He shakes his head. "I can't imagine anyone picking Lucie over *you*."

Jackpot.

I blow on my latte, pouting as I take a small sip. "You don't like her?"

He laughs. "I'm not into needy girls, thanks."

There's a tickle of delight in my chest. Caleb hates weakness. This is getting better and better. "Needy?"

He tips his chair back, not seeming to care that he's hitting the woman behind him. "You haven't heard? They had this big merger in the works, and he backed out of it because of her and the kids. I think she was bitching about the hours he worked or something."

I wince. It's a tiny splinter edging its way into my heart, the fact that Caleb was willing to do this for Lucie and her kids but not for me and our daughter. Then again, maybe it's a lesson he learned from our failure: that if you commit to a family, you need to put them first. I just wish he'd learned that lesson a little sooner. "To be fair, it doesn't sound like that's necessarily needy. I'm guessing any woman he was dating would want him to work fewer hours."

"Oh she's needy, believe me." His chair lands on its front legs again as he leans forward. "I heard she also made Caleb fire the receptionist yesterday. Some bullshit about Kayleigh being rude to her, but everyone says it's just that Kayleigh's hot and Lucie was jealous."

I fight a smile. If this was vaudeville, I'd be rubbing my hands gleefully beneath the table. "I think I remember her. Kayleigh Spencer?"

"Hutton," he corrects. He reaches across the table and slides a finger along the outside of my hand. "I guess it's no secret that I'm a little biased toward you, though. We should get drinks tomorrow. You never know—I might be able to make it worth your while."

What kind of fucking asshole asks an addict out for drinks?

I keep the thought to myself in case I need Wyatt down the road. "I'm just not ready yet. It's all happened so fast."

"I'm happy to wait," he says. "And my offer still stands if you want something less serious." His gaze drifts below the table.

Ugh. I should have let Caleb kick your ass when I had the chance. If he'd heard the offer you made me last time, he'd really have let loose.

It's only as I'm leaving the coffee shop that I remember it wasn't Caleb who wanted to kick Wyatt's ass at that holiday party.

It was Beck.

7

KATE

Thanks to social media and the second fake profile I created on Instagram (Nobu_girl_657), I know plenty about Kayleigh Hutton. I know she photographs every fucking thing that happens to her and manages to make it sound enviable, even if it's just a walk to work or a veggie bowl from Chipotle. I know she's the type to post a quote about kindness, then make fun of a celebrity's sudden weight gain five minutes later. And I know that every evening, after she leaves her new job, she heads to yoga on Main Street. #Namaste #GoodForTheSoul #GoodForTheAss.

Girls like Kayleigh want to sell you a story. They want to convince you they love yoga and treasure a pretty cappuccino and didn't take twenty selfies before they got a decent one to post. They think you'll envy them, and you probably will, but they also think your envy will make you like them more, and I'm not sure that's true.

Yes, I envy Kayleigh's veggie bowl and her yoga habit and those pretty cappuccinos sparkling in the morning light, but my envy doesn't leave me wanting to be her friend—it leaves me eager to watch her fall from grace.

I refuse to contemplate the fact that this moron with her duck-faced selfies appears to have a fuller life than I do. I go, instead, to Lucie's profile. She's accepted my request at last, and I'd expected a thousand photos of her showing off those D cups, but instead her feed is full of *them*. Her twins. Two tow-headed little kids living their best lives, playing on Caleb's dock, sitting on Caleb's boat. Of course he loves them. How could he not?

I slam the phone face down, swallowing hard. The itch in my chest, the one that started with Kayleigh, is now an ugly, raw wound.

I wish I could numb it. I am clinging to a windowsill in mid-air, and I'm so fucking tired of clinging.

I pace the room. I should probably call Ann, but I'd have to describe the meetings I've attended and claim I've found a local sponsor. I'm too goddamn frustrated right now to tell that many lies.

Which leaves Beck. Beck, who *must* want me gone. All the cleaning and cooking in the world won't change that. And he sure as fuck doesn't want to be hearing from me while he's at work, but he's all I've got.

"Fuck it," I sigh, snatching up my cell phone as I open up my texts.

> I'm bored.

BECK
> Maybe you should get a job like the rest of the world.

> Naughty Vixens it is. Should I wear a red bra to the audition or will it clash with my hair?

> I'm pretty sure it's not your hair they'll be looking at.

I snort. What a perfectly Beck response.

> Are you okay?

I start to tell him I'm fine, but then I delete the words. I wrote him for a reason, and it wasn't because I felt like lying to one more person.

> I'm struggling a little today.

I stare at my phone, waiting for his reply, and my stomach sinks when none arrives. He's getting ready for their busiest time at the bar, sure, but it's not like I asked him to come hold my hand. He could at least have said *"hang in there"* or *"you've got this."*

Whatever. I knew I should have kept it to myself.

I open my laptop and shut it. I turn on the TV and flip through the channels, embarrassed and pissed off and too fidgety to remain still. I start watching some documentary about life in the trenches during World War I. It looks pretty fucking miserable, sleeping in a foot of muddy ice water, being eaten alive by lice, but at least they had company.

A roar in the distance makes my spine go straight. It sounds like a motorcycle, and it can't be Beck, not at this time of day, but it's coming closer and then stops outside the house, followed by the *thump, thump, thump* of boots on the stairs.

The door flies open and Beck stands there in all his over-sized glory, helmet tucked under one massive bicep.

Beck came home. He came home for me.

My jaw falls open. "You didn't need to leave work. I wasn't gonna use."

He runs a hand through his hair. It doesn't look as casual as I'm sure he intends it to. "Lawrence is managing. There's no band tonight, so it'll be slow."

I sigh. He's lying. His bar is never slow. "Still. You didn't have to come home for me. I feel guilty for texting you now."

His eyes glint, and the corner of his mouth tips up. "Oh, you're going to make it up to me."

My mind immediately goes somewhere it should not. I imagine him stalking toward me, pushing me to my knees, telling me in no uncertain terms what he wants me to do as he tugs at his belt and unzips his jeans.

"What did you have in mind?" I'm breathless. And guilty. But more breathless.

He grins. "*Game of Thrones*. You and I are the only people alive who haven't seen it."

He crosses the room and flops onto the other end of the couch, holding his hand out for the remote, shaking his head at the black-and-white footage currently on the screen. "So, let me get this straight: you're depressed, so you put on a documentary about World War One to cheer you up?"

I grin. "Evil queen and all that. It was this or a doc about nine-eleven. I couldn't decide."

A rumbling laugh escapes his chest while he types the show title into the search bar. "So, how are you struggling?"

I shrug. "I'm just bored. Other people are going to yoga or hanging at the beach. I feel like I don't have a life."

It's not the whole truth, but I can't exactly admit to cyber-stalking Lucie and the girl she's gotten fired.

"You *don't* have a life," he replies. "You should get one. Problem solved."

I kick him. "You're so helpful. Just like a therapist. But, you know, *mean*."

"I'm serious. Why are you hanging out here all day? Go to yoga. Go to the beach. I'd kill for a fucking day at the beach."

Beck surfs, and surfs well. All the guys do, though it seemed different for Beck, as if it satisfied some need he has that few other things did. Who might he have become if his mom hadn't died? If he could have chosen a future for himself?

"It's not that simple," I reply. I wait for him to challenge me, and it's a relief when he doesn't.

The show begins. The Jon Snow kid I've heard about for years walks onto the screen and I frown.

"He doesn't seem like star material to me," I tell Beck. "I'd assume he was gonna get killed off in the first episode if I didn't know better."

"Watch the show," Beck says.

A few minutes later, a kid runs across the screen. "That's Bran?" I ask. "I thought he was, like, paralyzed or something."

Beck places his hand over my mouth. "Watch. The. Show."

I'd rather not. So far, it's just a whole lot of knowing glances and treachery, *blah, blah, blah.*

Beck's just put his hand down again when Khal Drogo comes onto the screen. Khal Drogo, who reminds me a *lot* of Beck. There are similarities in their coloring, but it's more that they are both huge and commanding, two qualities I seriously appreciate in a man. Caleb has those things too, but it's different in him. Caleb's command is all suave, Ivy League charm—a boulder polished until it gleams like a gem. Beck and his doppelgänger have a roughness to them, sharp edges they'd never allow you to erase.

"You think he's hot, don't you?" Beck asks, glancing over at me.

I narrow my eyes at him. "Oh, *now* it's okay to talk? Just because he looks like you?"

His eyes return to the screen and one brow raises. "I don't look like that guy. He's wearing eyeliner, for Christ's sake."

"Warrior kings have to wear eyeliner. That's just history, dude."

There's the start of a smirk on Beck's face. "So you think that guy, who apparently looks like me, is hot."

I roll my eyes. "*I* didn't say I thought he was hot. *You* said that."

"Well, do you?" he persists.

I glare at him. "I lost my husband, not my vision. Of course he is. What's your point?"

"That you are capable of wanting something other than Caleb."

The mere suggestion starts that panic in my chest swirling. Even considering someone else means shutting the door on the one thing that got me clean.

I force a laugh. "Are you offering, Beck? Me and Audrey are about the only girls in the state you haven't slept with, so I guess I shouldn't be surprised."

He smirks. "I'm not offering. You're okay-looking, but you're way too much trouble."

I round on him, the show forgotten entirely. "*Okay-looking*? Did you really just call me *okay-looking*?" I know my flaws, but my freaking looks have never been among them.

He fights a smile. "You're a solid five. Maybe a six with makeup."

I dig my toes into his thigh as hard as I can. "Fuck you."

This makes him laugh, a real laugh, and for a moment his face is transformed. He's been through nearly as much shit as I have, and in this half-second I see who he might have been before his life fell apart. "Shut up," he says. "You know you're hot. Too skinny for me, but you're hot."

We've been joking until now, but that last bit cuts so deep I'm impaled by it. I jerk my gaze back to the TV, seeing nothing.

"You know I was fucking with you," he says.

"What, about the skinny part?" I ask quietly. Because Lucie is not skinny. Lucie is all curves, all tits and ass like a reality TV star. She's never worn a padded bra in her life, and after these days spent wondering what she has that I don't, I've latched onto this like a life raft—a *barbed* life raft that's intensely painful to cling to.

He pauses the show. "Kate," he groans, waiting until I look at him, "I'm going to say this once and then we are never going to discuss it again. The first time I saw you, I thought you were the most perfect thing I'd ever seen, and I still think it. I wouldn't change a single thing about you. Now shut the fuck up and watch the show."

He turns back to the TV, where yet another couple is having sex, a couple I believe might be siblings, and even that barely gets my attention.

You were the most perfect thing I'd ever seen.

We've never addressed that night. We've never even alluded to it until now. But when I saw Beck from a distance, before I knew he was Caleb's friend, I thought he was the most perfect thing I'd ever seen too.

There was a minute there, before we'd ever even spoken, when I wished I'd met him first.

8

KATE

Another week passes with little change. Every few days there's a text from Ann—always far too early in the morning—and otherwise, it's silent.

It's barely light out when Ann texts today. I need to mute her.

ANN
How's the job hunt going?

Not so well at the moment.

It's still early. You're going to meetings?

Yep.

Have you gone to Hannah's grave yet?

She really needs to work on her six AM conversational skills.

Instead of replying, I go to Instagram. It was "raft night" for Lucie and Caleb on Saturday, apparently. The two of them are pictured floating in a pool with Lucie's smiling twins, all of them decked out in glow-in-the-dark paint.

Relationships are always easy at the start. Lucie's undoubtedly thrilled to have someone stepping in to pay her way, to parent her children. She's devoting every free second to showing Caleb how wonderful she is. She probably gets up hours before him to do her hair, apply subtle makeup. She's never too tired to spread her legs when he wants her to, and he's a fool in the same way all men are because he assumes it'll last.

Their relationship is a Jenga tower, and it's time for me to remove a piece or two from its base. It's only six AM, but no hour of the day is too early for the evil queen.

I begin by creating a website, one that lists signs that don't *necessarily* mean a guy is cheating but are things I have no doubt Caleb is doing.

Does he claim to work long hours?

Does he keep a password on his phone?

Does he insist he's over his ex, but you have doubts?

Is he unwilling to break ties with his past?

At the bottom of the website, I link to the dark corners a paranoid girlfriend might investigate if it got bad enough—spyware, keystroke trackers, other articles on cheating, the National Association of Private Investigators.

Then I move on to the ads. It's easier than you might imagine to target ads to just one person or a small handful of persons.

I take every single thing I know about Lucie—her location, that she's between the ages of twenty-five and thirty, and the mother of twins—and this becomes my audience. I grab a stock photo of a guy whispering into a phone. Then I add a headline: *"Is he cheating?"*

The ad links to my website.

I doubt it'll have any effect whatsoever, but it's a small

bright spot in my day, and I really need a bright spot or two right now. I go to the kitchen to start breakfast with my good mood restored, waiting for Beck to finish his insane workout in the backyard.

When he comes in, he scarfs the hash browns and bacon I've made as if he's being timed. I knew kids like that in foster care, the ones who always acted like you would steal the plate right from their hands. In his case, he's just so hungry he can't help himself. I want him to slow down. I want him to stay for a while. I wish breakfast involved multiple courses.

He gets a text and when his glance shoots guiltily to me, I know who the sender was. Beck and Caleb text almost daily—usually about sports or just to give each other shit. He turns the phone face-down on the counter and swallows the last of his hash browns. "How's the job hunt going?"

I shove the bacon around in the pan simply to avoid his gaze. I have no clue if he's asking because he wants me out or because he's worried I'm not doing shit to move my life forward. It's probably both.

"I've sent my resume to thirty places and haven't gotten a single call."

I wait for him to suggest that I'm aiming too high, that perhaps I should forget about the jobs I'd like and aim for the ones I can actually get: working in a fucking mail room or some entry-level bullshit where a coke habit hurts no one but myself.

"It's only been a few weeks," he says instead. "Give it time. You should come out to the yard with me tomorrow. There's nothing like a good workout to make things look brighter."

I raise a brow. "You and I have very different feelings about exercise."

"Wednesdays are usually pretty slow," he adds, walking around the counter to slide his plate into the dishwasher. "I'll try to get home early."

You don't have to. It's on the tip of my tongue. Except the

minutes I spend talking to him are pretty much the only break I
get from the shit inside my own head.

And I guess I sort of like having him around.

BECK RAISES a brow at the two throw pillows I splurged on
today for his couch, but says nothing as he takes a seat beside
me and turns on *Game of Thrones*.

I'm beginning to see why this show was so popular. There's
a *lot* of sex.

"You know what makes no sense?" I ask.

He laughs under his breath. "Here we go."

I ignore this. "There's a covenant between the King and the
Great Houses, right? The Great Houses are the source of all his
power since he's got no dragons. So why are they kissing his
ass? He needs them more than they need him."

The corner of Beck's mouth twitches. "So what are you
suggesting?"

"I'm just saying that if I was Ned Stark, I'd have started
talking to the other houses and making some fucking demands
years ago."

He laughs again. It's clearly *at* me, since I'm not laughing.
"Of course you would, Evil Queen. Just watch the show."

I continue to mentally tally the ways I'd handle power
better than everyone in Westeros and list who I'd kill and in
what order. I plan to share all this with him the minute the
show ends. But he's got an agenda of his own.

He turns to me as the credits roll. "Did you ever try to look
for your dad?"

Pretty much everyone on *Game of Thrones* appears to be ille-
gitimate somehow, so I should have anticipated the question.

"Why would I look? He never lifted a finger to help me, so
fuck him." I have no real memory of my mother, and on my

birth certificate it simply says "John Doe" for the father. People are always shocked by my lack of interest in the man responsible for fifty percent of my DNA, but it makes perfect sense to me. I've known enough terrible people who *theoretically* had good intentions . . . a man who abandoned his own child never had them in the first place.

Beck's lips press together as he pauses for a second. "Maybe he never knew you existed, though."

He can't believe my father would be the kind of asshole who'd abandon a child because he himself would never be that kind of asshole. I can very easily believe it because, well, look at me. I'm a jerk. I got it *somewhere*.

"You think my mother *chose* to drop out of college and parent me alone, with no financial assistance whatsoever?"

"From what you've described, it sounds like your mother made any number of illogical decisions."

I suppose he has a point. When I was small, I put my mother on a pedestal because when you have a huge hole in your life, you want to fill it with something, even something illusory. But over time I faced facts—my mother wasn't better than a single foster parent I'd had. She wasn't better than the ones who ignored me or mocked me or even the ones who hit me. At least *they'd* never abandoned me. I was three when someone called protective services on my behalf because they'd found me wandering a city street alone.

She overdosed a month later. She didn't deserve a fucking pedestal, but there's zero reason to hope my father does either.

"I just don't see anything good coming out of it," I reply. I toy with the hem of the blanket, suddenly uncomfortable. "Thanks for coming home early again. I know you had better things to do."

He gives me his almost smile. "It's possible your company is slightly more entertaining than that of a bunch of drunk guys hitting on girls and talking about high school a decade later."

I laugh. "My company hasn't been entertaining in a long time."

"You seem to be under the impression that everyone only likes the coked-up version of you."

I lie back on the couch, staring at the screen. "The coked-up version is the only one that's palatable. I'm sour and mean inside without it."

He's quiet for so long I've almost forgotten what I said when he finally replies. "No, you're not. You're a porcupine. A sharp and occasionally painful exterior to protect the vulnerable spots."

He's giving me too much credit. In truth, that's an apt description of *him*.

He comes off as harsh and even frightening to people who don't know him. But he actually has the biggest heart of anyone I've ever known.

9

KATE

There's an email in my inbox with "Interview" in the subject line. I'm on the cusp of opening it when Caleb texts, and the sight of his name is enough to make me forget every goal I've ever had that wasn't related to him.

CALEB

The separation agreement is ready for your review. Where should I drop it off?

My heart squeezes tight. It's not what I was hoping he'd say, obviously. And while I'd like to drag my heels for weeks, or even months, that would make me Bad Kate, the troublemaker, and it's necessary that Caleb sees I'm no longer her. When this stupid thing with Lucie starts to wither, I need to be a viable replacement, and Bad Kate is not. She's pulled too much shit in the past. Unfortunately, that leaves no option but to sign the fucking agreement.

I tell him I'll come to the office, but regret it the moment I remember Lucie works at TSG too.

I shower, dry my hair, and apply careful makeup, followed

by fifteen minutes of choosing an outfit, which is sort of ridiculous given how little I have to choose from. Caleb liked me in a suit, but my work clothes are in storage. I do my best with what I have, then get in the car.

TSG is on the other side of Elliott Springs, down toward Santa Cruz. I slide into a parking space and rub my palms over my skirt as I exit. This feels like an audition, and in a way it is. I'm auditioning for my last part, reminding Caleb that I was once someone he wanted, that I can be presentable when I need to be presentable and filthy when I need to be filthy. It isn't entirely authentic, but that doesn't bother me. Being yourself is a seriously overrated concept. At least half the people I know should *strive* to be someone else.

I enter the lobby and smile politely at the receptionist when she asks for my name. *Mrs. Lowell*, whispers that voice in my head, although I never actually took Caleb's last name. "Just tell him it's Kate."

A few minutes later, she leads me back to his office and tells me he'll be in momentarily.

I glance at his desk. We had sex there once. Will he think of that when he comes in? Will he think of my legs wrapped around his neck with my heels still on, both of us trying to be quiet so no one would hear?

Or perhaps he'll be looking at the framed photos that sit there instead—are they of Lucie? The twins? I walk to the large window at the end of the room so I won't be tempted to check.

"Kate," Caleb says, entering quickly and shutting the door behind him—*alone*, thank God. "I appreciate you coming in."

I've missed his face, but it's his eyes that make me want to weep with homesickness. I'm stunned anew at how thoroughly I managed to ruin the best thing that ever happened to me.

He's out of his jacket, wearing a dress shirt with the sleeves rolled up—the tie slightly askew. I itch to reach out and fix it but hold back.

He leans over his desk and grabs a file as I cross the room to him. He's barely even looked my way.

"The paperwork's all here," he says, handing it to me, perching on the edge of his desk. "I divided everything down the middle. The bank accounts, the investment portfolio—all of it. You'll probably want a lawyer to look it over."

When I disappeared, I cleaned out our checking account. What I did to him was terrible, yet here he is being generous, being fair. Even when I was gone, he tried to help me with that stipend I received. It was supposed to be anonymous but had his fingerprints all over it.

There was always something dirty and restless inside me while he was busy doing the right thing. It's why I've never felt like I was good enough for him.

I stare at the carpet, unable to face him. "I don't want anything," I whisper. *I just want you back*.

"I'm trying to do the right thing here," he says gently, *politely*. As if I'm an employee to whom he's handing a generous severance package after letting her go. "I want you to have what you need going forward."

Going forward. My stomach drops. Each word out of his mouth says this is a foregone conclusion, and it *can't* be a foregone conclusion because everything I want in the entire world hinges on him taking me back.

My eyes sting. "You've already done too much for me just this past year alone. And I don't deserve any of it after what I did."

"Kate," he croons, placing a hand on my shoulder before he stiffly pulls me toward him. I go willingly, pressing my face to his shirt. My tears are real, but I relish the fact that my mascara will run and his insecure little girlfriend will see it.

"It's okay," Caleb soothes, giving my back a small pat. "We endured something no one should have to go through. You, in particular. It's okay."

His chest, beneath my head, is firm, perfectly formed, his heartbeat regular, unaffected by me. I could move my mouth to his neck so easily, to the spot just below his ear, and change that. I know the precise words that would make him hard in two seconds flat. But if it failed, he'd go out of his way to avoid me afterward.

I need to wait until things start to fall apart with Lucie, until he's not sure he's got that much to lose. *That's* when I will bring out every trick I know...and I know a whole lot of tricks.

He releases me, his arms falling to his sides. I miss the heat of him immediately. "It's all behind us," he says.

No, but it will be. I kiss his cheek, making sure my soft pink lipstick grazes his shirt collar. "Sorry. I'll get back to you about this."

He frowns. "Is there anything you need? You found a place to stay?"

There's a small pinch of guilt right at the base of my rib cage. Beck hasn't told him, and he must fucking hate lying by omission.

"Yeah, I'm good. Applying for jobs."

He shoves his hands in his pockets. "I'm surprised you're sticking around. I thought you hated it here."

I did. I do. But everything I love is here. I shrug. "It's as close to home as I've got."

He nods. I'm not certain he believes me. "Let me know if there's anything you need."

I need you back. Nothing more.

And if I have to do something shady to make it happen, I will.

THAT AFTERNOON, I pay for a single session at Main Street Yoga and loiter outside the entrance, pretending I'm on the phone.

When Kayleigh enters, I follow and casually set a mat up next to hers.

She's even prettier in person than she is on Instagram—the kind of girl men picture while fucking the wives they've grown bored by—yet Caleb fired her for Lucie. It irks me.

People are stretching, so I do the same. Kayleigh appears to be taking a picture of her new pedicure, the one she already posted about over lunch.

I bend at the waist and stretch toward my own non-painted toes. "You look really familiar," I say, turning my head toward her. "Have we met before?"

She glances up from her phone. "I don't think so."

I scrunch my eyes, as if I'm trying to remember. "I feel like it was a work thing."

She takes one last shot of her toenails. She wishes I'd leave her alone. "I just started at McKinnon and Lieb down the street. The architecture firm?"

I shake my head. "No, it wouldn't be that. This is going to drive me crazy."

There's a tiny pinch of her lips, a hint of displeasure. "I used to work at TSG."

Thank God she finally got there. I was worried I'd need to be obvious.

My sigh is heavy with misery. "I'm extremely familiar with TSG. I guess that explains it."

I have her attention at last. She folds her feet beneath her and puts her phone off to the side. "Oh?"

"I *was* married to the CEO."

Her head swivels, eyes wide. She looks me over from head to toe, wondering how this pale, unpedicured woman beside her could *ever* have bagged her former boss. "*Caleb?* I'd heard he was married, but . . . when did you split?"

"We split when he met his new *girlfriend*." I swallow and

force a smile. Today I'm playing the role of the brave ex-wife done wrong.

Kayleigh rolls her eyes. "Ugh. I hate that girl. She's the reason I'm not working there anymore. She complained to Caleb and suddenly, I'm out of a job."

I'm guessing the three work hours Kayleigh must spend each day trying to capture the sun's reflection off her cappuccino for Instagram didn't help either, but facts matter little to me.

"Sounds about right," I reply, just as the teacher walks in and sits cross-legged on the mat. I resent her appearance just as the conversation is getting good, but maybe this is God's way of helping me out, reminding me to play the long game, not to appear too eager.

"Breathe out stress," the teacher instructs, placing her hands in front of her as if she's praying, "and breathe in peace."

I'm pretty sure I'm breathing out stress and breathing in vengeance, but following fifty percent of her instructions is better than none.

"Set your intentions for your time on the mat today," she tells us with a beneficent smile.

I close my eyes and set mine: *Figure out how Kayleigh can ruin Lucie for me.*

10

KATE

"I have a favor to ask."

Beck sets his fork down and waits, his eyes light.

"A favor beyond letting me live here rent-free and putting up with my shit all the time, that is."

I get the tiniest, grudging movement out of his mouth —*victory*. When I'd bring some new client to the firm at my first job, my boss would act like I was Joan of Arc and Eleanor Roosevelt combined. This is better.

"I need to get some stuff out of storage."

Any hint of a smile fades completely, and his gaze grows more focused. Beck is always assessing me, reading my expressions, parsing my words. It's a bit tiresome, the way he always suspects I have an ulterior motive. Especially since he's usually right. "Why?"

I huff in exasperation. "This isn't some diabolical plot. Why can't I say anything without you assuming I'm trying to fuck with Caleb?"

He acts as if he hasn't even heard me. "What do you need?"

"I have an interview Friday, and showing up in a tank top and cut-offs is frowned upon. I might need some help lifting boxes. If it's a problem," I add with my sweetest, most patently fake smile, "I'll just ask Caleb."

It occurs to me too late that maybe I *should* have asked Caleb. Maybe going through our old stuff would have triggered something for him. Lord knows we had sex on pretty much every piece of furniture we owned.

Unfortunately, my threat appears to have worked. "We can go tomorrow. Mueller can open the bar for me."

My heart starts to race, and not in a good way. I liked the idea of going to the storage unit better when it was something I wasn't doing within the next twelve hours.

Shit.

THE NEXT MORNING, we climb into his truck and drive toward Santa Cruz. I was too sick to eat, which I hid easily enough, but I can't control the jiggling knee, the fidgeting fingers that twist my hair as we turn on to the highway.

His gaze cuts over to me, curious. For once, he just leaves it alone, thank God.

We arrive, and I force myself to move, one step after another, to the first of the two storage units, the one Caleb thought my clothes were in. Beck's watching me like a hawk the whole time. As I enter the code, I force a grimace—it's the closest I can get to a smile—but I'm holding my breath as I flip on the light.

The room is unnaturally still, slightly surreal. I recognize our stuff and yet I don't. It no longer feels as if it's mine, outside of our home. I wish Caleb hadn't rented out our place. Even if I couldn't stay there, I'd like to have seen everything the way it was, revisited the days when I'd felt like I had something, like I belonged somewhere.

I'd never had that before. At that fancy private school Mimi got me into, I'd be ridiculed for hand-me-down uniforms from the school store and my off-brand sneakers. And then I'd return to the foster home, where they treated my attendance at private school as a slap in the face. *"Since you're so smart,"* my foster mother would begin every acidic criticism while the other kids snickered. My books would be defaced while I slept, the school-issued laptop hidden.

I'd dreamed of college, of a time when the playing field would be level, but it was never fucking level. Ever. Not until I got pregnant with Hannah. I'd thought, maybe, that God had finally decided to give me something of my own. But then He snatched that away too.

"This mostly looks like books and furniture," Beck says, placing a hand on my elbow.

I take one more cursory glance around the room, and we move to the second unit. The tall wardrobe boxes that hold my clothes are off to the left, but I don't move toward them. I instead move to the other side, toward white wood slats that rest against a wall, railings that curve, still smooth to the touch. A crib we didn't end up needing. I slide between stacks of furniture and reach my hand through, gripping one of the slats. That ache, the one that always rests in my chest, blooms until it's all I can feel.

The pregnancy was an accident, but I'd wanted her fervently from the instant those dual pink lines appeared. Before we even knew the gender, I was dreaming of a daughter with her little hand in mine as I walked her to school, a big Christmas tree loaded with gifts beneath it, camping on Shelter Cove.

Every bit of darkness seeped out of me when Caleb and I decided to get married, replaced by light. For months afterward, I felt like I was made of it.

Beck is behind me suddenly, resting his hand over mine

before he gently pulls me to his chest, his mouth pressing to my hair.

He doesn't try to distract me. He doesn't tell me to stop crying, the way Caleb did or act as if I'm sick and fucked up for not being over it yet, though I know it's true. He just stands there, waiting, solid and unhurried and whole, willing to be whatever I need right now.

It's kind of him but useless. There's no end to my grief. No bottom. Eventually he, like everyone else, will need me to stop, to pull my shit together. So I might as well get on with it.

Clenching my jaw, I pull away and cross the room, wiping my face hard. I find the boxes that say "Kate's closet" in Caleb's precise hand. "I think I probably just need that one," I say, pointing at the wardrobe box, my voice cracking.

"Scoot," he says, nudging me out of the way. "Go lower the tailgate."

He closes the door behind us and locks it, ending any thoughts I had of going back for one last look.

I wait in the car while he ties the box down. On Instagram, Lucie has posted a photo of the twins heading to tennis camp.

It's as if she's trying to get in my head as much as I'm trying to get in hers.

BY THE TIME I reach Santa Cruz for my interview on Friday morning, my inner thighs are damp with sweat, which I'm certain is pooling at the bottom of my skirt—nothing like the appearance of a urine stain to impress potential employers. I've been fumbling around my neck for my missing locket so much that I have a red spot there, and I've bitten a hangnail until it's bleeding. I should have gotten a manicure. I should have gotten a haircut. I should've tried to find my briefcase in the storage unit.

I should have recognized that I'll be lucky if anyone ever hires me again. Especially in a job overseeing their money.

Once upon a time, people would hear about my background, about foster care, and they all saw someone who deserved a chance. A professor once called me "a flower that bloomed in a desert" in a letter of reference. It's nice being the underdog—no matter how poorly you perform, you're still exceeding expectations.

That changed after I graduated. Then people saw an Ivy League MBA on my resume and they expected a fucking Ivy League MBA, not an addict with chewed-up nails wearing a suit two sizes too big.

Today's interview is not in the best section of the city, but I guess I'm probably not the best MBA looking for a job anymore either. I park and walk down sidewalks that need to be repaved, the heel of my shoe catching in a crevice, tweaking my ankle as I stumble. I greet the receptionist and sit in the lobby, staring at the threadbare carpet as nervous sweat dampens my shirt.

It takes nearly thirty minutes before I'm led to the CEO. He has one of those generic business-guy faces—jowls, a slight wave to his thick, overly styled hair, an off-the-rack suit hiding what is undoubtedly a middle gone soft. Surrounding the tables behind him are photos of himself and his family doing expensive shit—sailing, playing golf, standing in front of the Colosseum. The kids I went to school with had families like that. I assumed I'd have one too, as an adult.

He greets me but doesn't apologize for the delay.

"So, Wharton?" he asks, squinting at my resume. "And then Envirotech...that one didn't last long. And you haven't had a job for several years?"

Sweat beads along my hairline and I run my hand over it. "Yes." I swallow. "I was pregnant, but my daughter died shortly after she was born. It took me a while to get back on my feet."

"How'd that happen? How'd she die?"

My teeth grind. A decent person would be horrified, would at least offer some rote apology. This asshole, however, just wants to sate his idle curiosity. "It's called meconium aspiration. Sometimes it gets into the baby's lungs during childbirth."

He nods and moves on. Apparently, Hannah's death didn't prove as exciting as he'd hoped. "Even so, taking *years* away from the workforce seems excessive, does it not?"

I could lie, but it's a small world. This guy will undoubtedly know someone at one of the jobs I left off my resume, someone who will describe how I turned up at a work event high as a kite, how I was led by security out of the building. My only hope of this lasting is to come clean, as little as it appeals.

"I had some issues with drug usage." I steel my voice, aiming for *blunt* rather than *ashamed*. But how could I possibly not be ashamed? I spent my whole life exceeding expectations only to fail my own so miserably. "It took a while for me to complete rehab, but I did, and I've been clean for four months."

His smile is the sort you'd give a small child who thinks she's Picasso—patient, a bit condescending. "I congratulate you on your success, Ms. Bennett, but you do realize we're trying to hire a CFO here, do you not?"

"I was promoted to CFO at my last position after six months, and I—"

"I need to stop you," he says firmly. "If you'd been more forthcoming in your letter, this interview would not have taken place."

"As I was saying, I've been clean for—"

He sighs. "I can't entrust my company's finances to an addict."

I want to punch him right in his smug, self-righteous face, sitting there in his cheap fucking suit with his unattractive family in photos behind him. But I somehow rise from the chair, sticky with sweat and disappointment, and thank him for his time.

He stands as I walk to the door. "In the future, Miss Bennett," he begins in that unbearably smug voice of his, "I'd suggest you—"

I pull the door shut hard behind me before he can finish. The only victory of my day so far.

BECK TEXTS in the evening to ask about the interview. I wish he'd forgotten. It's humiliating that it went as badly as it did.

I tell him it didn't go well and that honesty is not, as it turns out, the best policy, and then I go on to Instagram, which does not improve my mood, as I'm apparently the only person in the freaking state who's got nothing going on tonight. Kayleigh is heading to Vegas with "the girls"—I assume the roommate she called a "fat c*nt" on TikTok one day after posting a quote about kindness is not among them. Beck is at work. Caleb and Lucie are probably having a romantic dinner for two while they talk about how much better Lucie is at giving birth than me.

I put on a horror movie and watch with growing impatience. What female goes into the creepy basement of a haunted house, finds a hidden passageway, and decides to investigate on her own?

"You deserve to die," I announce to no one as she grabs a conveniently placed flashlight.

My voice in the quiet cabin isn't loud enough to shout down the one in my head, the one saying, *If you're so much smarter than everyone else, Kate, why are you alone on a Friday night?*

The girl on the TV starts banging on the door that's just shut behind her when a motorcycle roars in the distance. It can't possibly be Beck. It's one of the bar's two busiest nights of the week.

Yet only a moment later, the cabin door opens and he fills the space with his massive frame.

"You have a swimsuit?" he asks, putting his helmet down on a chair.

I blink, astonished. Nothing about his presence here, or the question, makes sense.

"A swimsuit? It's nine at night."

"Yeah, Kate, I've got a watch," he says. "You always used to want to go night swimming. It's not like you've got anything else to do."

I frown. I have a long list of bad qualities, and my need for excitement is somewhere on there. Nowhere near the top, obviously, as there are far worse things about me, but it's something Caleb never liked, and it led me into a lot of trouble.

I swallow. "You think it's okay?"

He folds his arms across his chest, his mouth a flat line. "Why wouldn't it be?"

Because one form of fun leads to another.

Enjoying myself will create a craving for more. We'll swim, and I'll want to go to a bar. We'll go to a bar, and I'll decide one beer can't hurt, and when that beer's gone and all hell hasn't broken loose, I'll decide smoking some weed won't hurt either, and then I'll wake up to discover I'm at Kent's again—my mouth dry and my hands shaking for more of whatever I passed out doing the night before.

My fear is that fun is like cocaine—something I'm incapable of enjoying in small quantities—but it sounds too crazy to be said aloud.

I hitch a shoulder in lieu of answering. "Yeah, let's go."

After I've slipped a bikini on under my clothes, I follow him outside and he hands me his helmet.

"We're taking the bike?" Back when Caleb and I were just dating, I must have asked Beck to take me out on his bike a hundred times, and he always refused.

"No," Beck replies with a quiet laugh. "I just thought you

might like a helmet for swimming. Of course we're taking the bike. Why? You scared?"

I put the helmet on. "I think you know better than that. I've never had a logical response to fear."

He doesn't smile, but there's something heated in his slow appraisal that makes my stomach tighten deliciously. "Yeah. I remember."

He sits and I slip on behind him. As I wrap my arms around his waist, I picture being beneath someone his size. He'd probably crush me to death if he was on top, but there'd be worse ways to go.

He's careful on the gravel, but once we hit pavement, he accelerates so fast that I gasp. It's not the gentle ride you'd normally give a guest. We're flying, taking corners fast, weaving between cars.

My heart races and my brain—with its nonstop stream of insults and warnings—is silenced. There is only Beck—his size, his smell. The bike tilts and he's still there, solid and warm. It swerves and I press my cheek to his broad back so hard it'll probably leave a mark. My body molds to his, my grip on him tight, but I let myself relax a little, following Beck's lead, trusting him while the bike rumbles between my legs.

I love every fucking minute of it.

He comes to a screeching halt along the road and parks.

"What'd you think?" he asks as I pull off the helmet and climb to my feet with unsteady legs.

He looks so fucking good sitting there with that smirk on his face. Better than he should to a woman desperately trying to win her husband back, but Beck is hot, and I haven't had sex in a very long time. *Anyone* in my shoes would feel the same.

"I loved it." My voice comes out breathy, high with adrenaline.

He takes the helmet from me. "I knew you would." There's something quiet and unhappy in the words.

"If you let me drive us back, I can check it off my bucket list," I say, following him through the bush-lined path to the beach.

"Not happening. Choose something else off your bucket list."

He sits on a rock to pull off his boots, and I kick off my sneakers. "Camp at Shelter Cove? It's hours from here. You might want to just let me drive the bike."

He glances up with a single brow raised. "Of all the possible things, *that's* what you'd choose?"

It was Mimi who told me about it. I remember the photo she showed me of her and her kids camping there. The little boy in the photo was dead, she'd told me, but that was okay because she had me. I'd really believed I could replace him. Maybe she had too.

I shrug. "It's just one of those dumb things you hear about as a kid and think is special. I'm sure it'd be disappointing."

He walks a little ahead and begins to undress. I do the same. Except there's no swimsuit under his shorts—just boxer briefs, and he promptly removes those too. Not that I'd have expected anything different, but he has an amazing ass. You could eat a bowl of cereal out of that curve coming off his hip. Regrettably, he heads toward the water before I can check out what he's packing in front. He wades until he's waist deep, every line and curve in his back delineated as he dives in.

"Why do I have to wear a suit, but you don't?" I call from the shore as he emerges.

He pushes the hair out of his face. "Because you're a girl and you don't care, whereas I'm a guy, and I don't need to see one of my friend's wives naked."

"You're sure?" I tease, running a finger under the bottom of my bikini top as I wade in. "They're small but spectacular. You might never get this chance again."

He won't agree, but I could spin a whole lot of fantasies out of what might occur if he did.

A muscle flickers in his cheek. "I've already heard more than I ever needed to about how you look naked. You went skinny dipping with a bunch of our friends, and Liam continued discussing it for months just to torment Caleb."

I laugh quietly. "Caleb's kind of a prude where nudity is concerned."

His eyes drift over me. I'm not sure he even knows he's doing it. "If you were my wife, I'd be the same way." There's a hint of a growl to his voice, a growl that hits right between my legs. The sudden snap of desire is so intense it's almost painful.

I want to feel that growl against my neck as I reach below the surface of the water to palm him. I could, too. I could do it so easily.

My eyes flicker to his waist, to that trail of hair leading from his belly button. I sink into the water, drawn toward him unwillingly, and come to a horrified halt, stepping hard into the sand beneath my feet.

What the hell are you doing, Kate? You really think you can fuck Beck without ruining everything? You'd lose every goddamn thing you want from life.

"It's too cold for me," I announce abruptly, my heart thudding in my chest.

I turn and walk straight out, ignoring his objections behind me, my breath coming too fast. *Jesus, what was I thinking?*

I turn away and pull my clothes on.

"Well, that didn't last long," he grouses, walking out after me.

I look intently at the moon from under damp lashes, trying to ignore the sound of a zipper behind me as he dresses, waiting until I'm reasonably certain he isn't naked before I turn. "Sorry. And, uh, thanks. For doing this."

He pulls his shirt on. The wet fabric clings to muscles I'd be better off not seeing in the first place. "Why were you so hesitant to come, anyway? You were always trying to get Caleb to go night swimming."

My teeth sink into my lip. "Caleb thought I was too wild, and maybe he was right. Maybe needing something crazier than everyone else does is how I ended up where I did."

His mouth turns down. "There was nothing wrong with your idea of fun, Kate. The two of you are just different. I like riding a motorcycle. It doesn't mean I'm going to shoot heroin. You like to skinny dip and play ridiculous pranks. You *should* like those things. There's nothing wrong with them."

I wrap my arms around myself. "I'm worried that I'm not going to know I've gone too far until it's too late."

He places his hand on my shoulder. "I'm not going to let you mess up."

It's a promise he really can't make, but my heart swells anyway. His kindness has always come as a surprise. He is the gruffest, the most frightening one in his entire friend group, yet he's always been far better to me than I could possibly deserve.

I just hope he doesn't hate me when everything I've planned comes to pass.

11

BECK

On Tuesday night the guys all come in, since it'll be slow enough that we can hang out a little. These get-togethers used to be a weekly thing, but they're less frequent now that everyone is so busy, and I wish we could have skipped tonight's too—the longer Kate stays with me, the worse I feel about keeping Caleb in the dark. I never set out planning to deceive him to this extent—I figured Kate would take off once she saw Caleb was serious about the divorce. And Caleb and I have been texting every goddamn day about the 49ers preseason games, so it's going to be hard to justify my silence, if it all comes out.

Liam is the first to arrive. He takes a seat at the bar and is immediately eyeing me a little too closely, like a bloodhound who's just picked up a scent.

I slide him a beer. "What's with the face?"

He leans back, arms folded across his chest. "I could say the same to you. You look like you're waiting for test results. Have you heard from Kate?"

I'd demand to know why he thinks *I'd* have heard from her,

but I guess we already established that the last time he was here.

I rub the back of my neck. "Yeah, I've heard from her. She needed a place to stay."

He lets out a heavy breath. "Fuck, dude. You didn't."

I was sort of hoping he'd tell me it wasn't a big deal. "It's just temporary."

He shakes his head. "Are you sleeping with her?"

I set the pitcher in my hand down with a thud. "What the fuck is wrong with you? Of course not."

He laughs under his breath. "Let's not pretend it's your *high morals* that kept that from happening."

Am I pissed because I'm offended? Or because he's right? "Fuck you, Liam. She's still married to one of my closest friends. I can't believe you'd even suggest it."

"You've definitely thought about it," he says.

I start scrubbing down the bar more vigorously than is necessary. "Every man who's ever laid eyes on her has thought about it, asshole." It's almost impossible to look at her and *not* think about it.

"Not the way you have. By which I mean obsessively."

Yeah, maybe. It never occurred to me that I'd been so obvious. And if I've been obvious to Caleb, the fact that Kate's living with me will go over even worse than I'd thought. "Does Caleb think that too?"

"No, because if he did, he'd have already kicked your ass. You might have three inches and forty pounds on him, but I guarantee that if he thought you were after his wife, he'd find a way to make up the difference."

"Ex-wife. And I'm not after her. She asked if she could stay and I let her. That's it. She wants him back—I'm trying to avert a disaster."

He lifts his beer, taking a large gulp. "She's delusional, then.

I'm not saying Caleb wasn't into Kate, but what they had wasn't what he has with Lucie. It was less like love and more like...the sex was so good he couldn't stop himself."

Just the idea of Caleb with Kate makes my blood boil. He was never right for her, or her for him. I'd probably have done the same thing in his shoes, but I wish to God he'd left well enough alone.

Once Harrison arrives, I tell Lawrence to cover the bar and we head to a table in the back. I've just set a pitcher down when Caleb walks in.

I tip my chin at him. "Look who finally decided to show up."

He grins, dropping into the chair beside mine. "I've turned into the pussy who ditches his friends for a girl, haven't I?"

I lean back in my seat. "You were a pussy long before you met Lucie."

"How's it going with her anyway?" asks Liam, as if we're suddenly contestants on *The Bachelor* with nothing better to do than discuss our feelings.

Caleb's smile falters. "Good. You know—there are ups and downs, but it's good."

I stiffen. Maybe Kate's getting her way after all, which is in no one's best interest— especially not Kate's, despite what she thinks.

"I thought you guys were skipping through meadows and riding unicorns into the sunset," says Liam. "Is her ex causing problems again?"

Caleb lets his head fall back against the chair and closes his eyes. "He's always causing problems, but no, she's just having some issues with Kate being here."

My hand grips the edge of my seat. "When did she see *Kate*?"

"Only that first day on the dock. But there's just been some other stuff. Kate came to the office to get the separation papers and accidentally got lipstick on my shirt collar when she hugged me goodbye. With everything Lucie's been through...it unsettled her."

Caleb's the only guy here who'd believe Kate did it *accidentally*. Liam glances at me. *Trouble*, that look says. And now that we've established Kate's causing trouble, how am I going to tell Caleb *I'm* the reason she's able to cause it?

"She should trust you at this point, though," argues Harrison. "I mean, you blew off the merger for her."

"She trusts me. But, you know, she's *seen* Kate," he adds. We all understand what he means. Kate isn't just pretty. When she enters a room, shaking all that long red hair, looking around with those dangerous feline eyes, women watch like she's a tiger on the loose while the men they're sitting with just wonder how she can be trapped.

"Why's she back, anyway?" asks Liam. "I thought she hated it here."

Caleb frowns. "I'm not sure." It sounds to me like he *is* sure, he just doesn't want to admit it to himself or us.

Harrison scrubs a hand over his face. "Did you ask where she's staying?"

Liam's eyes shift toward me again. If he keeps this up, the whole fucking bar is going know where Kate's staying.

"I don't want to know," Caleb says. "If I find out she's with those junkies again, I'm going to get involved, and I just can't. For Lucie's sake, I've got to make a clean break."

It's my chance to step in and tell the truth. Instead, I go refill our pitcher.

Suzanne's by the bar with her friends, watching me out of the corner of her eye.

"You want to come to my place and hang out once your friends leave?" she asks.

I'd planned to get home early enough to see Kate, but I'm too fucking pissed off to even consider it now.

"Sure," I tell her. *Fuck Kate. Fuck the whole thing.* None of it's my problem.

I want my old, uncomplicated life back already. I want Kate out of my head.

12

KATE

I get home from yoga on Tuesday night and stumble into the shower. My arms hurt so much that it's hard to shampoo my hair.

Beck said he'd be home early, but even after I've eaten dinner and watched two stupid shows in a row, he's still not back.

I force myself to go online and look at my dwindling checking account. My lifestyle, at present, is funded by a magical grant I received during rehab, one I hadn't even applied for, intended to help "addicts who've suffered a loss." A grant whose paperwork was filed by *Caleb's* attorney.

It was unbelievably kind of him, but it won't last forever, especially given the money I'm spending on yoga with Kayleigh and ad campaigns targeting Lucie. So what's going to happen if no one will hire me? I guess I could start over in a new field. I could get a PhD in economics, simply so the years I lost won't be so glaring on my resume.

But . . . I'm *good* in my field. Really good. I don't want another degree, and I don't want to do something else, and how many people can say that about their chosen profession? How many people would choose to stay in their field over any other?

I glance at the clock again. It's after ten, which isn't early at all. Maybe Beck got held up, but he could have fucking texted.

I pull up my mother's college yearbook online while I wait. It's been a long time since I've done this, but Beck's questions about my father the other night have been floating around in my head ever since, irritating me like a bruise I can't stop poking at.

She was in two different clubs—Students Against Apartheid and the Berkeley Drama Club. Though we aren't all that similar physically, even at the age of eighteen she already *exudes* sex, something I've heard said of myself far too many times. And, of course, she liked drugs. We've got that in common too. She doesn't look like an addict, though, so what the hell happened between her arrival at Berkeley and her departure at the end of that year that could have changed everything? Maybe it was me.

Beside her in each of the photos is the same girl. I expand the page large enough to get her name: Sarah Dow. Sarah Dow was good enough friends with my mother to join two clubs with her. Maybe that means she was good enough friends to know who my mother slept with that year too.

It's after eleven when I start messaging all the women named Sarah Dow on Facebook, and I'm officially pissed. Doesn't Beck understand that I *count* on him showing up when he says he will? Doesn't he understand how fucking isolated I am without him?

I slam my laptop shut just after midnight, too angry to even face him if he manages to come home.

I don't expect much from people, but I thought Beck kept promises.

Idiot. No one keeps promises.

It bothers me, when I finally go to bed, that I care as much as I do.

~

I'M MAKING coffee and checking my phone when Beck's bike rumbles up the next morning. I throw my phone in my purse. He wouldn't have known I was checking for a text from him, but *I'll* know.

When he walks in, I'm staring out the window, hip pressed against the counter. I don't turn around to greet him but instead seethe quietly, fantasizing about throwing the glass coffee pot at his pretty face.

I can't believe he didn't come home *at all*.

His keys rattle as they hit the table. I turn toward him and wait for an apology, but instead he stomps into the kitchen, coming to a dead halt as his eyes run over me, head to toe.

"Do me a favor," he snarls, "and start wearing some fucking clothes around the house, huh?"

My eyes narrow. "Sorry. Should I stay fully clothed twenty-four hours a day just in case you *happen* to come home?"

His jaw goes tight. "This is the first night since you got here that I haven't come home."

"You *told* me you were coming home early."

"Does it matter?" he asks, closing in on me, his voice low and dangerous. What is it about that voice? Beck scares a lot of people, but Beck at his scariest turns me on like nothing else. He rests a single hand on my hip. "Did you *miss* me?"

The air grows thick and my pulse races, the hair on my arms standing on end. He's being a dick and my nipples are diamond-hard, as if he's doing something else entirely.

I push his hand away. "Piss off. You get to go hang out with your friends. You have a whole bar full of people you can talk to. You know who I speak to? You, and the checkout girl at Safeway. She asks if I want bags and I say *yes*. So, one word aside from talking to you."

"You seem to be forgetting a conversation," he says. "A nice long one you had with Caleb the week before last."

It's as if I'm ten again, caught stealing food from a foster mother who already had it in for me. Knowing I was about to get hit—and deserved it.

Except I'm a grown-ass adult and I don't owe anyone a fucking apology.

"I didn't realize I was supposed to be reporting all my conversations to you, *Herr Commandant*. It wasn't a big deal. We barely said ten words to each other."

His hand lands on the counter beside me. He's still too close. "Yet you managed to get some lipstick on his collar, which he actually believes was a fucking accident."

My pulse triples, but weakness could be fatal in a situation like this. "It was," I reply, walking away.

"*Bullshit*. I asked very little of you staying here. Two things. And you've already blown off one. So how long 'til I come home and find you comatose on my couch?"

I round on him. "Don't you dare say that to me because no one alive is trying harder not to use than I am right now. *No one*."

His arms fold across his chest. "I thought you had it all under control."

I swallow. If I tell him it's getting harder every day rather than easier, he's going to want me to go back to rehab. If I tell him nothing is going according to plan with Caleb, he'll point out that I'm not supposed to have a plan in the first place. "I'm in a town where the only people I can safely see all hate me. I have a degree from the top MBA program in the *world* but can barely get a job interview, and my husband—the only thing that got me clean—wants a divorce. So don't sit there with your job and your social life and all that pussy you get on demand

and talk to me about my failings. Staying clean requires a level of restraint you can't fucking imagine. I could drive to my old dealer's and be welcomed with open arms, but instead"—my voice starts to crack and I have to grit out the last words—"I stay in this hovel waiting for you, and you don't show up like you said you would."

I hate that I sound so needy, and I refuse to cry in front of him after his bullshit accusations. I go to my room, slamming the door behind me. Moments later, his bike roars as he leaves.

They told us in rehab to admit when we were struggling, but I told Beck and he couldn't run fast enough. They told us the lapses in our job histories wouldn't be a problem, but I've only gotten *one* interview, and it barely lasted three minutes. I'm beginning to wonder if anything they said in rehab was based on reality and not some Utopian society where an apology and good intentions solve every problem.

I rise from my bed and start packing. I've just alienated the only friend I have other than Ann. I have no idea where I'll go, but it's clear my time at Beck's is done.

13

BECK

When my mother was dying, she told me that I'd know the right girl when I met her, but I knew with Kate before we'd ever even met.

My bike hadn't even come to a full stop outside the club when I'd noticed her: long red hair whipping in the wind, an angel's face, *don't-fuck-with-me* eyes.

I knew. I fucking knew it was her...until Caleb walked up. That's when I realized this was the girl he'd been talking about for the past two months. I've spent years trying to forget how I felt that night, trying to separate myself from her, but it's never worked.

I was the one who was with her during her pregnancy, helping with all the shit Caleb was too busy for. I was the one who fought with him after Hannah died, who insisted that he couldn't throw himself into work when Kate needed him. I was the one who told him she was using and the only answer he ever came up with was rehab, because it was so much easier than being there with her himself.

She was suffering and the world said, *"You'll figure it out."*

And now she is drowning, and the world says, *"Hey, you brought it on yourself."*

It's time she had one person willing to take her side, and for that to happen, I need to come clean to Caleb.

Come clean about *some* of it, anyway.

I text and discover he's at his house, not the office . . . unheard of for a Wednesday morning, so I head out to his end of the lake, to the house I practically lived at during the summers growing up.

"Your timing is perfect," he says when he opens the door. "Give me a hand with this drywall."

"Can't believe you've taken a day off to work on the house," I say, placing my helmet on the foyer table and following him to the pile of drywall in the corner. "Didn't know you were capable of it."

He bought the house late last winter, planning to fix it up for his mom. We all took bets on how many decades it would be before he got around to the renovations. Looks like I'm out fifty bucks.

He grabs one end and I grab the other. "Garage," he grunts. "I'm just taking the morning off to get it ready for Liam's crew to come in."

"You're actually hiring him to finish this up?"

"My weekends and evenings are better spent with Lucie and the kids," he says, flinging open the garage door with one hand and twisting the drywall to get it through the narrow opening. "What's with the surprise visit, anyway?"

I wait until we've dumped the drywall onto the garage floor before I reply. "I have to tell you something."

He frowns at me, brushing his hands off on his jeans. "No one ever says *'I have to tell you something'* and then delivers good news." He turns to go back inside. "We'd better sit for this."

I follow him to the kitchen and take the seat across from

his. "Kate showed up at my house a few weeks ago, needing a place to stay," I announce. "She's been there ever since."

A muscle in his cheek flickers. "You're shitting me."

I don't think he's jealous—he's too whipped over Lucie to even notice other females. But it's not an especially good look when your best friend is shacking up with your ex, whether you've got feelings for her or not. I'd be pissed too. "She needed a place to stay, Caleb. It might have escaped your attention, but she's not exactly flush."

"Are you sleeping with her?" His voice is calm—*too* calm—and entirely without intonation.

I raise a brow. "No, and why would it matter if I were, unless you've decided you want her back?"

His mouth falls open. "That's not it, and you know it. It's just fucking disloyal. And you couldn't mention it *once* instead of sending me memes about the Seahawks?"

"Yeah, I should have told you sooner, but I never thought she'd stay as long as she has. And it was either me or her dealer. If you're so fucking selfish you'd want me to turn her away in that situation, you don't deserve my loyalty or anyone else's."

His chair scrapes along the floor as he climbs to his feet.

I stand too. "You want to hit me, asshole?" I demand. "Go ahead. I'm begging you to hit me first."

He stares at me, his jaw open wide. "You've been living with my ex for over a month in secret! Why the fuck are you acting like *you're* the injured party?"

Because you never deserved her, and you didn't appreciate what you had. Because this whole fucking situation could have been avoided if you'd cared a little more than you did.

"I'm not the injured party, dumbass," I reply. "She is. She's still so damaged by what happened that she can barely function."

His eyes narrow. "I'm curious why exactly you care so much, Beck. Because I don't see you doing much to help anyone but yourself. So is this actually a good deed, or is it just that she's one of the very few girls in the county you haven't had a chance to fuck?"

I've wanted to punch Caleb in his smug face before—every time he tried to tone Kate down or asked her to be less of what she is. But my anger is different now, and worse. It's the kind of anger that could permanently destroy a friendship I've had since I was a little kid if I gave in to it.

I head toward the front door and he follows.

I snatch my helmet off the table. "I'm gonna leave before I do something I might regret, but let's get this straight: I'm not the bad guy here. You wanting a divorce threw her for a loop. That's not your fault, but she's worked too damn hard getting where she is to let it all be fucked up now, and she needs someone in her court."

"Let's get one more thing straight," he replies. "Any damage the divorce has done is minimal compared to the damage *you'll* cause by turning her into one of your meaningless fuck buddies."

I turn and walk out of the house.

Caleb's wrong. Because if I was sleeping with Kate, it could never be meaningless. Not for a second.

And *she's* not the one who'd be fucked up when it ended.

14

KATE

It only takes me a few trips to get everything into my trunk.

I still can't believe he just left. And I can't believe I packed *slowly,* hoping he'd return.

I go back up to grab my purse and toiletry bag but stop at the front door to look around one last time. I shouldn't have called his place a hovel. I mean, it *is* one, but it's also simple and uncomplicated and *right*. I've liked it here—at least when he was around.

"Bye, Beck," I whisper, my throat a little tight as I close the door behind me.

I trudge toward my car as if I'm wading through waist-deep water and when I reach the driver's seat, my face presses to the steering wheel, but I refuse to cry. *There are things worth your tears. Beck isn't one of them. Suck it up.*

I push the button to start the car, but nothing happens. I push the button again, and there's still nothing, so I finally reach over to my purse to grab the keys.

And they aren't there.

I stare at the place where my keyring normally clips on, not comprehending. I didn't remove the keys, but if they somehow fell off, then they're still inside his house—on the other side of the door I locked as I left.

Which means that now, after Beck took off like an asshole, *I'm* gonna have to call him and meekly plead for his help.

I reach into my purse for my phone. And it isn't there either.

I stare, dumbfounded, until it finally comes together:

Beck.

Beck took my keys and my phone, anticipating my steps in precise order like some kind of mastermind criminal profiler. I scream in frustration. *Fucking Beck.* Does he think this is *funny*? Is this how he plans to punish me for *accidentally* getting lipstick on Caleb's collar—making me sit out here all fucking day? We're at least seven miles from town, and even if I walked all the way to his bar, there'd be no guarantee he was even there.

"It looks like I'm walking seven fucking miles," I grit out, climbing from the car.

That's when I hear a bike—in the distance but coming closer.

I start marching down the gravel driveway, as if this is a chicken fight and my whopping hundred and ten pounds is any match for him on a motorcycle. I've only made it ten feet when he stops in front of me, pulling off his helmet, casual as can be. His face is impassive, unapologetic—not a care in the fucking world, and if I were him, I'd have *several* cares. He knows me— no one has ever suggested that I am even-tempered on the best of days.

I march toward him and hold out my hand. "Give me my keys."

He smirks. "Sure. As soon as you've settled down."

"Fuck you," I say, hitting his chest. He barely seems to notice. "You fucking stole my keys and my phone. I had no idea how long you'd be gone. Give me my shit so I can leave."

"No."

Rage makes my vision go black at the edges. "What do you mean, *no*? You're gonna hold me captive here?"

His mouth barely moves, but there's a glimmer of life in his eyes, as if he's thinking about it.

"I'm sorry," he says. "I had to take care of something."

I blink. That's not what I was expecting.

There's more there—I see shadows shifting in those eyes of his. Beck's so full of secrets I'm not sure he even knows all of them himself, but he isn't going to tell me a thing.

I hold out my hand. "Great. Give me my keys."

"I've got an idea if you would like to come in and discuss it." His tone is formal, but he raises a single mocking brow. "*Calmly*."

I roll my eyes. "Fine. Can I at least have my phone back?"

He walks to my trunk and grabs my bags. He knew every step I'd take. "It's in my nightstand."

"I'd better not find it on top of used condoms or something."

He looks at me over his shoulder as he heads for the stairs. "Why would I put *used* condoms in my nightstand?"

"I don't know. Because men are disgusting?"

"Well, yeah. But that's not even logical."

I follow him inside. He puts my bags back in my room. He apparently has a lot more faith in this little idea of his than I do, which probably involves more rehab.

I flop on the couch with an exhale as he reemerges. "So, what's your big plan?"

He sits at the other end. His tongue sweeps over his teeth. "You could work for me. Just until you find something."

Not where I thought he was headed.

And while I'd be fine working in a bar, I can't believe *he* thinks so. "Work for you?" I repeat. "Like...waiting tables?"

He laughs to himself. "God, no."

Irritation is a tiny pebble in my chest, grating. He's trying to help me, but that immediate, arrogant *God, no* makes me want to punch him hard in the face. "I think I'm *capable* of waiting tables, asshole."

"I don't see customer service being your strong suit. But I've got some paperwork that's, uh, kinda fucked up. I need help."

I wish I could hold onto my irritation, but it vanishes despite my best efforts, replaced with concern. If Beck is admitting this to me, his paperwork is not *kinda* fucked up. It's exceedingly, ridiculously fucked up. "I assume we're talking about the kind of shit that could get you put in prison?"

He leans forward, resting his elbows on his broad thighs, looking at the floor rather than me as he answers. "I've pretty much just been making up numbers when I file taxes. I've kept receipts, but that's it."

"For last year, you mean?"

He winces as he exhales. "For the last four years."

"Beck," I groan. "It's a sad day when I'm chastising someone else about responsibility, but Jesus. *Four years*?"

Both hands tug at his hair. "The accountant my mother used died, and everyone I talked with after wanted me to use fucking software and input stuff, and I just didn't have time. I should have hired someone to deal with it, but I was worried about entrusting my finances to a stranger." He leans his head back and closes his eyes. "I realize you're capable of doing much better things, but it's definitely something you *could* do if you were willing and if working near the bar isn't a problem."

I loathe the way that makes me sound, as if I'm some kind of loose cannon who can't control herself anywhere. Maybe I loathe it, though, because it could be true. Back in the day, I *was* a bit of a loose cannon.

"I'm not an alcoholic," I reply. "I can work near a bar without drinking as easily as you. Though I'm going to need a can of Lysol before I set foot in that office. I know what you do in there."

He frowns. "I'm not that bad."

"Bullshit. When was the last time you had sex in there?"

His tongue taps his upper lip as he looks away. He says nothing.

"Oh my God. Yesterday? *Yesterday?*"

When he gives me a halfhearted shrug, I force a laugh, but I'm weirdly . . . unamused. It's probably just that I haven't had sex that I was conscious for in nearly a year.

But it's strange how much it feels like jealousy.

THE NEXT DAY, we walk in through the saloon-style doors of Beck's Bar and Grill together. Beck is technically *Jacob* Beck, though I've never heard anyone call him "Jacob" other than Caleb's mom, and the bar has been in his family for forty years.

There's a new deck outside, but the interior is the same, and I have a sudden, sharp memory of the last time I was here with Caleb. We were fighting because I'd wanted to go to a concert later that night and he'd wanted to stay home.

I've been struggling so hard to get back to him...it's as if I forgot we had bad times too.

The rest of the staff isn't in yet, so Beck shows me to the office, which sits just past the bar. He swears he's disinfected it and to his credit, it does smell strongly of bleach.

Aside from its theoretical cleanliness, though, the room is a grim, windowless place, with two desks reflecting back the gleam of fluorescent lights . . . and file boxes lining the walls.

"What's in those?" I ask, pointing at them.

He stares at the floor like a kid who just got caught stealing. "Receipts, mostly."

My jaw falls. There are at least twenty boxes, which means

hundreds of files, and hundreds of files mean thousands of pieces of paper. "Jesus. All of them?"

"No, there are employee files in there too."

My brow furrows. "You didn't digitize all that?"

He just looks at me. *Of course he didn't.* Because Beck has spent the past four years only handling the parts of his job he considers necessary, and that does not include bookkeeping or responsible file management. He shows me the payroll software and the purchasing system, both of which are ridiculously out-of-date. Just the act of showing them to me seems to be suffocating him. He looks toward the door longingly.

"In a hurry?" I ask. "Meeting your ten AM hookup in the alley outside?"

He narrows a single eye at me. "I just hate being in the office."

"Yeah, four years of receipts and this computer from 1992 tipped me off."

He's already backing toward the door. "Just fix it and don't involve me. I'll pay whatever you want."

I laugh. "Here's a little tip they taught us in business school. Don't ever say '*I'll pay whatever you want*' to a new hire. And I don't want your money. You're letting me stay with you rent-free . . . It's the least I can do."

His arms fold over his chest as he stares me down. "You're not working for me unless I'm paying you. I need to be able to treat you like any other employee, which means I get to be a dick if I want to, and you've got to put up with it."

"Yes, that's so different from our normal arrangement," I reply with a grin as he walks away.

Any amusement I felt fades when I open the first of many boxes, however. The receipts aren't even organized by *year*. It's going to take me weeks to get this squared away.

Over the course of the next few hours, I begin separating the expenses by year and broad categories. By the time he returns, the floor is awash in piles of paper—with barely enough space for him to get inside. I've only made my way through four boxes, and I haven't even *begun* to input anything.

He edges inside the room. "You already want to quit, don't you?"

"Yes," I say, rubbing my eyes. "But I want to keep you out of jail slightly more."

"Come outside and eat. It'll make you like me again."

"I never said I liked you in the first place," I grumble as he leads me into the restaurant.

A group of women having lunch wave excitedly to Beck, urging him to come over. I enjoy a little too much the way they deflate as he shakes his head with a polite smile and keeps walking.

We take seats out on the deck and I gaze out at the gently rolling mountains, a pale purple in the early afternoon haze. "While your organizational skills blow, I've got to say this view is pretty impressive."

He grunts, glancing out, seeing nothing. Beck and Caleb both inherited a business from a dying parent instead of pursuing their own dreams. It worked out okay for Caleb. I'm not sure that's the case for Beck.

A waitress swings by, we both order the steak, and then I turn toward him again. "If you hate everything about owning a bar, why are you doing it?"

He hitches a shoulder. "It's been in my mom's family for two generations. What am I gonna do? Let some asshole turn it into a McDonald's?"

"I would." I guess that's easy for me to say, though. I don't have a single blood relative I can even remember.

"It would be like I was slapping my mom in the face if I sold this place." He shakes his head and for the briefest moment, I see that the loss of her is still hard for him, all these years later. "It was just the two of us, my entire life, and that changes things. She jumped through crazy hoops to make sure she was with me every afternoon and she'd drop everything the minute I walked in. She'd close the bar entirely if I was sick and there was no one to manage it. This was her gift to me. I can't just fucking give it away."

Of course she did those things. I only had Hannah for a matter of minutes, but I'd have given her everything. Which is how I know he's wrong.

"Beck, she gave you the bar because it was all she had to give. You say she loved you so much that she'd just close the bar entirely if you were sick? Then she'd burn this place to the ground before she'd let it hold you back. Don't confuse the gift with the impulse behind it."

"I can't," he says stonily.

"Well, if you refuse to change careers, maybe you just need to find fulfillment in something else."

He smirks. "You saying I should settle down?"

I laugh. Ever since I've known him, Beck has been someone without roots. No relationships; no permanence. "Fat chance. You're never with any female for more than five minutes."

"I last *way* longer than five minutes."

I grin. "Sure, that's what they all say."

He looks at me for a long moment. He doesn't speak and he doesn't need to—it's written all over his face: *He'd last way longer than five minutes.*

I gulp my water, waiting for this sharp burst of want to dissipate. Even the most happily married woman in the world has a hall pass list—the handful of men she'd sleep with if she could. My husband's best friend just happens, inconveniently, to be at the top of mine.

Our steaks are delivered, and the smell alone has my mouth watering. My eyes fall closed as I pop the first bite in my mouth —it's the closest thing to ecstasy I've felt in a long time.

"Mmmm, Beck," I say as I swallow. "I haven't had a good steak in ages."

I open my eyes. His gaze is on my face while he runs a thumb over his lower lip. "Do you always moan like that over a piece of meat?"

I laugh. "*Good* meat, sure."

"Maybe you've been barking up the wrong tree in finance," he mutters, sawing at his steak with unnecessary force. "Only-Fans might have something for you. In the meantime, try moaning a little less while you eat."

I hide my smile.

Maybe I'm on Beck's hall pass list too.

15

KATE

The next few days in Beck's office go much like the first. The work is tedious and definitely not what I went to grad school for, but it's good to use my brain again, and it's good to do something for Beck, who never allows anyone to help him.

I force him to buy a new laptop and get him set up with an online accounting program, something his future bookkeeper will require anyway.

"I can only submit amended returns for the past three years, by the way," I tell him as I navigate to the correct page. "You might want to double up your workouts so you can defend yourself in prison just in case."

He raises a brow. "I'm pretty sure I can already defend myself in prison. You *are* joking, right?"

"You're not going to prison." He'll be very lucky if I can find enough deductions that he doesn't get slaughtered in back taxes and penalties, but I'll save that news for later. "I just wish you hadn't let it all go for so long."

"I don't have any fucking time. You've seen what my life is

like. I'm always at the bar. I also have no fucking interest in dealing with accounting programs."

"Eventually you'll have a bookkeeper doing most of this. Right now, I just need you to set up a password for yourself."

He shoves a hand through his hair as I open the page for him. "Can't you just do it? I just use the same password for everything."

I glance at him over my shoulder with a sigh. "Don't give your passwords out, especially not to your bank information. Especially not to an *addict,* for God's sake."

His gaze rests on my face. "I trust you, Kate."

I swallow around the ache in my throat. It's been a very long time since anyone ever even *implied* they trusted me, much less said it aloud.

"You shouldn't." I rise from the seat and usher him into my spot. "Just enter your password in this box, and click submit."

I cross the room and wait for him to finish. His jaw is grinding the entire time, as if what I said pissed him off.

"Done," he says, stalking out of the office without waiting for my response.

I roll my eyes at his departing back. I have no idea what he's so angry about—I did him a favor by warning him not to trust me. Anyone who looked at my track record, and what I did to both Caleb and myself, would agree. Beck's the last person in the world I'd want to hurt, but that doesn't mean I won't do it.

His irritation, fortunately, seems to have vanished by lunchtime when he comes back to get me, the way he always does. And that group of women who come in for lunch still wave at him like children instead of grown fucking adults and insist he come over.

"You can't keep ignoring us!" cries the blond ringleader.

He glances at me and takes a single, reluctant step toward them.

"How's that bike of yours?" she asks coyly, tipping her head.

She's employing a Southern drawl, one that sounds deeply fake. I close my eyes so they won't witness me rolling them.

"Still running." His smile is polite and nothing more. He glances my way again, perhaps to remind her he was in the middle of something. She either doesn't notice or doesn't care.

"Talk to me," she coos. "How's life?"

This bitch can't take a hint.

"Can't complain," he says gruffly.

He starts to back away and she reaches out a hand to stop him, grasping his bicep. "Beck, stay. Come *talk* to us."

I've had it. I step forward, but Beck's already gently pulling from her grasp. "On my way to lunch," he says, looking pointedly to where I stand, "but thanks for coming in."

He walks over to me and places a hand at the small of my back to guide me away. "You should ban them," I mutter under my breath, shooting them a disdainful glance over my shoulder.

His mouth twitches. "And why would I keep paying customers out of my bar, O Financial Genius?"

I frown at him as he pulls out a chair for me on the deck. "They treat you like a piece of meat. Do you *enjoy* being objectified?"

He looks oddly pleased by my tirade. His mouth actually curves fully, if only to one side. "I'm a guy, Kate. I love being objectified. That's living the dream."

I flip the menu open with unnecessary force, holding it in front of my face. "You should get a new dream. One that doesn't suck."

There's a quiet laugh from his side of the table. I have no idea why he's enjoying this as much as he is. I'm sure not.

"You have plans tonight?" he asks.

"Yeah, me and the girls are going to happy hour, then we may go clubbing."

"Smartass," he says, balling up a napkin. I dodge and it still hits me. "I was thinking about what you said the other night, about being scared to do anything because you don't know what will end up being a bad idea. You need to start doing stuff."

I raise a brow. "Like what, Beck? You're the only friend I have now, and you're always working."

"I'll take off tonight. You need to get out a little."

I tear apart a roll from the basket in the table's center. "You don't have to do that. Judging by how many girls I saw you leave with back in the day, I assume I'm already cutting into your— well, I'm not going to call it 'dating,' but whatever it is. And as I recall, you start getting cranky if you go for more than twenty-four hours without it."

He chuckles, a low laugh I'm not sure he even means for me to hear. "I assure you I'm still not going long without it."

My stomach tightens. I've got no business being bothered by that, but I am, just a little. "Gross. That's more than I need to know."

"I just don't want you worrying about my *needs*," he says. "I wouldn't take off work if I didn't want to. So let's try something small. We can just eat dinner out. Baby steps."

I offer an ambivalent shrug.

But I smile as I raise my menu again.

HE GETS HOME AROUND SEVEN, appraising me in that way of his.

Tonight, I went for the rocker chick look—tall black boots, tiny skirt, leather jacket. It was never Caleb's favorite style, but it was Beck's. I quietly relish his obvious approval, even if I shouldn't.

"It's kind of far," he says. He hands me a helmet, a challenge in his eyes.

"I'm not scared."

His gaze lands on my mouth for a moment, lingers before he turns and walks out to his bike. "Figured you'd say that."

The ride takes us nearly a half hour, a half hour in which my heart speeds then soars as we skirt around cars and take corners too fast. I probably should be terrified, but I feel safe with him.

"Do I have helmet hair?" I ask as I step off the bike.

His gaze sweeps over me. "You've got eighties rock video hair. You look like you should be slithering naked over someone's Ferrari."

I raise a brow as he turns toward the restaurant. "It's a *good* thing, Evil Queen," he says.

I fight a smile. "I'm fine with being the evil queen as long as I'm the *hot* evil queen."

"Mission accomplished," he mutters, holding the door.

Inside, the restaurant is surprisingly nice—floor-to-ceiling windows, candlelight. It's the first not-fast-food place I've entered in at least eight months, other than the bar, which is weird even to me. I lost a huge swath of my life to drugs, and a huge swath of it recovering from them. Who goes nearly a full year without entering a restaurant?

I don't want to lose any more of it. I really, really don't.

Our waitress asks if we'd like a drink. I order a soda and Beck asks for water when I know he wants bourbon.

Ugh.

"You can drink, you know," I grumble. "I'm not some kind of vampire who can't help myself. Drinking isn't even my issue."

He studies me. "We have a thirty-minute drive home over a very windy, narrow road, and I'm the one responsible for getting us there in one piece. *That's* why I'm not drinking."

"You could still have a drink. I mean . . ." I gesture in his direction, "you're massive."

"If anything happened to you," he replies, his voice low and gravelly, "I would never forgive myself."

My heart gives a hard thud. That's Beck in a nutshell. He lives alone and does his best to eschew any connection to another human being, but he cares more about *me* than anyone else ever has, even Caleb. I'm not sure why that care of his sort of hurts, why I have to stare at the menu and act as if I haven't heard him.

"I want the steak. I want the Chicken Milanese. I want the pot pie. I'm never going to be able to choose."

"Pick one and I'll get the other so you can try it," he says. "And then I'll end up eating all of mine and take half of yours."

There's a hint of a sly smile on his face. Between my legs, something flutters in response, and I struggle to shut it down.

"I wouldn't suggest that. I got kicked out of one foster house for putting a fork in someone's hand during that exact scenario."

I expect Beck to laugh, or at least mutter about me being evil. Instead, an unhappy muscle flickers in his cheek. "I'm sorry that happened."

"I'm not," I reply cheerfully. "I got foster-home famous from that. No one ever tried to take my food again."

He doesn't laugh the way I'd hoped, but he gives me that partial smile of his—the one that says he'll play along. "To be honest, that sounds pretty mild for you. I'm kinda surprised you're not foster-home famous for something worse."

I laugh, grateful once more. I love that Beck does his best not to act like I'm some object of pity, even when he'd clearly like to.

We eat in easy silence because I don't need to impress him or win him over and he doesn't need to impress me either. He's okay with me exactly as I am, something I don't think I've ever had with anyone else. From the outside, I'd say that sounds boring. Sitting here across from him, though, it's simply a relief.

When the meal ends, the waitress clears our plates and he tips back in his chair.

"So," he asks, "was it enough?"

My head tilts. "Enough *food*?"

"Enough everything."

Am I happy enough, without dancing, drinking, drugs? Am I happy enough without the insanity? I'm silent—not because I don't know the answer, but because I'm surprised by it.

"It was." I meet his eye. I'm never particularly earnest, so I want him to understand that I mean what I say for once. "This has been a perfect night."

"Good." It's only when he holds my gaze for an extra moment, when my heart starts to flutter like a warning, that I need to look away.

I go to the bathroom before we leave. He's waiting in the lobby when I return, watching me cut through the bar as if I'm precious to him.

When was the last time someone worried about me? When was the last time someone watched me everywhere I went because it mattered whether or not I made it safely? Who even *wants* me to win aside from him? I start to smile just as a hand grabs my bicep.

I round on the owner of that hand, a spike of irritation surging through my chest. The guy is sitting on a barstool in an expensive suit and grinning as if this move is a harmless flirtation.

If I had a fork on me, I'd show him just how harmless I find it.

"You've got about five seconds to let go of my arm," I warn him.

"Let me buy you a drink."

This piece of shit *deserves* that fork to the hand. "I don't want a drink. Now you have two seconds."

"Come on," he croons, with what I'm sure he thinks is a winning smile. "You've got—"

His words are cut off by a large hand wrapped around his throat.

"Touch her like that again," Beck says, his voice quiet and lethal, "and I'll break every fucking bone in your body."

The violence, the suddenness of it, shocks me. But the goose bumps climbing up the back of my arms aren't from fear and neither is that stab of want in my gut.

I'm strung too tight, an instrument that might snap with a single pluck.

Maybe it's just been too long since I had a good pluck.

And Jesus Christ, I'd like Beck to provide one.

Beck releases him with a shove and the guy pitches backward over his seat. He's still on the ground, shouting, when Beck begins leading me away with his hand at the small of my back.

"I wasn't going to accept his offer," I tell him once we get outside.

He's got that familiar sneer on his face. It's dead hot even during moments when I'm *not* already turned on. "I know you weren't."

"Then why didn't you just let me—"

"Because no one touches you, Kate, without your permission. No one." He squeezes his eyes shut and pinches the bridge of his nose. "Let's just go, okay?"

I'm stunned into silence as we climb on the bike.

He defended me. He defended me as if his life depended on it, in a way even Caleb never did—as if I mattered to him more than anything in the world. I have no way to adequately thank him for his misguided, undeserved care, so instead I just nestle into his back more tightly.

Whoever he winds up with is the luckiest female in the fucking world. Men like him come by once in a lifetime.

16

KATE

The next morning, Beck emerges from his room fully dressed and more alert than normal. "Do you know how to fire a gun?"

I laugh as I pour his coffee. "A *gun*? Why would I need to fire a gun?"

His body is entirely still aside from those assessing eyes of his. "I don't like the fact that you're out here alone at night."

I shrug. "You're usually home by one or two at the latest. Besides, I thought you said no one ever came out here."

His jaw shifts, the hollow beneath his cheekbone going in and out again like the single beat of a heart. "No one *did*. But you draw attention."

I narrow my eyes as I slide him a plate of pancakes. I'm not sure what he's trying to imply, but I'm certain I don't like it. "Attention from whom? I spend the bulk of my day alone in your windowless office. I promise you, my daily jaunt to the grocery store involves no nudity or lap dances whatsoever. I don't even speak."

"You don't have to speak," he says, once he's swallowed his

first bite. "You draw attention just by existing. And not always from people you want noticing you. Like the guy last night."

I drop the pan in the sink. "He was just a guy, Beck. A stupid, overconfident guy who was taking his shot. That happens to everyone."

"But it happens more to you. What if he'd followed you home?"

I laugh. "I wish him luck with the way you drive."

"Don't act like it hasn't happened before." His jaw is tight. "Remember that guy a couple years ago? The security guard who followed you home after work?"

I vaguely recall this. "That happened once. As soon as he realized I was married, he disappeared."

"He didn't *disappear*, Kate. Caleb and I took care of him."

I try to remember if I ever saw that guy at work again. "Took *care* of him? You didn't...kill him, right?"

He laughs, a low rumble that starts in his chest and then fills the air. It's such a rare sound that I smile involuntarily. "You seriously think Caleb and I would *kill* someone?"

You would. After your reaction last night, I can't believe you're even asking the question. "Well, in mafia movies, when they say someone was *taken care of*, that's what they mean."

He shakes his head, still laughing. "You haven't answered me. Do you know how to fire a gun?"

"No, and I don't want to know. What if I flip out because I hear a noise and accidentally shoot you?"

A smirk hovers around his lips. "I'm assuming your aim won't be that good."

I agree, but still give him the finger. "No. No guns."

"You should take a self-defense class then. You need to be able to defend yourself anyway. Everyone should."

"I'm tough. If anyone laid a finger on me, I'd stab him in the eye with my keys."

I turn to tie off the garbage. He comes around the counter

and reaches out as if he's going to take it from me, but pulls my forearm instead. In the second it takes me to gasp, he's turned me, my back pressed to his front, his arm wrapped tight around my neck. Shock gives way to anger and to something else as well—something I intend to ignore. The trash falls from my hand. "What the *fuck*, Beck?"

His mouth rests near my ear, his breath rustling the nerve endings there, making heat pool in my stomach and sink lower. "*That fast*, Kate. It could happen that fast. Go ahead. Show me how tough you are."

I struggle against him, but he's got me held so tight I might as well be frozen. His skin is warm, his body immense and solid. My knees want to buckle in response. "Let go."

"Come on. I want to know what you're going to do, since you're so tough. How do you plan to stab me? Where are your *keys?*"

Jesus Christ. What's wrong with me that I find this so hot? If his arm slid from my neck to my breasts right now, he'd realize *exactly* how hot I find this. I bet if I squirmed a little against the bulge pressed to my lower back, I'd make *him* realize how hot this is too. "Okay," I snap. "You've made your point."

He releases me and I spin toward him, scowling. His eyes drift, for half a second, to what is very obvious given that I'm wearing a T-shirt and no bra. And then he grabs the trash and his helmet and stalks off without a word.

I slap a hand to my face and groan after the door shuts. *How humiliating.* It was okay when it was just me, fantasizing about Beck inside my own head. It's another thing entirely for him to know I'm doing it.

But...I'm not going to be stopping anytime soon either.

I can still almost feel the heat of him behind me, his absolute control. I'm used to calling the shots, but I suspect that with Beck, I wouldn't be.

I like the idea way too much.

~

HE'S NOT behind the bar or in the office when I get in. That's probably for the best. And when he doesn't come back to get me for lunch, I decide I'd rather starve than go out in search of him as if I did something wrong. They were nipples, for Christ's sake. They respond to loads of things—he can't say for sure it was him.

At five, I grab my laptop and purse and walk out. Though he's still in the wrong and I'm not, I'm hoping I can persuade him to come home early so we can watch *Game of Thrones*, a peace offering of sorts.

He's behind the bar, standing in front of a woman who's clearly mid-story, her arms wide as she gestures.

He's nodding, engrossed. I can't hear what he says in response, but it's clearly not his typical monosyllabic grunt of an answer. It's thought-out, his brow furrowed in concern. And I probably wouldn't think a thing of it if the woman didn't look like she was on her way to a *Playboy* shoot. She's beautiful and curvy in the ways I'm not, with lush blonde hair that falls abundantly past her rib cage.

Suzanne.

I remember meeting her once, long ago. She's one of several women Beck has been entangled with at some point . . . and apparently still is. I can't take a full breath, and I'm not sure why. He can fuck whoever he wants.

I walk straight to the exit with discontent scraping the inside of my chest, and pull out my phone when I get to the car.

Lucie is not a frequent poster, but today is the exception. She's uploaded a carousel of pictures of her kids at the beach with Caleb beside them. He never made it to a single goddamn sonogram, but now he's taking time off work to build fucking sandcastles?

I slam the phone against the steering wheel.

I hate that she has my husband. I hate that she's giving him what I didn't. I hate that she didn't just get one kid but *two*. Her profile picture is all dimpled smile, as if she's made of sugar and rainbows, when in actuality, she's the person who stole my entire world.

Fuck it. It is, according to Kayleigh, #TimeToGetMy-DowndogOn.

We haven't progressed far in our friendship, but one of us always manages to take a potshot at Lucie before we breathe out stress and breathe in peace. I've built the necessary foundation to move this shit forward, and today's the day.

"You want to get coffee afterward?" I ask Kayleigh an hour later, unrolling a mat beside hers. "Mountain Brew does the prettiest cappuccinos."

Everything about Mountain Brew annoys me. The coffee isn't good, and they've got all this outrageously priced, spectacularly shitty "local art" on the walls, as if Elliott Springs is just rife with people in the market for a ten-thousand-dollar watercolor of a gas station. They *deserve* to be run out of town by a huge conglomerate. I need to write Starbucks again, suggesting it.

"I love that place," she says.

I already knew this, of course. She tags them so often on Instagram, she must be on their payroll.

We walk down the street after yoga, and Kayleigh gets checked out as often as I do. It needles me, this reminder that Kayleigh is beautiful, that Kayleigh is the kind of woman men want, yet Caleb still chose Lucie of the perky ponytail and *"look at my twins being cute!"* social media posts.

We get coffee and tuck ourselves into a table at the back to bond. The simple fact that Kayleigh loathes Lucie makes *my* loathing feel justified, righteous.

Lucie is a bad person. She stole my husband. She got Kayleigh fired. She deserves what's coming to her.

"I'd love to get her back," Kayleigh says. "I just have no idea how."

Delight tiptoes through my chest. *Yes. This is what I've been waiting for.*

"Do you still have friends there? Someone who hates Lucie?"

She nods. "Yeah, but what good is that?"

I smile, tapping my lip. "I don't know yet. But I'll figure it out."

If Beck was watching, he'd make some evil queen comment and I'd laugh.

On second thought, if Beck was watching, he'd just be very disappointed in me. And fuck Beck, anyway. I'm disappointed in him too.

17

BECK

My mother's love for me was legendary. Her friends still mention the way she showed off pictures and reports cards and trophies to anyone in her vicinity. I couldn't enter the room without her trying to feed me or hug me or ruffle my hair.

I dropped out of school when she was dying. Her last words to me—slurred by pain and the steady drip of morphine, too detached to realize she was in a hospital—were, "*Let me make you something to eat.*"

Her bias toward me was legendary as well. Heaven help the teacher who sent home a critical note, or any bar patron who suggested I took after my piece-of-shit dad. She thought I could do no wrong, but even she wouldn't approve of what's happening here, between me and my best friend's wife.

I go to the backyard and work out longer and harder than usual, dragging a weighted sled across the yard, my head too full of thoughts I need to be rid of. I chop wood, dig a hole and refill it, carry sandbags from one end of the yard to the other.

But the moment I stop, I'm remembering the incident in the

kitchen—her tight against me, my mouth so fucking close to her ear, her ass pressed to my cock, our breathing erratic.

She will never fucking admit it, but she wants me too. She doesn't even *have* to admit it. I saw the goose bumps climbing over her neck when I grabbed her. I saw her nipples turn diamond-hard in a second flat. Jesus, the things I'd have done to her in that moment if she'd just fucking let me. And that's the problem here...I keep hoping she will.

I really need it to stop. I just don't know how.

EARLY SATURDAY MORNING, on four hours of sleep, I meet Liam and Harrison at Long Point to surf. Once upon a time, this was a daily event and required no communication at all. Now multiple texts are exchanged and several alterations are made to the plan, which starts late because I was at the bar until two and will end early because Harrison has to get into work. I'm still waiting for the part of adulthood that lives up to the hype.

It's seven by the time we're in the water. We're no longer here enough for anyone to consider us locals and the teenage punks at the break are already getting territorial as we start to paddle out.

"We've turned into the old guys we used to hate," I grouse.

"Yeah, and just like the old guys we used to hate, I have no problem beating the shit out of anyone who gets in my way," Liam replies.

I groan. Being six-five means I don't get in a lot of fights, but they go pretty fucking badly for the other guy if I do. "Don't get us in a fight, dude," I reply, glancing back at him as my arm does a long sweep through the water. "Harrison can't bail us out of jail if he's in there with us."

"From what I hear, you're the only one of us I might be

bailing out of jail," Harrison says with a quiet laugh, catching up on my right. "Heard you and Caleb got into it pretty bad."

I raise a brow. Harrison's a good guy—he's kept a lot of shit to himself, on my behalf—but I'm not in the mood for a lecture.

"Don't," I warn.

"I hope you know what you're doing," he says. "That situation...is tough. And no woman is worth losing friends over."

"You wouldn't be willing to lose friends over Audrey?"

He frowns, the only sign of his discomfort. "She's my wife. That's different."

"And he's already about to lose friends over his wife," Liam chimes in. He glances at Harrison. "Tell Beck about the move."

"Nothing's certain yet," Harrison says, frowning at Liam before he turns to me.

"Audrey was offered a job in London. She's talking about going out in January, right after the holidays. She'd stay for a few months, make sure it's a good fit, and then I'd join her."

My brow furrows with the effort to hold back what I'd really like to say, which is *why the fuck would you move to London for her? You two are miserable together. I bet you haven't gotten laid in a year.*

"What about your job? And you just bought the beach house."

He looks away. "We'd rent the houses for a year and see how things go, I guess. And it would be pretty easy to find work there."

"Bro," Liam groans. "I'm going to be blunt: if you're not happy together here, what makes you think you'd be happy together *there*?"

There's the briefest clench of Harrison's jaw as he swallows down what he really thinks. He's a loyal guy—no matter how miserable she makes him, he's not going to say a word against her.

"She moved out here for me even though she hates California. She deserves to feel like she's *home* when we start a family."

I'm about to point out that Audrey isn't from London, so that's not home either, but I get distracted by the thought of Kate, back at my place, sleeping on a mattress on the floor. That can't feel much like home either.

"You really think she's going to be ready to start a family if she's just changed jobs?" asks Liam, which is a fair point. And kids bring a lot of great things to your life, but they aren't known for their ability to fix a broken marriage.

Who the hell am I to comment on his stupid decisions, though? I'm letting myself get sucked in a little more every day by a woman I will never, ever fucking have—and I don't plan to stop.

It doesn't get much stupider than that.

18

KATE

Breakfast on Saturday, my day off, is a new creation: egg quesadillas. Even if it sucks, I'm sure Beck will eat it as if it's his last meal.

He regards me over the kitchen counter when he gets back from surfing, which seems to have released some of the tension that's lingered since the incident with the trash.

"How was it?" I ask as I flip a quesadilla. My arms hurt so much from yoga that I can barely hold the spatula in mid-air for more than thirty seconds. I need to make less of an effort there going forward.

"Good. Just wish we could have stayed longer. You have no idea how much I envy your day off," he says.

I glance over my shoulder. "If you refuse to sell the bar, hire someone to manage it and go do something else."

He frowns, running a hand through his hair. "I don't even know what I'd do instead."

I don't either. I can't really picture him doing anything else, perhaps because he's owned the bar since we met. "What were you studying in college when you dropped out?"

He hitches a shoulder. "Engineering. Surprised?"

My teeth sink into my lower lip. "I did picture it being something dumber."

He laughs, leaning back in his seat, stretching his endless limbs. He's impossible to insult. Or maybe he just doesn't give my opinion much weight. "It's fine. Engineering wouldn't have made me happy either."

"So if you didn't have the bar, what would you do?"

He runs a hand through his hair. "Something with exercise, probably. Anyway, I was thinking you might want some furniture."

My glance flickers to him. "Furniture?"

"Yeah," he says, "it's the stuff you use to put clothes in, to keep your mattress off the floor, etcetera."

Obviously, it would be nice not to sleep on the floor and move my clothes out of suitcases, but furniture makes it seem like I'm staying. "I wouldn't want you to do that just for me."

He does not like this answer. I'm not sure how I know this, given that his face doesn't move. I just do. "Though it might make you appear less suspicious and creepy when some local girl goes missing," I add.

He grins. "Suspicious and creepy?"

"The only thing keeping this house out of a horror movie is the lack of bloodstains on the floor."

"Why would there be bloodstains?" he asks. "Baking soda and hydrogen peroxide can get blood out of anything."

I laugh. "Well, there's the kind of statement that screams '*I'm innocent*' to the cops. Furniture would be great."

After he leaves for the bar, Ann calls. I've told her so many lies by now that it's hard to keep them all straight: I've told her I have a sponsor, I've told her I've gotten a real job instead of working at Beck's bar, and I've told her I've stopped focusing on Caleb.

The one thing I haven't lied to her about is Hannah's grave because I *can't* lie about that. It sickens me that I haven't gone, but I just can't take the risk.

"It's important, Kate," she says when I admit, once again, that it hasn't happened yet. "You're stronger now. It won't be like it was last year. You need to see that for yourself. It's why you left rehab, right?"

"Yeah," I admit with a sigh. "They really shouldn't make it so easy to leave."

Her laughter is quiet and slightly pained. "They don't make it easy, hon."

Maybe. But given how sneaky addicts are, they shouldn't make it quite so *obvious* the doors are left unlocked for the six AM shift change every morning.

"Fine. They don't make it hard enough to get out for someone who really *needs* to leave."

"We've discussed this—you didn't *need* to leave either."

I don't argue, because this is something no one understands —the way it ate at me every night, knowing Hannah's birthday was approaching and she'd spend it alone. Was Caleb going to go to her grave? Of course he wasn't. He hadn't been once since we buried her.

Except...going there broke me in ways I hadn't expected, and I had nowhere to turn. Caleb had already refused to see me again until I'd completed rehab. I guess I could have gone to Beck, but Kent felt like the easier answer, an answer that bled into weeks, then months.

If I go to her grave again, I know where I'll wind up.

"You're right," I tell Ann. "Yeah. I'll go."

So I guess I've now lied about every fucking thing possible. Because I'm not going to Hannah's grave yet. I'm better, but I'm not *that* much better.

～

BECK ARRIVES that afternoon with a truck full of furniture—bed, dresser, nightstand. Even a mirror.

"You need help?" I ask.

I'm rewarded with that smirk of his. "Kate, my hand could probably circle your bicep twice."

"If your hand can circle *anything* twice, you belong in a circus. Actually, if your hand can circle something twice, I'm not sure what you need a girl for. No one could compete with that."

I'm sure he wants to laugh, though he provides no visible sign of this. "Just hold the door."

He saves the biggest box for last, hoisting it overhead with his arms flexing, though he doesn't appear to be struggling in any way.

"I should take a picture of you lifting that," I say as he walks past. "For your fan club."

"What fan club?"

I blow out an irritated breath. "I've seen those girls you hook up with. They're the type who dig your whole half-man, half-beast thing, and you look like The Incredible Hulk at the moment."

He sets the box on the floor of the living room. "I'd rather be with a girl like that," he says pointedly, "than the kind who only wants a pretty boy in a suit, flashing his platinum card around."

I shoot him a look. I've never heard him criticize Caleb until now. "That's nothing like Caleb."

A muscle flickers in his cheek. "Sorry. I thought we were offering each other completely unfounded generalizations about our exes. And speaking of exes, are you going to sign the separation agreement?"

I start to ask how he even knows about that and then I remember. "You and your friends gossip like teenage girls."

"You didn't answer the question."

"I still need to get a lawyer to look it over," I reply. "I've got to make sure there's nothing crazy in there."

"Caleb would never in a million years put something crazy in there, and you know it. Lie to whoever else you want, but don't try to bullshit me too."

"Fine," I say, raising my chin. "I plan to drag ass on signing it for as long as humanly possible. I'm *married*. I'm not going to apologize to you or anyone else for the fact that I want to *remain* married."

He walks to the door, and then he turns back toward me. "Seriously, Kate. I don't understand you. You and Caleb weren't fucking soul mates. You were only together for one reason. Why can't you let this go?"

No, Caleb and I were not soul mates. Our relationship was based mostly on our shared love of sex. We didn't like the same music or have the same interests. He never entirely got me, and I didn't get him.

But then we were married, and I was so ridiculously, sickeningly happy. I'd give up my entire life to have a few more of those minutes, and those are minutes that can only exist if Caleb takes me back.

"If you'd ever loved anyone deeply," I snap, "I wouldn't have to explain it to you."

His jaw is set hard, but there's something sad in his eyes when he looks at me. "Yeah," he says, grabbing his helmet, "I guess you've nailed it, Kate."

I DON'T SEE him again all weekend and he's not at the bar when I arrive on Monday. I hate that what I said hurt him, but it's easier to be angry about the fact that he's been gone, so I focus on that.

I spend the morning waiting for him to come back to the

office. He can't avoid me forever. By one, when my stomach is growling and the tension is no longer bearable, I go in search of him and come to a shocked halt. He's already sitting at *our* table with another woman. I can tell, even from behind, that she's beautiful—her dark hair falls in soft curls, her delicate hands gesture in the air with the confidence of someone who doesn't get shot down. She's in heels and an *expensive* baby-blue suit, which has me glancing down at my own ensemble in dismay— the black skinny jeans and boots that seemed cool when I left the house now look like the choice of a fourteen-year-old girl rebelling against her mom.

I bet she's sweet and bubbly, something no one has suggested of me even once in my life—not when I was sober anyway. She's the kind of girl who'd probably make Beck smile, who might actually make him happy.

I hate her.

"Who's that with Beck?" I ask Mueller.

He glances toward the deck. "Rachel," he says casually, as if she's here often. I like this even less. "She's a friend of Beck's. She helps him with marketing for the bar sometimes."

Friend my ass. No one is *friends* with a girl who looks like that. Suzanne bothers me because she's simply not *worthy* of Beck, but Rachel might be. She's not a one-night-stand kind of girl—she's a move-in kind of girl. And I don't have to question her interest in Beck—you'd have to be *dead* not to be interested in him.

He reaches out a hand to help her to her feet—*when the fuck does Beck ever help a female to her feet?* I'm irrationally angry, but when she turns my way, everything inside me goes cold.

She's about seven months along, I'd guess. And for some bizarre reason, Beck's steering her right toward me.

"Rachel," he says, placing his hand at the small of her back, "this is Kate, who's helping me get our financial stuff in order. Kate, Rachel does some marketing for us."

Rachel seems to know exactly who I am already. She gives me a wide, sunny smile as she extends her hand. I accept it stiffly, trying not to stare at her stomach. "It's so nice to finally meet you," she says.

"You too," I mumble with far less enthusiasm. "I'm sure I'll see you around."

I return to the office. Beck follows me in a moment later, raising a brow.

"Looks like you told her all about me," I say, typing with unnecessary aggression.

He leans against the wall. "I didn't even mention you. But Caleb is one of her husband's investors, so maybe he has."

I sigh. "Great. One more person in this town to treat me like I run a prostitution ring just because of my past."

"She was perfectly nice to you. You'd actually like her if you gave her a chance, and you could use a friend or two."

I glare at him. "I don't need friends."

His nostrils flare. "Good to know."

He walks out, letting the door slam behind him, and I pick up my phone.

Today, Lucie has posted a picture of herself holding the twins as newborns. She has that drowsy, dreamy look on her face, the kind universal to new mothers. There's a little bundle under each arm, both wrapped tight in hospital blankets, their mouths puckered in sleep. My heart twists, then splinters. God, I fucking hate her.

"Can you believe these two are about to be in first grade?!!!" she asks.

Everyone seems to have these vast stores of sympathy for Lucie because she was married to a dick. Do they realize how much she has in its place, though? She's got a job, she's got my husband, she's got those kids...it's *bullshit*.

I wasn't planning to go to yoga, but sacrifices must be made.

"This is what we do," I tell Kayleigh that evening, drinking another ridiculously overpriced post-yoga cappuccino. "Caleb still travels constantly for work, right?"

She hitches a shoulder. "He did when I was there. Lucie probably cried about that until he stopped."

I flick my hand in the air, dismissing her concern. "His job requires travel. He'd have to sell the company before that changed. So you find out where he's going, and then we start a rumor that he hooked up with someone during the trip. Lucie's super insecure, clearly. This will tip her over the edge."

Her nose scrunches. "I'm only friends with two people there. It's not like I can tell the whole company."

I wrap my hands around my coffee cup. "You won't need to. Tell your two friends—you said they hate her, right? I guarantee they each tell at least one other person, in theoretical secrecy, and so on. No human is capable of truly keeping a secret, especially with something like that. No one's even going to know where it started."

She shakes her head, dismissing it. Kayleigh's the sort that thinks she's smarter than everyone else but never has a fucking idea of her own. "They might tell each other, but it's never getting back to Lucie."

"Eventually, after a couple of these trips that everyone's talking about, someone's going to pull her aside and she'll understand what all those pitying looks were about. And if they don't, we'll make sure she gets an anonymous note."

She spins her plastic coffee lid under her index finger. "Lucie will just ask him and he'll deny it."

"Don't worry," I reply. "Get me his travel schedule. I'll make sure there's proof."

I drive home afterward and stop short at the sight of Beck's bike in front of the cabin. My pulse starts ticking, fast and light, the way it did as a child when I knew something was about to happen, and I wasn't sure if it would be good or bad.

Would he kick me out simply because I wasn't nice enough to his fucking friend? No, he wouldn't. But he might kick me out because he's tired of the incessant tension in his own home.

I'd kick me out, under the circumstances.

I climb the stairs warily and walk inside. His eyes land on me in my yoga attire and remain there a beat too long.

"I have an idea," he says, looking away. "The next step in your return to society."

I curl up on the couch, wrapping my arms around my knees. "So far, your ideas have involved me doing your taxes and searching for my deadbeat dad. So forgive the immediate lack of excitement."

"Infinite Zest is playing at The Midnight House tonight. And I can get tickets."

My eyes open wide.

Yes.

Wait. No.

God, I haven't seen a show in so long, and the mere idea of it makes my heart take flight. But I also associate concerts with a fair amount of drinking and at least a little something stronger. If it were anyone but Beck making the suggestion, I wouldn't even consider it.

Except...it *is* Beck.

"I'm not going to let anything happen to you," he adds.

I don't deserve him. No one does. "Yeah, I know."

I take a quick shower and emerge from the bathroom in black jeans and a low-cut tank. His gaze sweeps over me. He says not a word but somehow leaves me glad I made the effort.

We take his bike and park in front of the bar, exactly where he parked the first time I saw him years ago.

It's a moment I've returned to in my head again and again— me, leaning against a brick wall waiting for Caleb to return, Beck pulling off his helmet and taking me in as if I was something he intended to devour, sloppy and voracious and unrepentant.

He wasn't just hot—he was a black hole, absorbing the light around him until he was all I could see. The mere sight of him was enough to wipe my mind blank.

What would have happened if Caleb hadn't called my name at that exact moment? What if I'd crossed the street to Beck and said, *"Let's just go?"*

Occasionally, when things were bad with Caleb, and sometimes even when they were good, I wished I had.

Beck walks ahead of me and I follow. Inside, the opening act is just clearing the stage. We fight the crowd to reach the bar in the back, where I get a soda and he gets a beer.

"This is where I was sitting when we first met." I toy with my straw. "God, you hated me."

I loathed the visits here when Caleb and I began dating. It was Beck who noticed how bored I was, *Beck* who seemed to know exactly how dark I was on the inside and who'd frown at my jiggling knee like a parent giving his child a silent warning.

His mouth pulls down at the corner. "I didn't hate you." He sounds angry.

"Yeah, you did. You never thought I deserved Caleb. You had a sneer on your face from the instant you saw me, like you'd already decided I wasn't good enough."

"That's not what happened at all," he says. "And it was the first time we were *introduced*, but it wasn't the first time I saw you."

I frown. He's messing with our official history, the one we've always stood by. It's dangerous to start bringing up the truth now.

"It doesn't matter where we first saw each other," I tell him. "My point stands."

The lights dim, and Beck wraps his hand around my forearm, pulling me toward the floor. "And what point is that?" he asks over his shoulder, still keeping me close.

"That you were never nice to me once until I came back here, married. I guess you'd just given up hoping Caleb would change his mind."

"Yeah," he says, ushering me in front of him and wrapping himself around me as the crowd surges forward. "I guess I did. Except I wasn't waiting for him to change his mind. I was waiting for you to change yours."

My breath stops. The noise in the room is deafening, but I can't hear anything at all.

I was waiting for you to change yours.

I'm glad he can't see my face. I'm glad the room is dark and people are squeezing in around us, like water flowing between rocks, so he can't see how absolutely thrown I am by what he just said.

He was waiting for me to change my mind.

And I did. So did Caleb. We were ninety percent over when I found out I was pregnant. I'd rewrite that part of my story, later. Now I'm wondering how different my story could have been if it had taken place with Beck instead.

He pulls me tight to his chest as the crowd continues to push, closing in around me like a brick wall with his hands resting on my hips and the steady, patient beating of his heart just under the back of my head.

He's so big. So certain of himself. No one could feel endangered with Beck standing guard behind them, the way he is with me. You could drop me in the middle of a battlefield and I'd shrug as long as Beck was at my back, as illogical as that is.

The lights stay low as the band begins to play. The room is so dark and the music so loud that it makes my mind go to places I don't normally allow it to go—not with him so close anyway.

It's as if Beck and I temporarily exist in a space where there are no consequences. Where we could do anything we wanted and it wouldn't hurt our friendship or ruin my chances of getting back with Caleb.

We sway with the crowd. I'm held tight against him, and every single thing I've ever imagined doing to him pulses inside me, expanding until I contain nothing else.

If there were really no consequences, I'd want his hands to move from my hips. I'd want them to span my rib cage before trailing under my shirt. I'd reach behind me, my hand sliding into his waistband, and it would remain there until he shuddered against my palm, his groan hot against my ear.

I think of it throughout the entire goddamn show, and even as we ride home, I can't shake that want of mine. My arms are around his waist, and it's a struggle not to slide them lower, not to dig into his thighs, climb up, ask him if just once we could forget who we are entirely. By the time we pull to a stop in front of the house, I'm strung so tight my skin can't even contain me.

We walk inside, and each of us heads to our respective doors. God, just once I want to see that intense focus of his as he hovers above me, taking me in just the way he is now, his eyes burning a path, catching on my mouth.

If I crossed the distance between us, if neither of us spoke . . . could we wake and pretend it hadn't happened? I want it almost too badly to listen to any voices that argue against it. It's a siren singing in my ear, promising that one time never hurt anyone.

Beck might be the most tempting, dangerous drug I've ever considered trying.

My hands go to my neck the way they always do when I'm upset or anxious, as if that empty space is a cross, or a rabbit's foot. "Thanks for tonight."

"What happened to your locket?" he asks, staring at the spot where it should rest, where my hands even now still search.

"I lost it. I can't believe you remember that."

His eyes flicker over my face, dancing across my mouth one extra beat. "I remember everything," he replies, turning away.

I remain in place as his door closes behind him. I wish he hadn't left quite so fast.

19

KATE

When I wake in the morning, I'm dumbfounded by all the urges I had the night before, by how close I came to acting on them.

But it's not entirely behind us, either. When he walks inside from his workout, shirtless, gleaming with sweat, there's a sick twist of desire in my gut.

"Rachel's coming in today," Beck warns, pulling out a chair at the counter while I slide his breakfast in front of him. He gulps a scalding cup of coffee like it's ice water. "So try not to be a dick this time."

"I wasn't a dick," I mutter. "No more so than I usually am."

"That's plenty on its own," he replies just as my phone chimes.

It's probably Ann, but I check anyway. One of these mornings it will be Caleb, telling me he misses me. Telling me the world is too G-rated without me in it.

The message isn't from either of them.

UNKNOWN NUMBER

> Hi, Kate! This is Sarah Decker (it was Dow in college). I got your message on Facebook. Yes, I was roommates with your mom. I'm so sorry to hear she passed away. We lost touch after she left Berkeley, but she was a lot of fun.

I'm guessing there are many people who thought my mother was *a lot of fun*. Including, I suppose, my father . . . for a few minutes, anyway.

"What's up?" Beck asks.

"It's from my mom's college roommate," I reply, already typing a response.

> I'm actually trying to figure out who my father might be. She would have been pregnant by the time she left school. Do you know who she might have been dating?

> I don't remember her dating anyone specific. There was this professor she was obsessed with and possibly seeing, though for obvious reasons, she never gave me his name. He was in economics, maybe?

There's a whisper up my spine.

Economics. My major. It could be a coincidence, of course, but...it came so easily, felt so natural, was so consistently fascinating to me. Maybe it's not a coincidence.

Beck waits patiently until I finally glance his way. "My mom was spending a lot of time with some economics professor."

He frowns. "I wonder if you can still get her class schedule?"

I lean against the counter behind me, defeated already. It's a total crapshoot and even if they have her schedule, who's to say he's my father? My mom was, after all, '*a lot of fun*.' For all I know, she was even more fun than I was at my worst. Maybe she slept with the entire economics department.

"It seems like a waste of effort. I'm sure they haven't saved a schedule from 1995."

He narrows one eye. "A waste of effort or are you just getting uncomfortably close to the truth?"

"I'll just..." I shrug. "Maybe I'll take a DNA test."

He laughs. "Sometimes I can't tell if you're lying to me or lying to yourself. Just fucking call the school and ask."

I flip him off, but once he's gone, I reluctantly place the call. In a turn of events *no one* could have predicted, the woman who answers scoffs at my request.

"That was nearly three decades ago," she says. "You seriously think we keep students' schedules that long?"

I don't know if I'm disappointed or relieved. Both, I guess. There was always this possibility that my father was some great human being who didn't know I existed, who'd be thrilled to hear from me. The much greater possibility is that he's a scumbag who heard my mom was pregnant and disavowed all responsibility, especially if he was a professor sleeping with a student.

I walk into the bar, hoping to bury my head in numbers and forget the whole thing. I've got amended returns ready for two of three possible years, but there's so much more to be done. Beck's getting robbed blind by suppliers—it's as if he didn't even know he could negotiate—and he *should* be running a lot of expenses through the corporation instead of paying them on his own.

I walk into the office and discover Rachel at Beck's desk, with him in the chair across from hers.

I can't even see her baby bump, but I still want to walk straight out of the room. I'm jealous, yes, but mostly...I'm terrified. I want to warn her not to get her hopes up and tell her all the things that can go wrong, things they never even suggest in pregnancy books or Lamaze class, so she can watch for them. I want her to know that if she counts on the baby too much and it doesn't work out, she'll be so crushed she'll never fully recover.

It's crazy. It would be an awful thing to do. So I simply give her my least-encouraging smile and go to my desk.

Beck frowns—I guess he thinks that was dickish. He has no idea how much worse it could have been.

"Did you call Berkeley?" he asks, as if I really want to discuss my shitty background in front of perfect Rachel with her perfect pregnancy.

"No luck," I mutter.

He looks from me to her. "Kate's trying to get ahold of her mother's course schedule from college," he explains.

I shoot a glare his way and catch a twitch at the corner of his mouth. He's doing this *intentionally*. "She's trying to find her father," he continues, "and she thinks he may have been her mother's professor."

Even Rachel is narrowing her eyes at him. "Wow, Beck. Remind me not to tell you any of *my* family shit."

"I already know your family shit." He turns to me, grinning now. "Rachel's father just went to jail for his third DUI—he ran a family off the road on their way to church."

I shake my head. "You're such an . . ."

"*Asshole*," Rachel concludes before turning to me. "Anyway, did you ask the school for a list of faculty in that department during that year?"

I sigh. "They didn't seem particularly inclined to help. They wouldn't have it anyway, probably. It was years ago."

"Oh, they'll have it," she says, grabbing her phone and looking something up. She dials a number and puts the phone on speaker. "Hi," she says briskly when the line is picked up. "This is Rachel Brown with the *San Jose Business Journal*. We're doing a cover story on the incoming CEO of"—she scans the room, her gaze settling on a stack of printer paper—"Paper-source. He was discussing how influential one of his professors at Berkeley was and blanked on the name. We're wondering if you can help us out."

"Oh, of course," the woman replies. "What department and year?"

Rachel's eyes go wide and she looks to me for the answer.

"Economics," I whisper. "1994."

"Economics," she repeats. "1994."

"I'd have to do some research, but I may be able to send you a list of all the department faculty from that year," the woman says. "Would that help?"

Rachel grins at me after she's ended the call, then rests a hand on her stomach. "You didn't hear that, angel."

Ping. It's as if she's plucked a sharp string in my chest. I used to talk to Hannah that way too.

I swallow hard, forcing a smile. "I would not have expected you to be such a good little liar."

Beck rises. "I may have created a monster, introducing the two of you." He smiles at me quickly as he walks out the door and I smile back. Yes, he's an asshole, but he meant well. Which makes him a better person than me.

Rachel laughs quietly. "That's *messy.*"

I look around the office in confusion. My desk is neat as a pin. "What's messy?"

She leans back in her chair. "You know, the whole thing with him liking you while you're still married to his best friend."

"He doesn't like me. Not like that."

She rolls her eyes. "Oooookay. But just for the record, I'm not judging. I was engaged to someone else when I fell for Gus, who *was* my fiancé's best friend."

My mouth forms a small "O" of surprise. *And here I thought*

Rachel was so angelic. "That *is* messy. But that's not at all what's going on here."

She smiles again, but this time it's as if she knows something I don't.

20

BECK

Caleb called over the weekend and apologized for doubting my intentions—no doubt at Lucie's bidding. *"I know nothing would happen between you and Kate,"* he said. *"I overreacted."*

I accepted the apology, but as Kate walks into the bar on Monday, I'm reminded that *I'm* not the reason nothing has happened. I want her. I've always wanted her. And when she's having a good day—and today is quite clearly a good day—she's impossible to resist.

There's something in her eyes—the thing that caught me the first time I saw her—as if she's been lit up inside. That pretty little mouth of hers is soft, and she seems to have to fight to keep it from curving into a smile. She attempts to walk past me with an insouciant little wave. I'm not having it.

"Kate," I bark. "Come here."

She hitches a shoulder as she sashays to the bar and takes a seat at the counter. "It's a little early for drinks, but I'm game. Sex on the Beach sounds good. Of course, that's always good, come to think of it."

She fucking said it just to make me hard, and she succeeded.

I raise a brow. "We're all smiles this morning, I notice. What evil have you unleashed on the world today?"

"I ran a bus full of orphans off the road on the way here," she replies, "but I do that a lot."

"I wasn't aware Elliott Springs had that many orphans. And what else has happened?"

She smiles fully at last. "I got an interview with this company down in Santa Cruz—Zavatello. They import shit from India. I'll have to research them some more, but honestly, I don't care what they import as long as they're willing to hire me."

"Sex slaves? Heroin?"

She hitches a shoulder. "That's actually even better—no storefront and minimal advertising costs mean less overhead."

I laugh, but in my chest, something rises and dips like a roller coaster. I'm happy for her. I know she needs to move, but at the same time I wish she didn't have to. I like knowing she's a few feet away. I like having her waiting for me at night. I've spent years claiming to relish my independence only to discover that I'm entirely dependent on the sight of that long red hair splayed over one end of my couch, her feet tucking beneath my thigh when I sit, and her nonstop criticism of the battle strategy on *Game of Thrones*.

Having her around has proven how little I like my life without her. It's going to be hard to go back to what I had when she leaves.

"When's the interview?" I ask.

A shadow comes over her face. She stares at her nails. "Friday."

"What's wrong with Friday? That's five days from now. You've got plenty of time to get ready."

She swallows. "Yeah. I just need to get a haircut and shit."

I turn away, more irritated than I should be, but I wish to fucking God she'd stop lying all the time. Whatever problem she has with Friday, it's not about the haircut.

And I guess whatever problem I have with this situation . . . the lying is the least of it.

21

KATE

I'm able to get a haircut appointment that afternoon. When the stylist asks me what I want, I mean to tell her a bob—a nice *I'm a responsible adult* cut.

But then I picture Beck's gaze on me as I pulled off that helmet the other night. He's into the long red hair—not that it matters.

"Just a trim," I tell her. "An inch at most."

I'm tempted to look through the storage unit for my briefcase afterward, but decide against it. That unit has a siren's call for me not unlike the one I hear from Kent's house, and I'm never sure which call will be the one to send me crashing into the shore.

I head back to the bar afterward, eager to see Beck. I want to watch his gaze dart over my freshly blown-out hair, see that spark of desire in his eyes before he playfully grunts something about my life of leisure.

I'm halfway across the parking lot when a guy steps in my path—douchey hair sweeping over his brow and a smug, punchable face. He's got a flashy gold Rolex on his wrist and a calculating smile on his lips and I loathe him on sight.

I mostly loathe that he jumped in my path—if he knew me better, he'd realize that's a bad fucking idea.

"You're Kate, right?" he asks. He extends a hand. "I'm Jeremy Boudreau."

The name is familiar, but I don't want to stand here long enough to figure out why. I glance past him, to the bar. "Can I help you with something?"

"Your husband is sleeping with my wife." The words are crisp, angry. "So I thought we should have a little chat."

Lucie's husband.

He'd be a good resource in my battle to get Caleb back, but I resent the way he seems to be putting the blame for their union on me. "I can't imagine what there is to talk about."

"You came home hoping to reconcile, right?" he asks. "So we both want our spouses back, and two heads are better than one."

I don't like this guy, and I suspect getting to know him won't change that fact, but I'm not really in a position to turn away help and my own paltry efforts don't appear to be working. I was certain Caleb would tire of Lucie, that her small insecurities would go from fault lines to deep crevasses, but that's not happening.

So perhaps I've been working the wrong angle. Maybe instead of waiting for Caleb to tire of Lucie, I should have been waiting for Lucie to tire of *Caleb*. I love my husband, but he has his failings, especially for someone who wants—or already has —a family. I bet he's still spending long hours at the office and that she can't get him to sit through an entire movie without taking a work call or going on his laptop. When she finally gets him to take a day off, he insists on spending it on that boring fucking boat.

Maybe she's starting to see the grass isn't greener in Caleb's backyard, and if something about her husband appealed to her again and she could be persuaded to go back,

Caleb would have no reason to divorce me. Which means that, punchable face or not, Jeremy may just be my new best friend.

"Have you ever been to Mountain Brew?" I ask. "They make a nice cappuccino."

"Love that place. Nice art there too." His disingenuous smile is mistimed. He's not a great liar, but I appreciate his lack of ethics—it'll come in handy going forward.

I get back in my car and follow him down the hill to the busiest part of town. He swerves his Audi into the only spot near Mountain Brew and it takes me five minutes to hunt for a space. He's got a cappuccino waiting for me by the time I finally walk in. I accept it without thanking him—he should have given me the fucking parking spot.

"So," I say, grabbing two sugars and ripping them open, "I assume you have some dastardly plan to make our spouses break up?"

He hitches a shoulder. "I'm batting some ideas around. What was your plan?"

"My plan is to wait until he gets sick of her."

"Have you seen them together?" he asks. "Because if you had, you'd know that your plan blows. He was after Lucie from the minute she moved next door to him."

There's a bitter taste in my mouth. I'm not sure if it's jealousy or just anger that my dream was slipping away long before I realized it. "So what's your big plan there, *Ocean's 11*? And why do you want her back anyway? I heard the reason she left is because you were cheating."

He sighs. "Don't believe everything you hear. Lucie has been playing the victim card to the hilt."

I'd love to believe the worst about his wife—and I generally *do* believe the worst, if the worst is that Lucie is weak and ineffectual and someone lacking even minimal raw intellect—but I have a deep, inexplicable distrust of this guy that makes me want answers. "That still doesn't explain why you want her back."

"She made mistakes, and I made mistakes. I'm willing to own my part in it even if she can't own hers. But the important thing is our kids. We need to put them first. For their sake, if nothing else, I'm willing to leave the past in the past. This would have ended months ago if your husband wasn't so hell-bent on making *my* family his."

Is that what this is? Is Caleb only with her because he's trying to recreate what we lost? In spite of the fact that Jeremy's words sound rehearsed, they also resonate.

"You need to make him dislike her," I reply. "Caleb despises weakness. If Lucie thinks he's cheating, she'll get suspicious and clingy, and the more he argues, the more she'll wonder."

He pushes his coffee away from him. "And how do I do that?"

I lean back in my seat, chewing on the stir straw from my cappuccino. The more people I bring into Operation Screw Lucie, the higher the odds are that someone will spill all of it. Jeremy could rush off and tell Lucie and Caleb everything—he's definitely someone who would throw me under the bus when he no longer had a use for me—but right now, he needs an ally, and I'm all he has.

Plus, I could really use someone to *fund* my plans.

"Caleb's going to Miami for work on the twentieth," I tell him, sharing the intel I got from Kayleigh. "Hire someone to photograph him walking through security."

"What the fuck?" he asks. "What good would that do?"

I don't trust Jeremy enough to spell everything out. "I assure you they'll be interesting pictures."

He studies me for a long moment. Whatever he finds, he appears to be satisfied with it. "Get me the flight info," he says. "I'll take care of the rest."

I'm not as relieved by his agreement as I'd have expected to be.

BECK'S BIKE is in front of the house when I pull up, though it's far too early for him to be home for the day.

Why is he always home early when I've done something wrong?

Maybe I'm just doing something wrong more often than I'd like to believe.

I open the door to find him waiting on the couch—legs apart, elbows resting on his thighs, his jaw set hard. Only his head moves toward me, and he sears me with a glance.

He's so angry that even I, someone never scared by Beck, am scared by Beck...and that pisses me off. I spent my entire fucking childhood scared of what I'd find at whatever "home" I was in at the end of the day. I've come too far to cower now.

"What the fuck are you doing, Kate?" he hisses.

I ignore him, walking toward the kitchen. "Well, I was planning to collapse on the couch, but you're once again taking up all the space. You really need some more furniture."

In a breath he's on his feet, blocking me, and my heart explodes in my chest. *I guess I'm not done cowering after all.*

"Did you just go out with Jeremy Boudreau?"

Jesus Christ. It was a half hour at most. This is why I hate small towns.

I brush past him to drop my purse on the counter. "I didn't 'go out' with him. We got coffee. And since when is it any of your business? Are you not only my boss and my roommate but my *father* now too?"

"It's my business because there are only two possible reasons you're getting coffee with that asshat, and both of them suck."

I round on him. "Let me see if I've got this straight: it's okay for you to hang out at your bar, see all your friends, go off with that little slut who's always there when I leave, but the only friend I'm allowed to have is *you?* It's taken nearly two months for anyone else in this town to even *speak* to me, and you're telling me to stay away from him."

His nostrils flare. "You have a number of flaws, but stupidity isn't one of them. He does not want to be your *friend,* and you know it. If it wasn't about Lucie, then he's trying to get in your pants."

I shrug. "Maybe I should let him. Seems only fitting since his ex and mine are doing the same."

He's got me pressed to the wall so fast that there's barely time for me to gasp. His breath is coming fast, but when our eyes meet, it's not rage there...not entirely. He wants to kiss me. He's *going* to kiss me.

And I want it so badly I can already feel it on my lips. I can already feel his beard abrading my skin and the weight of him as he leans against me. Everything inside me grows soft and pliant, experiencing the moment before it's even begun.

His nostrils flare. "Fuck," he hisses, pushing away and walking out of the house.

I slump, letting my head fall backward, closing my eyes so I can picture it: that breathless half-second of waiting for his mouth to descend. The desire is so pointed it's painful, jabbing into my gut like a small knife.

For the rest of the night, I can't feel anything else, and I'm not thinking about anyone else.

Not even my husband.

～

THE SLAMMING doors when he comes home the next morning warn me that he's not here to apologize. I remain in my room because I'm sure as hell not planning on an apology either.

He isn't behind the bar when I get into work, and he's busy when I leave for the day—chatting to customers, not a care in the world.

My simmering anger fires into a boil as I climb into my car.

At home, I iron my suit for tomorrow's interview, then watch the next episode of *Game of Thrones* just to spite him. Halfway through, I turn it off and fling the remote onto the coffee table. It slides off the other end and hits the floor, its batteries rolling in different directions.

How dare he? I did nothing wrong, as far as he knows, but he still held me against the wall. How fucking dare he? So much for his whole "*no one touches you without your permission, Kate*" thing.

The fact that I *was* actually doing something wrong is completely irrelevant, as is the fact that I liked the way he held me against the wall.

I snatch the batteries off the floor and throw them onto the coffee table.

I'm allowed to have friends who aren't him. I'm allowed to date. And he can pretend otherwise, but I'd stake my life on the fact that he wanted to kiss me. Badly. He wanted it every bit as much as I did.

"I don't need this shit right now!" I yell to the empty cabin walls as one of the batteries rolls back to the floor. "I really don't!"

It's not entirely about him. It has far more to do with the interview and what tomorrow reminds me of. But it shouldn't be about him at all, and it is.

When I wake the next day on very little sleep, I remain in my room, waiting until the door slams and his motorcycle roars away before I emerge to shower.

I go through all the motions of getting ready, but it still seems as if my head is in the wrong place. It was always going to be in the wrong place, though, whether I'd fought with Beck or not.

No tragedy has a single anniversary, not when you're the reason it happened. Because there are all the times preceding it when you could have chosen differently, all the times when you took a path and it turned out to be the wrong one.

Almost every month of the year holds some small tragedy, but this month...it holds the most, and those anniversaries seem to hurt more now rather than less.

Time heals all wounds, people say, but mine simply fester.

Today's tragedy has a photo marking the date. I couldn't forget it if I wanted to. *August 18, 2020*, it reads, beneath a picture of Hannah in utero. The profile of her face is crystal clear. She is sucking her thumb.

It was the day my doctor suggested a scheduled caesarian— not because Hannah was breach, not because there was any kind of problem, but because Caleb and I worked so much. *"Women in your position sometimes prefer that,"* she said, *"simply for planning purposes."*

I turned her down and called Caleb immediately afterward, stunned by how unethical the suggestion was. But what if I'd said, *"You know best"*? What if I'd said, *"That's really thoughtful of you, and yes, actually, it would be nice to know my water isn't going to break in the middle of a meeting"*?

If I hadn't been so goddamn sure I was smarter than everyone else, my daughter would be approaching her third birthday right now. I'd be planning her party and giving her all the things I'd promised her while I was pregnant. God, I made her so many promises back then.

Caleb was always gone, but it didn't matter. I'd sit in the nursery Beck had helped me decorate, swaying in the white painted chair I'd already bought her, and dream of bringing her home, of the weight of her in my arms and the way she'd really be mine, something no one could take from me. I was going to give her every single thing I hadn't had.

Camping at Shelter Cove. Christmas in Hawaii. Dance classes. Tennis lessons.

I guess, really, I was just promising her the same future Mimi had laid out for us, the life she said we'd have after I started at my new school. How fucking pathetic that all I could offer my daughter were the same lies some bitch offered me.

When I tuck the photo into my purse as I walk out the door, it's not because I hope it will bring me luck. It's just a reminder that no matter how badly today goes, I deserve worse.

ZAVATELLO IS LOCATED in San Jose. It's not a great commute back to where Caleb's living now, it's manageable.

I park in a garage and walk through the green space between the buildings while all the office dwellers walk briskly by—phones in their right hand, coffee in their left. Yes, people are getting shit done here, and even if it's not my dream job, it's an opportunity. A place where I can prove I'm okay again.

I wait in the lobby until my name is called, and then I'm taken to a corner office similar to the last one I had.

The man behind the desk rises. He's middle-aged, big and doughy, like a former football player who let it all go after college. His face is familiar, though, and he's smiling as if he expects me to know him. *Was* he a football player? Those guys always seem to think they're celebrities, even if they never saw a second of game time.

"Kate," he says, clasping my hand tight in one meaty paw. "Todd Stanich. You used to work with my wife, Lisa?"

A tiny spark of hope darts through my chest. Lisa Stanich and I got on reasonably well and he must be okay with my past, because there's not a *chance* he doesn't know.

"Of course," I say, though I don't recall any specific interaction with him. "It's good to see you again."

He indicates the seat across from him and I take it.

"So, how have you been?" His face is open and friendly, his smile gentle. His way of saying *I know, and it's okay*. His gaze drops to my legs and lingers there too long, but whatever. He's still a guy, even if he's a sort of friend. I can't expect him to be Jesus.

"I've been well, thanks. Just getting back on my feet."

"And I assume you're out of rehab, and that's all behind you?"

"It is," I tell him. "I've been clean for several months."

"That's really amazing. You went away for that, right?"

I nod. I'd rather not spend the whole interview talking about rehab as opposed to my qualifications, but as long as I wind up with a job, who cares? "Yes. I was outside Portland."

He rocks back in his chair. "Love Portland. Did you get over to Cannon Beach? Fantastic place."

This guy clearly doesn't understand how rehab works. I force another smile. My jaw is starting to ache with the effort. "No, I didn't. I've heard good things, though."

He seems to sense, at last, that it's time to wrap this shit up. He leans forward, pulling a file toward him. "You've got an impressive resume, obviously. I imagine it's been hard finding something, in spite of that, with your job history?"

I wipe my palms, now slick with sweat, over my skirt. We've moved on to the portion of the interview where he tries to make me think I'd be lucky to get hired.

"I only started looking a short time ago, so I can't say for sure, but I still have an MBA from Wharton and graduated at the top of my class. I imagine that will help."

His smile is patient but nothing more. "I certainly hope you're right, but to be honest, I have my doubts."

I swallow. He already knew my background when I came in,

so if he believes it leaves me unemployable, why the fuck am I here? "I'm a little confused. I'm here to interview for the CFO position, am I not?"

His gaze drifts to my tapping foot and lingers a little too long on my legs again before he gives me a sympathetic frown. "Well, when I saw your name, it occurred to me I might be able to offer some help until you find something. A position you can put on your resume and a letter of recommendation, perhaps."

I grip the edges of my seat, steeling myself to be New Kate, the one who doesn't immediately ask this fucking asshole why he thought he could lure me in like a used-car salesman. He basically promised me the new Mercedes out front and thinks I'll be okay with a banged-up Chevy instead.

I can't believe I got an eighty-dollar haircut and drove forty minutes for this utter bullshit.

"What did you have in mind?" I ask between gritted teeth.

"A mentorship." His grin is sly. A smug president-of-the-frat, I-date-the-hottest-girls-on-campus grin from a guy who hasn't set foot on a college campus in thirty years. "We wouldn't necessarily need to call it that on your resume. We can work out the title."

It would be an insulting offer even if it was a genuine one, and based on the way he keeps looking at my legs...I strongly suspect it's not.

"A mentorship." My voice is flat. "What would that entail?"

"You'd work directly under me. Maybe *mentorship* isn't the name for it. Let's call it...a special friendship. Essentially, I help you and you return the favor." His eyes meet mine. "If you know what I mean."

I glance at the calendar behind him as he speaks and am reminded, once again, of the date. I should be sending out invites to Hannah's preschool playmates right now. I should be off ordering a *Mulan*-themed cake and renting a bouncy castle.

I've lost so much, and the solution is not to keep losing things, but I don't really care at present.

I smile and cross my legs. He watches that too, and now there is ownership in his eyes, as if I've already agreed to the sale and we're just haggling over the price. "And how soon would we start this, uh, 'friendship'" I ask, letting my voice drop low, "where I'm *under* you?"

He leans forward eagerly. "Obviously, we want to get you back on your feet. So, the sooner the better."

I rise and walk around to his side of the desk, perching on its edge. His eyes widen as I rest my foot on his thigh, allowing it to slowly slide upward. "I assume this is the kind of friendship we're talking about?" I purr.

He groans. "God. Let me just lock—"

I jab my heel in his crotch as hard as I can.

"I don't need a friend, special or otherwise," I tell him, rising from the desk as he falls forward with a cry of pain, "but I hope you've got a good lawyer."

"Fucking bitch," he gasps.

"You think?" I ask, walking out the door. "It's possible, but let's get your wife's opinion first."

I march out of the office and make it to my car before I crumple, letting my face press to the steering wheel as the tears begin.

My phone chimes with a text from Stanich, but there's nothing he can say to make this right...and I know he's unlikely to *try* to make this right.

TODD STANICH

> Kate, I'm very sorry you misinterpreted my meaning to such an extent. I'm willing to let it go, but your behavior today concerned me. I really hope you're not using again.

I'm too defeated to even get mad. He's doing damage control

and he'll get away with it, because being a female puts you at a disadvantage anyway, but being an addict? It offers douchebags like Stanich a get-out-of-jail-free card for just about anything. No one would ever take my word over his.

I don't want to return to the empty cabin or go to the bar and have to explain how it went wrong to Beck. I just want to go to the chair in Hannah's nursery, back to a time when our whole future lay ahead of us.

The only place I want to be is one that no longer exists.

22

BECK

I fucked up the other day. I know that.

And I nearly made things so much worse.

I've had no idea how to set things right, and I still don't, but Kate had her interview today, and the resulting silence has me worried I might have missed my chance. She's got to be done by now. I doubt they'd have offered her the job on the spot, but if they did, she might be home packing her shit, and if it went badly, well, that's an even bigger worry. Kate can take a hit. She takes hits so well you convince yourself she can't be toppled and then you discover she's shattered, suddenly and without warning.

Pregnancy healed something broken inside her and losing the baby cut her off at the knees. I'm wondering if she's been shattered again as the minutes tick by.

By three I've sent her a text, to which she does not reply. At four I call, something I only do in life-or-death situations, and when she doesn't answer, I begin to panic. Kate would answer if I called, no matter how mad she was.

I leave Mueller in charge of the bar and head home. The house is empty, her morning coffee cup still on the counter. I doubt she's come back since the interview, so where the hell did she go?

It could be nothing. Maybe her interview went spectacularly and she's spent the day in HR, filling out paperwork. Maybe she celebrated by looking at apartments.

Or maybe it went horribly, and she decided to give up. Why the fuck didn't I ever ask where that dealer of hers lives? I'm on the cusp of calling Caleb to ask when I remember the storage unit, and Kate's hand wrapping around the curved rail of the crib.

It was hard to watch. I know Caleb had to move on, but I wish he could have done it without dismantling their old life in the process. Without shoving every memory of Hannah into a cinderblock room as if it were meaningless.

I drive past Elliott Springs and south toward Santa Cruz until I reach the storage unit. Her car is one of the few in the lot. I'm relieved, but also...not.

The door is ajar and she's sitting in the rocking chair, holding a photo in her hands. Her eyes are red-rimmed and vacant as they meet mine.

It's as if she's pushed her hand into my chest and squeezed. Kate, who does not cry, has been crying for a long fucking time today.

I take a single step toward her. "Kate, what are you doing here, sweetheart?"

"I don't know." Her voice is raspy from disuse or tears.

When I'm only a foot away, she glances down to the photo in her hands and swallows. "This was three years ago today. Look how big she was."

I squat in front of her so I'm at eye level and take Hannah's sonogram from her hand. Kate's face crumples, her shoulders shaking as she releases a sob.

My eyes squeeze shut briefly, the same way they did when I heard Hannah had died. As if I can close myself off from the pain. Except that's what Caleb did for years, closing himself off from his pain *and* hers—and look how that turned out.

I rise, and then I scoop Kate into my arms like a child.

I expect her to fight this—because when does Kate not fight *everything*?—but she doesn't. She curves into me as if she can't hold herself upright any longer. She has such an oversized personality that I forget, sometimes, just how tiny she is.

I settle back into the chair and she rests her cheek against my chest.

"She was totally healthy then," she says. "If we'd just known..."

Kate's spent her entire life outwitting things, and she's still trying to outwit this too, to somehow find the loophole that will bring her daughter back.

I bury my face in her hair. "You're just opening doors that lead nowhere. There isn't a single possibility—true or otherwise—that can bring her back."

"I know," she whispers. "But when is it going to stop being this hard, Beck?"

Her voice—so young, so raw—is a punch to the throat. Nothing in my life, not even the loss of my mom, prepared me for this kind of grief, for its depth and its length. She's always been alone in the world and a little lost—even with Caleb, she was alone and lost—and for the first fucking time, she thought she wasn't. Of *course* she can't stop wanting it back.

I pull her closer. "I don't know, but it will, eventually. I promise."

She nods, her hands gripping my shirt as if she'd fall straight to the floor if she didn't hold on and then her head rises slowly. "I should let you get back to the bar."

My arms tighten, pulling her right back where she was. "I already told Mueller I was taking off." It's a lie, but I'll text him once we're home. "Let's go watch some dumb TV and order pizza."

Her body relaxes once more. She takes one shaky breath, then another. "I don't understand why it's so easy to discuss this with you. I can tell you things I can't say to anyone else."

She's not ready to hear the answer to that and I doubt she ever will be.

Kate and I are the same on the inside—nothing but jagged pieces held together by raw hope. I felt it in my bones the moment I laid eyes on her, and of all the things I wish I *hadn't* felt for Kate Bennett, that's probably the hardest to disregard. Because how many times in your life will you ever meet someone who was made for you?

And how do you possibly walk away if you find her?

WE ORDER pizza and put on a movie. She doesn't want to discuss the interview, and goes to bed no better than she was when I found her at the storage unit, looking small and alone. I tell myself she just needs a good night's sleep, but as I walk to my room, I hear a noise that wraps around my heart like a fist. She's crying again.

After a second of hesitation, I cross the hall and knock on her door.

"I'm fine," she calls, but her voice wobbles, so I walk in anyway. She's curled up in fetal position with that fucking sonogram picture in her hand.

"*Kate*—" I start to plead before I catch myself. I'm no better than Caleb—I want her to stop crying because it's hard on *me*, which is bullshit. "Is there anything I can do?"

She shakes her head. "No. But thank you."

I return to my room but leave the door open. And not a minute after I've climbed into bed and shut off the light, the hardwood floor is creaking beneath her feet as she crosses the hall to my room.

She stands in the frame of the door wearing only a T-shirt, lit by moonlight.

"Beck." Her swallow is audible. "Can I stay in here?"

I still. Jesus. The last fucking thing I need in the world right now is Kate Bennett sleeping in my bed.

"I'm sorry," she says, turning. "I shouldn't have asked."

"It's fine," I tell her. "Just don't hog the covers."

She walks to the other side of the bed, barely meeting my eye. It's hard for her, admitting weakness. "I won't."

I pull the blanket over her after she slides in. "Your promises aren't worth shit."

She laughs. The sound is more tremulous than joyful. "Yeah. True."

She's grieving and in need of comfort. I know this. My body, however, only knows that Kate Bennett is in my bed, wearing a T-shirt and not much else.

It's going to be a very long night.

23

KATE

Today really went off the rails.

I shouldn't have gone to the storage unit. I knew it even at the time. I just wanted to relive those moments of sitting in that chair, talking to my daughter, planning out our future.

I wanted to imagine her weight in my arms again.

I shouldn't have come to Beck's room either. It's pushed the boundary of our friendship beyond any reasonable point. But when he picked me up and pulled me in his lap today, I was the safest I'd felt in a very long time. And I want to feel that way again.

What would have happened if I'd met Beck first? A chill runs down my spine at the thought, but I'm not sure it's a *bad* chill.

He slides his arm under my head and I let my face rest against his bare chest. He always seems to run about ten degrees warmer than everyone else, while I'm about ten degrees colder. I wonder if he could warm me all the way through if I were just near him long enough.

My hand unfurls from its tight fist, pressed to his stomach, splaying over his warm skin.

He's only wearing boxers. I should have realized it sooner. Now that the chill has left me, the sharp sort of grief, I get why he hesitated when I asked if I could sleep in his room. My hand moves to his rib cage—his body is taut as a bow, tense. He's as painfully aware of me as I am of him. Sleeping with Beck—how many times have I imagined that? Countless. I never felt bad about it, but I was also never lying beside him in bed when I did it.

My hand stretches, trying to reach as much skin as possible from a single spot, his ribs under my forefinger, my pinky brushing the trail of hair just below his belly button. His breath comes in a short burst.

"Kate," he warns, his voice hoarse.

I raise up so that I'm half over him, my head slightly above his, and he searches my face for a breathless second before his hand digs into my hair, slides to the back of my neck and pulls my mouth to his.

It's soft, and slow, and perfect—the kind of kiss that promises it won't be stopping anytime soon. There's no haste to it, but a fire spreads through my blood anyway, several years of repressed want bursting to life.

His free hand travels down my spine and inside my waistband until his rough, large palm is against my bare skin. I move slightly and let my weight settle atop him. He groans as his very long, thick erection wedges against my abdomen. It makes my mind go blank. *Yes. I want to do so many things to you that I don't even know where to start, Beck.*

"Shit," he says suddenly. He withdraws his hand from my panties and gently rolls me off him. "We can't do this." He sounds winded, as if he's just finished a long race.

Or as if he's struggling to do the right thing when he

shouldn't have to be the one struggling. *I* should have been the one to stop this.

I climb from the bed. "Sorry."

"Don't apologize," he says gruffly. "This is on me. You were upset and I—"

"You didn't do anything, Beck," I say, stopping him. I walk to the door before I turn toward him. "Can we forget this happened?"

"Pretty fucking unlikely." His voice is more gravelly than usual. "But we can try."

EVERYTHING IS TOTALLY normal the next day. I make breakfast. He goes outside to drag tires and dig trenches or whatever it is he does in his yard, then he sits at the counter, shower-damp and half-dressed, and I pretend I'm not ogling him. Just like normal.

Except now I'm also remembering that kiss. I'm remembering his mouth and the warmth of his skin, how fucking *hard* he was, the way his hands knew exactly where to go and were not hesitant in any way. I'm remembering it so much that when his eyes find mine, he knows exactly where my head is.

"You okay?" he asks. Unperturbed. As if nothing happened at all.

"Yeah." My voice is slightly too breathless to be convincing. "We're out of syrup."

He nods, as if these two phrases make sense back-to-back, which they do not. "I can get some," he offers.

"That's okay." I turn away, swallowing. "I'm going to the store later."

This mundane exchange troubles me more than any post-hookup conversation I've ever had because this is not me. I've never been awkward with men. I am not hesitant or breathless or uncertain. I've never said *no* to something I've wanted and I've never had someone tell me *no* when I've wanted it. I'm no longer sure about anything anymore. I only know that the sight of him reaching for his helmet—the small pulse of his tricep as it happens—makes my core clench.

And that, an hour later, his smirk as I walk into the bar makes it clench again.

We eat lunch together, and I drink him in like a lovesick teenage girl with her long-term crush each time he glances at his plate. When I glance up from *my* plate, his eyes are on me too.

And nothing about any of it is new. It's always been this way with us, hasn't it? I just wasn't willing to admit it until now.

It doesn't help that the memories of me and Caleb together seem to be fading a little, as if I'm recalling a movie about two other people, one I saw long ago. I try to force myself to remember being with him—the long Saturdays we'd spend in bed when he'd visit me in San Francisco, the time I convinced him to have sex in a store dressing room—but it sparks nothing inside me that comes anywhere near those seconds with Beck last night, his mouth soft under mine, one hand fisting my hair while the other palmed my ass. I should be relieved that he stopped things when he did. Instead, I'm disappointed.

Jeremy's name lights up my phone screen, an unwelcome intrusion into my thoughts.

"Caleb arrives in Miami Thursday, right?" he asks. "Nothing's changed?"

"Right." I got the text from Kayleigh a few days prior: *Operation Screw Lucie still on target.* I don't appreciate the paper trail she's leaving, but it's not like we're planning to *murder* Lucie. Yet.

"And you did your part?" he asks.

My part, really, was simply a phone call to an old coke buddy who now lives in Miami—a girl I suspected would do anything for cash. But I love how this asshole, with the job he got from daddy, thinks he has to check up on me. "Of *course* I did my part. It was *my* fucking idea, remember?"

I'd almost forgotten the plan entirely, though, until I got Kayleigh's text, and a part of me wishes I'd never set the ball rolling. Not that I don't want to fuck with Lucie until the end of time, because I absolutely do, but there's a brick in my stomach when I imagine Beck learning I had a hand in it.

I WAIT in the evening for the sound of his bike, and when it comes, there's this *charge* in my spine, as if I was half-asleep without knowing it until now.

I was watching *Grey's Anatomy*, but that stops the instant he sits beside me on the couch. He settles without a word, legs spread wide, and I'm incapable of focusing on anything but him.

The air crackles with something that wasn't there a day ago, and I can only think of the way his hands felt on my skin, of his smell and his sounds. My breasts ache for the roughness of his palms. I'm wet just from the *idea* of it.

I slide my toes under his thigh, which is boulder-solid. It's probably for the best that nothing happened last night. He's too heavy. My bones would shatter like fine-blown glass if he landed on top of me.

But Jesus Christ, I'd like him to try.

I jump off the couch. "It's late," I say breathlessly. "Good night."

I go to my room with a hand pressed to my face. I'm not sure what happened to the grown fucking woman I was a week ago, but she's been replaced by the world's most awkward preteen.

I strip to my T-shirt and curl up in bed, but sleep eludes me.

I'm sweating and feverish while every fantasy I've ever had about Beck is playing on repeat in my head.

I need air. I need a change of scenery. What I really need is to get laid, but I'll have to settle for the first two.

It's pitch-black in the hallway. I creep past Beck's room, walking blindly through the darkness. I stub my toe on the couch and wince at the creaking of the front door as it opens. Except all my efforts not to wake Beck were pointless. He's already out here, sitting on the porch stairs—and wearing nothing but a pair of shorts.

Fuck my life.

"Oh." I'm frozen in the frame of the door. I can't just turn and walk away.

His eyes drag over me, top to bottom, resting an extra beat on places they should not. My nipples harden under his gaze.

"Are you going out?" he asks.

"No." The desire to act casual makes it sound like a lie. "I just couldn't sleep. I thought I'd sit out here instead of the couch so I didn't wake you. Why are you out here?"

He tips his chin. "Same reason."

He rises from the step, his eyes burning in the dim light, and my desire is a palpable thing, spreading though my bones. My lips swell at the mere thought of him and I close my eyes, wishing I could somehow tune him out.

The porch creaks beneath his heavy footfalls as he goes back into the house.

I got what I wanted, yes? I'm out here alone. But his absence and the cool breeze offer no relief. My blood bubbles and boils, chants and pleads for something I'm not providing it. When I rise and follow him inside, it isn't a conscious decision.

My body has simply staged a coup.

I cross the floor to his room, where the lights are off but his door is ajar.

And it's never been ajar before.

My palm presses to it and it swings open.

He's sitting in the darkness, leaning against the headboard. I approach slowly, and he simply watches. He might appear bored to someone who doesn't know him the way I do, someone who can't feel the tension that pulls each sinew and tendon of his body tight. I stop at the foot of his bed, waiting for him to be the better person. To say, '*Kate, go back to your own room.*'

"Come here," he commands, and his hands reach out, gripping my hips as if I've moved too slowly. He pulls me atop him, my knees planted on either side of his broad thighs, his thick erection wedged between us like a promise.

His kiss is not soft the way it was last night—it's the kiss of someone who has been tortured for too long. He breaks away only to rip the T-shirt over my shoulders, flinging it somewhere to the side, and then, with a low growl in his chest, he rolls me beneath him, working his way along my skin with his lips. I run my fingers through that wild, unruly hair as he goes, pulling hard on it when he takes a nipple into his mouth.

His tongue flickers, followed by the sting of his teeth. I gasp and he glances up at me with a smirk, my nipple still pulled tight.

I knew you'd like it, that smirk says. And he's right. I do. I like that he's rough and unapologetic, that his focus on me hardly seems as if it's *for* me but simply because it gets him off.

His hand trails over my ribs, between my legs. I'm drenched. His thick fingers slip inside me easily.

He thrusts against my thigh. "So fucking wet for me already," he hisses. "I knew you would be."

"Fuck me," I demand, and he laughs.

"You're not in charge, Kate. I'll fuck you when I'm good and ready."

His mouth moves from my breasts to my ribs, then my belly button. It presses to the sensitive skin of my inner thigh, and then his teeth sink in, hard enough to mark me, and I bow off the bed.

"Beck," I cry, but he ignores me, yanking my panties off before he spreads my thighs wider and lets his rough tongue slide over my clit.

It flickers; it glides. His fingers push inside me and that tongue of his keeps right on going.

He is everything I imagined and more, reading every desire before I have a chance to voice it. Ignoring what I ask for, making me wait, and then rewarding me for waiting.

His tongue flickers, his fingers thrust, and there's a sharp tug in my gut. Before I can even tell him I'm coming, I'm gasping and wordless, my back bowed off the bed. "Oh, Jesus," I whisper, once I'm finally capable of speech.

I'm nowhere near done, and—thank God—he's well aware of it. He leans over to grab a condom from the nightstand and tears it open with his teeth. Just the way he grasps himself to put it on—his cock thick, already leaking—has me breathless with impatience, fighting myself not to demand he hurry the fuck up.

He hovers above me, so hard that I gasp at the pressure before he's even pushed in.

Caleb was large. Beck, some might argue, is too large. As wet as I am, he has to go slowly, inch by inch, waiting for me to adjust.

And then, at last, he thrusts, bottoming out, releasing a single, harsh breath. "*God.*" He swallows. "You okay?"

I have no idea if I'm okay because I can't feel any part of my body aside from the place where he is lodged, but I nod, digging my fingers into his back and down to his ass, urging him to move.

He does, watching my face with feverish eyes. It's the first time in my life that I have no instructions to give, no demands for *faster* or *harder* or *more*. I have no words at all, only the press of my fingers warning him not to stop, which he already seems to know.

"Fuck," he grunts, his eyes falling closed. "I knew it would be like this."

I did too. Lying under him, the object of his desire, is everything I anticipated. From the moment I first saw him outside that club, I knew exactly how intense it would be. My skin burns for more, and he gives it, slamming into me as my hips rise. I gasp as my orgasm crashes down on me, squeezing him so tight it must hurt.

"Kate," he groans. "*Fuck, fuck, fuck.*" With a single, violent thrust he stills, gripping my hips, holding me tight against him, capturing my gasp with his mouth.

He thrusts twice more, jerkily, and then finally stops.

We are slick with sweat, pressed together. I've never felt this close to anyone in my life.

I don't want to have a single conversation about what just happened. I only want to lie here, breathing him in, until he's ready to do it again.

Eventually, he pulls out, tying off the condom and crossing the room to discard it. When he returns, his gaze meets mine, and I catch the briefest flicker of guilt.

"What's the matter?" I ask.

His eyes widen as if he's been caught at something. He pulls down the covers and climbs back into bed. "Nothing."

I push myself upright. "Bullshit. You think I can't tell when you're bothered by something?"

He stares up at the ceiling. "This is basically the one thing Caleb asked me not to do."

There's a tingle along my spine. I sit up straighter, pulling the sheet to my chest. If Caleb doesn't want me with someone else, it means some part of him still cares. And still wants me for himself. "Caleb asked you not to sleep with me?"

His eyes darken. "Oh, I get it. You think he asked because it's not over for him. You just fucked his best friend. Don't you think *that* made it over?"

Dread hits me like a fist. *No. Fuck. No. I can't have ruined everything, can I? Fuck.*

I climb from the other side of the bed, reaching for my panties. "I'm not going to feel guilty about this," I snap. "Caleb's sure as hell not respecting our marital vows anymore, so why should I?"

His nostrils flare. "And is that what this was? You spreading your legs because it's the best way you had to get back at him?"

"Fuck you, Beck!" I snatch my shirt off the floor. "Don't try to make this my fault. You were there too."

His arms fold across his chest. "I'm not making this anyone's fault, Kate. I'm just pointing out that it wasn't the behavior of a woman desperate to win back her husband."

My stomach sinks. It *is* different than just sleeping with a random guy. Even if Caleb ends things with Lucie, the fact that I've now slept with his best friend might be one step too far for him.

I've lived and breathed this dream about Caleb and the family we will have for the better part of a year, and I threw it off to the side as if it meant nothing at all.

I turn on my heel and walk from Beck's room into my own, slamming the door hard behind me before I climb into bed with my face pressed to my hands.

Fuck, fuck, fuck. What am I doing staying with Beck? Working with him? Fantasizing about him and losing my focus?

And this could also destroy Beck's oldest friendship. It will mess things up with his entire friend group if it comes out. Did I even consider that before I went into his room? Of course I didn't. But it's typical of me to take what I want without considering who I might hurt in the process.

There's motion across the hall. I'm not surprised when he knocks on my door, then opens it.

I hate what happened, that I fucked everything up, yet my core clenches at the sight of him all over again. I've salivated over him for *years*, and he's only more appealing now that I know what it's actually like to be beneath him, to have him inside me.

God, it's going to be a struggle not to think about *that*.

"I'm sorry," he says.

I stare at my blanket. "I am too."

He crosses the room. I scoot my knees to my chest and he sits in the space I've made for him.

"Did we just fuck everything up?" I whisper, not quite able to meet his eye.

He runs a hand through his hair, hesitating. "I hope not."

He took too long to answer. I'm not sure he means it. "Can we just forget it happened and move on?"

He rises. "It won't happen again, and I've managed to lie to Caleb about enough shit that I guess I can add this to the list. But no. I'm not going to forget. And neither are you."

When he leaves, I roll onto my side and cover my face with my hands. Was it disloyal to Caleb that I did it? And if I want my husband back so badly, why can't I stop replaying every single second I just spent with his closest friend?

24

BECK

I'd really like to avoid her entirely the next morning. I just swore it was behind us, but I've already jerked off twice thinking about it. Except she's doing her best to act like things are normal—from the kitchen there's the sizzle of bacon, the crack of an egg breaking open against a bowl—so the least I can do is sit down and pretend alongside her.

I emerge from my room. She's wearing jeans and a hoody instead of that fucking T-shirt that reveals a lot most of the time and nearly *everything* at the best of times, as if I can't be trusted.

She's right. I can't.

I took advantage of someone too vulnerable to know what the hell she was doing and enjoyed every fucking second of it. If she gave me a single *come hither* look, I guarantee I'd take advantage of it all over again.

I pull out a chair at the counter. "You're fully clothed."

She gives me an overly bright smile. "I know how irresistible I am. I figured I should tone down the magnificence."

There's a burning in my gut—guilt and rage both. I'm not a fucking animal.

Except with her...I sort of am.

I take the plate she's just set on the counter and pull it toward me. "You have nothing to fear. You know me—one and done."

The smile doesn't leave her face, but it dims a little, and I wish I hadn't said it.

She grabs the spatula tightly, and I shove half the breakfast sandwich she's made in my mouth, remembering that same hand in my hair last night. The way she gripped it hard as she came. I wasn't even inside her yet and I was worried I might fucking explode just listening to her moan.

I wince. *Stop thinking about it.*

"Are you okay?" she asks. Jesus Christ, she's treating me like some lovesick young pup she's got to let down easy.

My eyes open. "I'm fine." The words are barked, angrier than I intended.

She bites her lip, a flicker of concern in her eyes. "Do you want—"

I push away from the counter. "I'm going in early," I tell her, grabbing the other half of the sandwich. "Thanks for breakfast."

I'm making the situation worse. The way I always do.

The way she does, too.

There's no way this will end well.

I'D PLANNED to avoid her when she got into work, but it hardly mattered.

All it took was one whiff of her shampoo as she passed to plunge me into a memory of last night, long legs wrapped around my hips, so far gone that she couldn't even run her smart mouth for once.

One and done? She's opened a fucking Pandora's box, and I can't seem to close it. I can't enter the office without picturing my hand sliding through her hair as I pull her mouth to mine. I can't look at the bar without picturing her spread like a feast atop it.

And this is shit I've imagined many, many times, but it was vague before. Now I can imagine it so vividly it's as if we're actually doing it, so vividly that just the sight of her is enough to get me hard . . . a situation that isn't ideal at work or even at home, given she's staying with me.

Laura emerges from the kitchen, asking me to check how much steak we've got coming in. I give her a terse nod and force myself to go back to Kate.

The office is too full of her. Her scent, her bossiness, her smile, that filthy little knowing thing in her eyes. She's not even looking at me and she's definitely not smiling, but it's all here anyway, floating around the fucking room like a virus. Her hair is spilling around her shoulders—I picture it fisted in one hand as I sweep that computer off her desk and bend her over.

I pull up the order but make the mistake of another deep breath. I get a hit of her shampoo and my cock throbs in response.

I have to get the fuck out of here.

"I'm ordering lunch. Do you want anything?" I ask as I rise.

She stares at her computer screen, her mouth pursed. "No, thank you."

Maybe she's just focused on work. Or maybe I fucking ruined things last night.

I climb to my feet. *Jesus, this is awkward.* "I'll be running errands all afternoon, so I won't see you when you leave. I'll be home around ten."

She chews her lip. "You don't need to. I'm just saying you...can do whatever you want."

I guess she's trying to give me a free pass to go fuck someone else. And I probably should, because how else are we going to return to normal? Except I don't want to. I haven't wanted to in a long time and I'm pretty sure I couldn't even manage it right now.

I've got to get us back to where we were.

"I'm coming home," I say, meeting her eye.

She shrugs. "Okay. Whatever."

Mueller, who entered the room at some point during this conversation, watches the two of us as if we've gone insane. It feels like we have.

When I reach the cabin that night, after five solid hours away from her, I've convinced myself we're going to be fine. I'm not an animal...I can sit next to her for an hour and behave.

I open the door. She's on the couch watching TV, and before she's even turned her head, my first impulse is to pull her flat and bury myself inside her.

It's not going to be fine.

She curls up, making room for me. She's watching *South Park*, which has far less sexual tension than *Game of Thrones*, but the tension remains between us anyway. Her throaty laugh has me bracing my thighs. She runs her thumb over her lip—I stop breathing.

And when she stretches her arms overhead, revealing half her midriff, I rise from the couch, unable to take another second.

"I'm beat," I tell her, walking away without waiting for a response.

Nothing improves when I reach my room. I can smell her shampoo on my pillow. I fist myself, knowing it won't do any good.

I think we ruined things. We're never going back to the way it was.

∽

I CLOSE the bar a few nights in a row just so there's no weirdness at home. I ignore her and she ignores me. It's the only solution I've got.

On the third afternoon, she walks out of the office with her purse, something forlorn in her gaze. "I'm heading home," she says. The emptiness in her voice pinches my chest hard.

"What's wrong?"

"Nothing," she snaps. But her eyes are no longer bright the way they were.

That twinge of anxiety inside me expands. She's closing herself off, and that's when shit starts going very badly with her. "Kate, don't lie to me."

Her jaw shifts. I wait for her to lash out, but instead she simply releases a slow exhale. "I got used to hanging out with you. I guess I just need to get a life."

I'm such a selfish prick. It's fine for me to spend all my time in the bar and pretend I'm needed here, but what is she doing? The part of her life that I filled is empty again, the way it was when she first came back to town. "I'll come home early tonight."

She shakes her head. "You don't have to do that. I'll come up with something."

"Kate." I pause, waiting until she meets my eye. "I *want* to. You're not the only one who got used to hanging out. We can go see a band."

She hesitates before she nods in wary agreement. Of course she's wary: it's a terrible fucking idea. If I can't even sit on a couch with her watching *South Park*, how am I going to handle a whole night with her pressed against me like she was the last time, her tight little ass against my thighs, her rib cage rising and falling under my hands?

When I arrive at home, she's ready to go—her hair down and wild, wearing a black leather jacket, stiletto heels, and a denim skirt that ends just beneath her ass. If she was trying to choose an outfit more likely to get me off, she couldn't have.

Fuck. I can't spend the night with her looking like that.

"What's up?" she asks.

I open my mouth. *Please don't wear that.* "Nothing. Let's go."

I steer her toward the truck because it seems safer, but the moment I climb in, I discover my error. Confined to the small space, I smell nothing but her rose-scented shampoo and body lotion. In my peripheral vision, all I see is inch upon inch of bare thigh way too close to my hand.

The times when you cave to a desire you've been fighting are almost never when you're asking yourself if you *should* cave. They're when you've been suppressing that desire for too long, telling yourself the answer is *no* and that there won't be a discussion about it. That's when your primitive brain finally says *fuck you.*

She lifts her hips, smoothing her skirt under her ass, and only succeeds in making it ride up in front more than it was. I'm hard enough to break nails.

"Jesus Christ," I say, closing my eyes.

"What's the matter?"

She shifts toward me—her legs closer now, her mouth in a small pout and I can't stand it anymore. I lean over the console, placing my hand on her leg, letting my fingers press into the velvety skin of her inner thigh. "This," I tell her, my voice rough with yearning. "*This* is what's the matter."

She meets my eye, licking those strawberry lips while she considers what I've said.

"Good," she whispers, swinging her leg over my lap to straddle me. I grasp the sides of her face, my fingers digging into her hair.

It's not gentle; it's not romantic. It's simply tongues and teeth, my belt tugged open, her skirt pushed up, a grunt as her hand reaches into my boxers and wraps around me, circling her thumb over the moisture at the tip. She grabs my wallet off the dashboard and fishes inside it for a condom, rolls it down my cock, and raises up only to impale herself, her mouth open, her head thrown back.

The windows are fogged, the cabin of the truck damp as a fucking rainforest. I tug her jacket off and grab her hips, pulling her on me harder.

"Ride me, Kate," I growl. "Just like that. Don't fucking stop."

She does. She couldn't claim for a second to be a passive participant in any of this. She moves faster, her face flushed, her mouth swollen, and eyes dazed—so close to coming, so desperate for it. She's never looked more beautiful.

"I'm going to come so hard inside you," I grit out, my jaw tense with the restraint it requires not to let go entirely, and she gasps, arching backward against the steering wheel, clenching around me so tight as she comes that I couldn't hold back if I wanted to.

"*Kate*," I hiss as I fill the condom, barely conscious of the way she slumps against me. We're both breathing heavily, dripping in sweat. I want us to stay like this forever.

"I guess we messed up again," she whispers, her face buried against my neck. There's something strangled in the word "*again*." Because it's a mistake when it happens once. Twice, though? That's something else entirely.

My fingers, tracing her spine, still. "I guess we did."

Her lips tremble as she forces a smile. "I should probably go inside, I think." She slides off me, grabbing her jacket and purse. "Good night."

She walks away as if she doesn't have a care in the world, but I don't miss how straight her spine is, how stiffly she moves.

This is how Kate runs. How you know she's terrified even though she would never fucking admit it.

"Good night, Kate," I answer, long after she's shut the door behind her.

25

KATE

I spend every waking hour thinking of the way he groaned my name, the way he felt inside me as he came, and I am momentarily breathless, lost in the memory of it.

My ringing phone—Jeremy again—is simply an irritation, a distraction.

"The photos suck," he says, his voice a pointed finger of blame as if *I* were the photographer. "I just forwarded them to you."

In my head, Beck's mouth is still on my neck. *Ride me, Kate. Just like that. Don't fucking stop.*

With a sigh, I force the memory away to look at the photos Jeremy's sent: an unsuspecting Caleb walking out of security at the Miami airport, only to find the girl I hired basically attacking him, throwing her arms around his neck and kissing him on the mouth. That he's utterly stunned and trying to push her off him is plain as day.

"Anyone can see he has no idea who she is," Jeremy continues. "This is going to look like a fucking setup, and it's all going to point back to you and me."

I'm curiously detached from the whole thing. "I guess we can't use the photos."

"Easy for you to say—I'm the one who had to pay that guy almost a thousand bucks for an hour of work."

I roll my eyes. Jeremy probably has a thousand dollars in change lying around in his car. He's just mad it didn't work.

"We'll figure something out later," I tell him, but I've got no impulse to consider what's next. I don't care that this plan has failed, and I don't care about the next one either.

I hang up the phone, close my eyes, and return to imagining Beck's hands are on my hips.

RACHEL POPS her head into the office that afternoon and asks if I've had lunch. Since Beck and I are back to both pretending the other doesn't exist, I have not.

"Come on," she says, waving me out. "My treat."

I laugh. "I eat for free."

She grins. "Then I'll buy the booze."

We go to the deck where Mary—the new waitress whose crush on Beck irks me to no end—takes our order.

Once Mary leaves, I force myself to ask the polite question I should have asked a while ago. "So, how far along are you?"

"Thirty-two weeks," she says. An apology rests in her eyes—I guess Beck told her. Or perhaps Caleb told her husband. "It wasn't planned, but we're happy."

I remember that point in my pregnancy. I had the nursery set up in case Hannah came early. By thirty-two weeks, her room was painted and her name was hanging in wooden letters over her crib. Her closet was a sea of tiny onesies and dresses. I've never done anything halfway. I jumped in with both feet, never dreaming it could all go wrong.

Mary unceremoniously drops our drinks and a basket of

bread on the table and walks away. She appears to like me about as much as I like her.

"If I were Beck, I'd have already fired that girl," I mutter.

Her eyes twinkle. "Somebody's jealous, I think."

"I'm not jealous. But a little tip I learned while getting my MBA was *don't hire surly females for customer service positions*."

"I actually meant *she* was jealous." She tilts her head. "So you've got an MBA, but you're doing part-time bookkeeping?"

"Your father is an addict," I reply. "You, of all people, should understand what that does to your job history. I interview, but no one is willing to give me a shot once they hear the truth. It's gotten really old."

Rachel reaches for a roll and tears off a piece, slathering it with butter. "Loads of people in the world have made mistakes, Kate. Not everyone is going to shit all over you for yours. How many interviews have you gone on?"

"Two."

"Wow," she says with mock astonishment. "Two? My God, you must be *exhausted* from all that interviewing. I mean, that must amount to like . . . an hour of your life? I don't know how you do it."

I give her the finger and she laughs.

"Go get turned down from a hundred jobs and then come back here and cry to me about how no one will give you a shot. Beck said he thought you'd stopped sending out resumes."

I frown. Beck doesn't need to be talking about my job hunt to others. And it's not *entirely* true. It's just that the jobs I'm even vaguely interested in seem to have dried up. I could look in San Francisco or LA, but that puts me a lot farther from everything than I'd like.

I guess I *have* taken my foot off the gas a little bit. "The constant rejection was tiresome. I'm just taking a break."

"Well, now isn't the time to be taking a break because you've got a damn MBA and you're working part-time at a bar. Do you know how many times I had to sleep with Gus to get pregnant with this child?"

I cock a brow at her. "Your husband would be flattered by what a hardship you're making it out to be, and you said you got pregnant by accident."

She grins. "Yeah, okay, I was just trying to shore up my argument about adversity. But we had to have a *lot* of sex to get pregnant by accident, let me tell you."

I laugh. She's the first person I've met here who I'd *choose* to be friends with, other than Beck.

Mary delivers our lunch with a heavy sigh, but Rachel doesn't appear to even notice the attitude—she's one of those women who just assume people like them, or *will* like them upon further acquaintance. I've always been the opposite, perhaps because very few people do actually like me upon further acquaintance.

"We're having a housewarming party Sunday," she says. "You and Beck should come."

I poke at my ravioli. It looks dry, which means Mary left it under the heat lamp too long. "We're not a couple."

She smirks. "Ooo-kay. Well, you're still welcome either way."

Housewarming parties usually suck and I'm not at the point in my life where I feel like oohing and ahhing over someone's new sofa from Pottery Barn. But if *I'm* invited, Caleb is. My crush on Beck notwithstanding, I need to take my openings when they arrive, and as Rachel unwittingly pointed out, I have taken my foot off the gas.

"I'd love to," I tell her.

New Kate will be at that party, her most adult and charming self. She'll shine so bright that Lucie shrinks a little under the glare.

$\sim$

BECK WORKS out in the yard the next morning, showers, and arrives at the counter fully dressed, to my chagrin. He got in late last night, but I heard him outside my door, hesitating as if he was considering walking in. I laid awake for hours after that, taut with desire for things he didn't provide.

His hand flexes as he grabs the plate from me, and in my head, his hand is flexing on my inner thigh the way it did in the truck.

He lifted me on and off him like I was made of air.

"Rachel said something about a housewarming party Sunday. Are you going?"

He stills, his fork suspended in mid-air. "I hadn't planned to. Are you?"

I hitch a shoulder before I pour the bacon grease into a can. "I might."

"Since when do you attend housewarming parties?" he asks, his voice icy.

I turn toward him. Yes, I've slept with him twice, but he needs to understand that nothing has changed. He didn't just *fuck* my life goals away in his truck the other night. "She's nice. Why wouldn't I?"

His eyes are nearly black. They hold mine a moment too long. "I've gotta go," he says, pushing away the plate of food he never ate and grabbing his helmet.

For fuck's sake. He's mad?

"I thought you wanted me to be nice to Rachel!" I shout as he slams the door behind him.

He didn't hear me, but it wouldn't have mattered if he did. We both know I'm not going there on Rachel's behalf.

I'm off today, so I spend the next few hours looking at the same litany of boring jobs I've seen for months, full of euphemisms. *Integration manager, operational restructure, employee efficiencies.*

The jobs are dull, but the bigger problem is that these are

companies I don't care about. No one has ever described me as an altruist, but I still need to work on behalf of a product I *like*, doing work that actually interests me.

Maybe that's been part of the issue all along, moving here. I agreed to let a part of myself die when I married Caleb—resigning myself to jobs I didn't care about and a town I didn't like—and there just wasn't enough alive inside me when things fell apart.

There's no word from Beck all day. I pick up my phone a hundred times wanting to fix this and put it back down, knowing I can't without telling him a lie—without claiming I'm over Caleb, that I'm cool with just letting Lucie take my entire life. I sleep fitfully, waiting to hear him pull up outside. All night, it seems, I'm dreaming of Beck above me with his hair falling forward, his control gone...but that ends at four AM, when his heavy tread finally shakes the outside steps.

It doesn't take two hours to close the bar, which means he went home with someone else. If it wasn't one and done with us before—or two and done, I guess—it sure as fuck is now.

My jaw grinds as I listen to him walk past my room. There's something underneath my irritation too, something like grief, but I'm ignoring that. I've spent enough time addicted to shit to recognize when I'm under the sway of something I don't want any part of.

The two of us are not going to be able to go on like this forever. I should already have left.

I give up on sleep a few hours later and go straight to the bar—I'm too angry to make Beck a breakfast that isn't poisoned. The front doors are still locked, but I'm able to get in through the kitchen, where they've already started prepping for lunch.

To the kitchen staff, I'm a curiosity. *The woman who lives with Beck.* They probably think I'm some pathetic bitch who doesn't realize he's sleeping with everything that moves, someone they quietly pity, which really sucks though it's exactly what I'm trying to do to Lucie.

I close the office door behind me and sink into my desk chair, pressing my hands to my face. *I can't believe he came in at four. I can't.*

I don't know why it matters, but I need to get the hell out of Beck's bar and his house because I can't keep feeling the way I do right now.

I open my laptop and start sending out resumes anywhere and everywhere. I'll find something entry-level and start over, prove myself. It sounds plucky of me, but what other option do I have at this point?

It's after ten when Beck strolls in, dumping his helmet on the desk with unnecessary carelessness.

I ignore him, focused on my laptop, hoping he'll realize I'm not in the mood for a fucking chat.

"Why'd you leave so early?" he asks.

"Figured you'd sleep in, given the hour you arrived home." I'm delighted by how emotionless I sound despite the rage spinning in my chest. "I decided it was time to get real about looking for a job so you won't have to employ and house me forever."

He scratches his neck. "You act like I'm doing you a favor by giving you a job."

I note that he didn't reference his feelings about me as a roommate in any way, and that was the part that actually mattered. The moments I've spent with Beck, until recently, have been the bright spots of my day and my year, but I can't be his charity case for the rest of my life. "Either way, I've gotten two paychecks. I can probably be out of your hair pretty soon. I'm sure you want your place back to yourself."

His shoulders sag. There are circles under his eyes that weren't there a week ago. "Whatever you want to do is fine," he mutters, a non-answer that makes me crazy.

Would it kill him to say, '*Kate, I like having you around*?' And why do I want him to say it anyway? This is why I need to get out. We're blurring too many lines.

"I'm sure it would smooth things over with Caleb if I weren't there," I reply.

His nostrils flare. "Smooth things over for *you* or for me?"

I sigh. *For us both, clearly.* I know better than to say it aloud. "For you, obviously."

He turns to walk out. "I don't give a fuck what Caleb thinks about you staying with me. But go if you want to go."

"Okay, I will," I tell the closed door. It's pretty clear it's not just in my best interest to leave but his too. It's also clear our friendship, or whatever it was, is probably over.

The bar is unusually busy when I come out of the office that afternoon, and Beck's alone. "Where's Mueller?"

"Stomach trouble," he says, without looking up.

"I'm going to look at an apartment, unless you need help?"

He sneers. "From *you*?"

I flip him off, but he's already turned his back to me.

The apartment in question is in the shittiest section of a rundown town that isn't near anything. It has a leaking sink and a stain on the carpet that looks suspiciously like blood, and a bunch of guys are lounging on the outside steps in broad daylight. The smell of weed as I walk out is so strong I'm probably getting a contact high.

It's as if, no matter how hard I try, I'm destined to wind up in the same gutter I started in. I'm destined to wind up alone, surrounded by addicts, and left for dead.

The happy hour crowd has already arrived when I get to the bar and Beck's still the only one back there. I'm tempted to keep walking since he was such an asshole before, but I stop. *Kate, you are so fucking weak.* "Why are you still alone?"

"Lawrence called in sick too." He glances at me from the tap, something at war in his eyes. He needs help, but he refuses to receive it from *me*, the addict. "It'll be fine. There's enough kitchen staff to cover food service and clean-up, and Melissa comes in at six."

They normally have three bartenders on a Friday, so they'll still be short. And Beck looks wiped—I guess he hasn't had a break all day, and God knows he didn't get much sleep last night, the bastard. But if he can't be bothered to ask for my help, I'm sure as hell not offering again.

In the office, I wrap things up for the week and have just ended my final call when Melissa walks into the office and drops her purse on Beck's desk. She looks like death warmed over.

"Are you okay?" I ask.

"I don't think so," she whispers, and then she grabs her purse, and vomits inside it.

"Go home and get in bed," I demand and she's so sick she can barely nod in agreement as she walks back out. I follow her out to discover people are now three deep at the bar, waving credit cards in the air, and Beck's still back there alone.

He watches in dismay as Melissa walks out and I give up. He's not going to ask for help and...whatever. He's being an idiot.

I slide behind the bar and turn to the woman closest to me. "What can I get you?"

Her mouth falls open. She glances toward Beck.

"Yeah, I know, you'd rather he waited on you," I tell her. "I wish he was waiting on you too, believe me." When she sees I'm about to move on to the next person, she orders a dumb girl drink and I groan audibly.

I knew I should have gone to the guys first.

"What the fuck are you doing?" asks Beck, watching me grab the Chambord.

"Pretending I know how to make a Cosmo."

He grabs the Chambord from my hand. "You can't be back here. And there's no Chambord in a Cosmo."

"Right. That's why I said I was *pretending* I knew how to make one. Melissa's sick, so you're stuck with me."

"Fuck," he hisses under his breath, running a hand through his hair in frustration. "Fine, but just wait on guys. They don't order complicated shit."

I grin. "Suits me. Men like me better anyway."

"The ones who don't know you, maybe," he mutters.

For the next few hours, orders come flying at me, cash and credit cards and empty glasses shoved in my face. Men try to flirt over the crowd, crushing the chicks waiting on espresso martinis in the process. But it's *good*—I'm *alive*. I'm challenged. It's a game to me, like those tests they gave as a kid, the ones that got me into private school. How much can I hold in my head? How much can I do at once?

"You love this, don't you?" Beck grumbles.

"What's not to love? Men are throwing money at me and I haven't even had to get naked yet."

His jaw pops. "You're not getting naked at all. And stop flirting with everyone."

I squeeze lemon into a gin and tonic, which might be the wrong citrus, but *I'm* not the one who has to drink it. "Why can't I flirt?"

Beck grabs a guy's credit card off the bar. "Because you're like a rigged contest at the fair that no one ever wins. Every one of these guys is taking their shot and you're letting them do it when you know they'll all go home empty-handed."

I slowly shift my glance to him. "Maybe one of them *won't* go home empty-handed," I taunt. "If you can stay out 'til four, I can too."

His eyes narrow and a muscle in his jaw pops again. I could stand here gloating over the way I've clearly hit a nerve, but why would I when there are men here *clamoring* for my attention? Men like the annoying guy at my end of the bar who keeps trying to make conversation whenever I'm near. He's one of those overconfident assholes who thinks every female will still spread her legs because of that one winning pass he threw a decade ago, but I bet he wouldn't go fuck some random barfly if he could have me instead.

"Why haven't I seen you here before?" he asks.

"I normally work back in the office."

He laughs. "Yeah, I'd want to keep you to myself if I were him too."

I cross the bar for the bourbon, and Beck moves beside me. "Is that guy bothering you?" he demands.

"He's harmless. And he's tipping hand over fist. If I'd known bartenders made *this* much, I'd have skipped grad school entirely."

He sighs. "Bartenders don't make this much. *You* make this much, and it has nothing to do with service. You haven't made a drink *correctly* all night long."

I laugh. "No one's complaining though, are they?"

"Yeah, that has nothing to do with your bartending skill either," he grumbles.

There's a tickle of pleasure in my chest. I find his misery delightful.

The next time I glance at Overconfident Former Athlete, I wink, and no sooner have I done it than karma comes around to kick me in the ass. Suzanne has pushed her way up, front and center, and she's leaning over the bar, letting her ample cleavage jut forward while she says something to Beck I can't hear.

He grins—that lopsided grin I love, high on one side—and fury spins in my stomach.

I decide, without ever deciding, to let Bad Kate out of the cage. The version of me who is game for anything, uninhibited, full of innuendo. It's not as if I can take it too far with Father

Beck here, holding my reins tight. But I can sure as fuck tug on them a little.

I strip down to the black tank under my flannel shirt. Maybe I don't have Lucie-sized assets, but the men around the bar don't seem to mind.

Beck steps away from Suzanne and moves toward me, his nostrils flaring. "Put your fucking shirt back on."

I laugh as if it's all a big joke. "Silly Beck. My tips are going to be so much better without it." That rage I felt earlier is now a wild animal, made vicious by the smell of blood.

Overconfident Guy buys another round of shots, then slides one back to me. "That one's yours."

I slide it back to him.

"Drink up, Katie," he says, pushing it my way once more.

Ugh. You've got to love a stranger who decides to give you a nickname.

I grin, slow and seductive. "You need to get a girl drunk first?"

He leans forward, both forearms on the counter, and I notice Beck has approached us though he's got no reason to be at my end of the bar. "Are you saying I *don't* need to get you drunk?" he asks.

I bite my lip as I start to turn away. "I'm saying I don't need to be drunk to do the things I want to do."

He rises, leaning closer, nearly knocking over a beer bottle as he does it. "Could I be one of those things?"

I walk away, smiling at him over my shoulder without saying a word. He *won't* be one of those things, but Beck doesn't know that.

"Stop leading that guy on," Beck growls, grabbing a credit card out of my hand.

I raise my eyes and look up at him from beneath my lashes. "Who says I'm leading him on?"

He slams the gin onto the shelf. "You're not going home with Pritchard. He's a douchebag."

This is ridiculous. "Funny how every guy who shows an interest in me is a douchebag, yet those whores *you* go home with are just fine. Why is that?"

We don't say another word to each other for the rest of the night and his mood is so foul that it's a relief to hear him shout for last call, since it means I'll finally be able to get away from him.

Overconfident Guy leans forward, his hands pressed together in supplication. "*Now,* will you do a shot for me?"

"'Fraid not. It's last call. You want anything else?"

He winks. "I want a whole lot of things, but for now, just let me borrow your neck for a body shot."

I have no desire to let this moron put his tongue on my neck, and am about to say so when I glance at Beck and see that lovely spark of fury in his eyes.

Good, asshole. Now you know how it feels.

"Okay," I purr, loud enough for Beck to hear. I hand the guy a salt shaker and a shot of tequila, and then I climb onto the bar, popping a lime wedge between my teeth as I lean back on my forearms to offer him my neck.

He hasn't even gotten close to me before I'm scooped up and thrown over Beck's shoulder. He marches toward the office, shouting at Liam to take over.

"You're done," he says, slamming the door behind us and setting me down. "If you're going to act like a whore, do it in someone else's bar."

He did *not* just call me a whore. My heart is in my throat, my blood rushing to my brain in waves.

"Fuck you!" I pick up a stapler from his desk and throw it at him. He catches it easily, so I hunt for something else to throw. "You've done nothing but tell me to forget about Caleb, but I do something that doesn't even *approach* what you do with your 'patrons' and *I'm* a whore?"

His jaw is locked, his nostrils flaring. "I didn't tell you to replace Caleb with a douchebag."

He's jealous. He's *so* fucking jealous.

Good. He should be.

I slam down the pencil cup I was about to throw. "There's a big difference between *replacing* someone and *screwing* someone. But you know all about that, don't you? You're *dying* to fuck me again, but instead you go home with Suzanne."

I expect him to lash out, but he does not. Instead, in absolute silence, he turns the dead bolt behind him. The fine hairs on the back of my arms stand on end as he approaches, so broad that he blocks my view of the door entirely.

His eyes glitter, dangerous and predatory, and the room is dead silent but for the scrape of his boots against the floor. With every step my heart is racing faster, my breath hovering uselessly in the center of my chest. He moves until he is pressed against me, until the edge of the desk is biting into my ass.

I don't know where the air in the room has gone. I brace myself, my hands curling around the desk's edge, and he leans down, his lips brushing my ear. "Is that why you were about to let Pritchard put his mouth all over you? *Jealousy?* I haven't slept with anyone but you since the first time we were together, but I guess it's safe to assume that if I had, you'd want to take her place."

His tongue flickers, his breath hot in my ear, his hands sliding up my thighs, pushing my skirt around my waist.

"No, I—"

He pulls the strap of my tank off my shoulder, sinking his teeth into my skin. His hand slides inside my bra to palm a single tight nipple.

"You're sure?" he asks, his mouth near my ear. He tears my thong in half as if it's made of paper, and his fingers slide between my legs to find me embarrassingly wet. "Because you don't seem sure."

When he starts to withdraw his fingers, I arch against his hand, silently begging him for more. I expect him to laugh or say something smug, but instead he reaches somewhere behind me, tearing a foil packet with his teeth while he wrenches his jeans open.

He rolls the condom on and steps close. My thighs spread as if he's demanded it, and with a single, sudden thrust, he's buried all the way inside me. It's so much, so good, that I collapse backward to my forearms.

"Oh God," I groan, wrapping my legs around him. Even my forearms can't support me. I fall flat on my back, knocking over the pencils in the process.

His hands grip my hips tight as he thrusts, his nostrils flaring, his eyes never leaving my face. Yes, he's still angry, but there's something more there too, something I've seen a thousand times when he's looked at me: *want,* dark and wrong and lethal, want he's contained for too long. He pulls out and thrusts back in, dragging the air from my chest. And then he does it again, harder. Again, harder still, with his thumb circling my clit.

I close my eyes, but he grabs my chin. "No. *Watch.* I want you to remember who made you come."

I obey as if I'm in a stupor, and the mere sight of him—his eyes glittering dangerously, his hair falling forward—is too much. I've imagined his face just like this, his focus on me, his mouth ajar and breathing heavy, too many times. Heat races up my thighs and down my spine, and my core clenches tight. "I'm—"

He winces. "Don't. *Don't.* I want it to last."

I can't help it. Everything inside me pulls inward, tight and sharp, as the world goes black. It's his name and no one else's in my head as it happens.

A torrent of profanity pours from his mouth and he comes, gripping my hips so tightly there will be bruises in the morning.

I remain exactly where I am when he slides out, rolls the condom off, and tosses it into the trash like this is something he's done every day of his life, which probably isn't all that far from the truth.

He turns away from me, buttoning up his pants. And I no longer know how I feel about anything, so I grab my purse, push my skirt down, and walk straight out the door.

26

BECK

The staff is already putting chairs up on the tables and the crowd has mostly cleared when I return to the bar. Pritchard is finally gone, which is in his best interest. I'd better not see him in here again.

"You want to tell me what just happened?" Liam asks.

"Not really," I reply, going to the register to close the last few tabs. "Thanks for taking over."

"She shouldn't have been back here, dude," he says softly, his brow furrowed.

Liam is the least likely of all my friends to offer a lecture, so if I'm hearing it from him, I'd be hearing *howls* of outrage from Caleb and Harrison. "It was an emergency. It won't happen again."

He opens the dishwasher and starts loading glasses, though he hasn't worked here in a decade. "She's a messed-up girl, Beck. I know she's been through a lot, but nothing good can come of this."

Yeah. I know that too. I've only ever wanted her, and she still wants her fucking husband. Nothing good is *already* coming of this.

I let the staff go home though the place isn't in perfect shape. I'll come in early tomorrow to tie up any loose ends, but right now, I've just got to get the hell out.

I climb on my bike, longing for an extended, reckless drive into the hills like the one I took last night, hoping to sort my shit out. Except my shit was still waiting at the cabin for me, and it'll be waiting tonight too, so I might as well get it over with.

She's watching TV when I walk in. I have no idea whether to expect silence or a projectile whipped toward me. Anything's possible where Kate's concerned.

She glances over her shoulder. "You're back early."

I pull up a chair and sit backward on it to face her, scrubbing a hand over my brow. *Man up, Beck. Apologize.*

"I'm sorry," I begin. "What happened at the bar...shouldn't have."

Her jaw clenches and her gaze returns to the TV. "I'm starting to find your guilt tiresome. If you feel so strongly that you shouldn't fuck your best friend's wife, then stop doing it. But I don't need your guilt. I've got enough problems of my own."

I still. She's completely misunderstood me. Maybe she's been misunderstanding me all along.

"I'm not guilty because of Caleb," I tell her, reaching out to let my hand rest on her knee. "The reason I shouldn't have done it is because I was mad, and because I went about it all wrong."

Her gaze slides back to me, guarded and uncertain. "So, how exactly should you have gone about it?"

"I'm still figuring that part out." I climb to my feet. "Let's go for a ride."

Her head jerks up. "On your bike?"

"No, on my magic carpet. Yes, of course on my bike."

She gives me the finger but still starts putting on her shoes.

Maybe this is what we both need: enough cold air and speed and danger to engage our brains, because nothing seems clear anymore.

We head outside, and once her arms are tight around me, I take off fast, the gravel spinning beneath the tires. I *need* fast. So does she. I can almost feel her excitement vibrating through my back.

I accelerate and she leans closer, her fingers pressing to my rib cage.

Yes, Kate, fucking cling. Just like that.

I bank right and she grips me tighter still.

How does she not understand that she needs this? That she's someone who wants to be thrilled and scared and challenged, and that these are things Caleb not only wouldn't provide, but would go out of his way to make sure she didn't get? He told me before I ever met her that he didn't want me to take her anywhere on my bike. *"She'll like it too much,"* he warned.

He thought she was a fire that might burn out of control. He thought he was protecting her when all he was really doing was depriving her of air.

Maybe I've been depriving us both of air too, with my insistence on not giving in to this thing between us. By the time I've pulled in front of the house, I've decided it's time to just let the fire burn.

I'll deal with the damage in the morning.

We climb off the bike. She removes her helmet and her eyes are gleaming, just like I knew they would.

I toss my helmet to the ground and march toward her.

"What are you doing?" she asks as I pull her against me.

My hands cradle her face, slide back into her hair. "First, I'm going to kiss you."

"And then what?" she asks, breathless.

I pull her lip between my teeth and release it. "And then I'm going to take my time doing all the things I should have done earlier."

Her hands slide inside my T-shirt. "I've got no complaints about earlier."

"Then I guarantee you'll have no complaints about this time either." If my mouth wasn't already back on hers, I'd probably be smiling right now.

27

KATE

I t's strange how very normal things are.

I slept in my own bed last night, but when I enter the kitchen in the morning, it's his T-shirt I'm wearing.

When he emerges from his room, deliciously bare-chested, his gaze consumes me, and his mouth lifts a quarter inch. There's an acknowledgment there, made silently: *I want you; you want me. No need to have a conversation about it, and we're probably not going to act on it again. Unless we do.*

When Ann calls, I don't mention this development, of course...adding to the slew of lies I'm already telling her: about how much I enjoy the daily NA meetings I attend, about how often I'm going to Hannah's grave, about how I'm *not* working at a bar. What's strange, though, is that when I tell her I'm starting to put Caleb behind me—which is definitely a lie—it sort of feels true.

I go into work although it's a Saturday and Beck's eyes linger on me as I walk past him. I'm fighting a smile as I continue to my desk.

God, the way he kissed me outside the cabin. And all the things he did to me once we got inside...

Jesus. He did *so many* things.

When he enters the office, we both look at his desk, where he fucked me within an inch of my life fifteen hours ago. If he suggests we try it again, I'll have my jeans off before he finishes the sentence.

I wish he would.

I have no idea why he's suddenly okay with this situation, but I don't see how I'll make it through the day without having him inside me, gripping my hips, doing his level best not to come before I do.

My services are not needed behind the bar that evening— not that I imagine Beck would allow me back there again anyway. I sit at home, overheated, my clothes constricting me. When the sound of his motorcycle wakes me at two AM, it's a struggle to stay in my own bed. I fall asleep dreaming of his head locked between my thighs.

He's up before me to surf the next morning and must head straight to the bar since he never returns.

I *need* him to return. I need a repeat of the other night like I need my next breath.

I'm in the kitchen when he walks out on Sunday morning, shirtless, with that fucking swagger of his. God, I love that swagger.

I picture his shoulders beneath my hands, his teeth sinking into my lower lip. If he's not going to fuck me again, he needs to start wearing more clothes around here.

"Let's go camping," he says.

"*Now?*"

He holds my gaze very deliberately. "It's on your bucket list, right? Lawrence can close. He owes me for Thursday night, and the bar will be dead anyway."

Camping isn't actually on my bucket list—it was just something I wanted to do when I was six. And today is Rachel's housewarming—my big chance to show Caleb I'm winning at life. But when I picture being in a very small tent with Beck—nowhere for either of us to scurry off to—it's as if the decision is made for me.

I fight a smile. "Yeah. Let's camp."

Beck hands me a grocery list on his way to borrow gear from Rachel's husband—an insultingly specific grocery list. *Buy four potatoes. If you come back with a fifty-pound bag, you, not me, will be carrying them.*

"I'm not an idiot," I huff as I read. "I wasn't going to buy a fifty-pound bag of potatoes."

"When you're the one carrying all our gear, you can determine whether or not you're an idiot. For now, let's just agree that you are."

When I return from the store, he's back too and carrying stuff to the truck. His gray T-shirt clings to him as he lifts, those biceps of his flexing. I picture them flexing as he hovers above me with that fierce concentration on his face, the almost pained look he gets when he's close and trying not to come. My skin *itches* with the need to see it again.

"See something you like?" he asks with a brow raised.

"Yeah," I reply. "That fifty-pound bag of potatoes you're lifting."

I *did* buy a ten-pound bag. Just to fuck with him.

He loads up the backpacks while I look at the clouds moving overhead. The weather is brilliant—sunny but crisp. "I hope Gus lent you some decent sleeping bags. It'll be cold tonight."

His glance flickers over me. There's a beat of silence. "I'm a furnace. You'll be fine."

So he plans to keep me warm. I'm beginning to see why people enjoy camping.

We climb in the car and head north to the mountains. Everything grows dense and green the farther we trek. I'm a city kid, but there's something about this—the clear sky, all the pine trees, the lack of traffic—that I don't mind, though I sort of suspect I wouldn't mind any trip if Beck was the guy at the wheel.

About an hour north of Elliott Springs, he swerves into a small gravel area off the shoulder of the road and I look around us in dismay. "We're camping *here?*" I ask.

He opens his door. "No, we're walking from here."

I jump out, meeting him at the back of the truck as he lowers the tailgate. "Uh, I thought we were going to like, put up a tent and then go look around."

He grins. "No. That's not what we're doing. Come on. Grab your pack."

I attempt to grab the backpack he's set against the tire and scowl at him. "This thing weighs roughly a million pounds. I thought *you* were going to do all the heavy lifting."

"I am. Lift your backpack and then lift mine. This would be a lot easier on you if you'd come into the yard to train with me like I've offered a hundred times."

"This would be a lot easier on me if you'd just carry all the stuff too," I counter.

The path he heads up once the packs are on is so narrow I'm not even sure it's actually a trail. He stops to hold a branch for me, which is the first gentlemanly thing he's done so far today.

A *true* gentleman would have parked at a fucking campground so we didn't have to lug all this shit around.

"How do you know where we're going?"

"Just guessing," he says over his shoulder. "If I'm wrong, we'll turn around."

"Well, how long is it going to take for you to figure out you're wrong? I don't want to walk three miles for nothing."

I hear his low laugh. "Don't worry your pretty head, *Kate*. Once in a while you've got to hand over the reins."

"Oh, I'll hand over the *reins*," I murmur. *Tonight. While we're sharing a tent.*

"What's that?" He smirks over his shoulder at me.

"I was talking to myself," I reply primly.

About twenty minutes in, we get to an overlook, and he tells me we're taking a break. My shoulders ache as I unceremoniously drop the pack and plop onto the large boulder in front of us. He produces a water bottle and I drain half of it immediately, silently thanking God I didn't bitch about the amount of water he was packing, which I definitely considered doing.

The sky is impossibly blue, the breeze just cool enough to be welcome.

I hold my face to the sun. I haven't thought about Hannah or Caleb until now. Should I feel guilty about that? I'm not sure.

When my eyes open, Beck is watching me. "How are you doing?"

I give him a small nod. "I'm good." It's only after I say the words aloud that I realize I actually mean them. I *am* good. I'm lighter. I can't stop smiling. I'm *happy*.

Not *almost* happy.

Not *less sad*.

Happy.

I've spent my entire life feeling as if I don't belong anywhere. And I don't know if I necessarily belong in the wilderness either, but when I'm with Beck, it doesn't matter. I know I'm not lost, and that's enough for now.

After a few minutes, he stands and helps me lift my pack. The weight appears to have doubled while we sat, and we've got a really steep climb ahead of us, but that's okay too.

I shift the weight of the pack as best I can, holding it up to relieve one shoulder, then the other, and I walk, and walk, and walk. It's funny, the way having so little to focus on makes the smallest things special: a cluster of wildflowers still growing despite the dry summer; birds chirping; a burbling brook we have to maneuver across.

It seems like hours before we stop again, at an overlook where the sharp peaks below us look like gently rolling hills.

"God," I groan. "I've never, in my entire life, appreciated sitting as much as I do right now."

He hands me my water. "It takes a little bad to appreciate the good."

"That sounds like some self-help bullshit right there," I reply, wiping my mouth on my sleeve.

He stares out at the view. "My mom always said that everything in life has a counterpoint, and you need one to appreciate the other. So you have to be hungry to appreciate being full. You've got to be tired to appreciate rest. Your fear of losing something makes you appreciate how much you love it. That's why it's better to go through the hard things than to avoid them...because it's going through that makes you grateful for what you have."

"That still sounds like self-help bullshit, but your mom sounds cool. I think I'd have liked her."

He looks over at me, a tiny smile on his face. "She'd have liked you too."

I laugh, the sound short and a little bitter. "Unlikely." His mouth opens and I wave him off. "I wasn't fishing for you to tell me otherwise. I'm bitchy and mean. I wouldn't like me much either."

"I would never in a million years use either of those words to describe you," he says, the words floating quietly in the afternoon air. "You lash out at the wrong people sometimes, but I've seen plenty of the other side of you, too."

Would he be so generous if he knew about the Facebook ads I targeted at Lucie? Or the way I've conspired with Kayleigh?

"If you think that," I reply slowly, "it's only because you don't know just how awful I've been."

He stretches out, using his backpack as a headrest. "What have you done that's so awful?"

I want to keep him talking because it means we get to rest longer, but I'm not sure this is a conversation I necessarily want to have. I can't tell him about the shit I've done to Lucie. I can't.

I guess there's a lot of other shit I've done, too, though. It festers, and I'm tired of it festering. I'm too exhausted—physically and emotionally—to keep lugging its weight.

I swallow. "I cheated on Caleb."

His jaw is knifelike in silhouette, his whole body tense. "When?"

I scuff my hiking boot along the dirt, unable to meet his gaze. "When I was using...Caleb was watching our money like a hawk. I could only withdraw small amounts at a time and I was desperate. And then I left rehab last year and started using again. It didn't even feel like a choice."

"Who was it?" His voice is gravel and ash. I wish I hadn't told him.

I grab a branch beside me and start drawing flowers in the dirt. "Kent. My dealer. That's where I stayed the second time I left rehab, when it looked like I'd just disappeared. I was barely even conscious for most of it."

The resulting silence makes my chest tighten. *Well done. You've proven to the one human being who liked you that you are truly awful.* "I told you I was evil."

He sits up. "That doesn't make you evil. You were an addict, and you were desperate. I fucking hate that you let him use you like that, but you're not the villain in that story. He is."

In foster care, I was always at fault. They expected me to have handled any situation that went badly in a different way, even if I'd seen other people do the same thing I had. No one, until Beck, has ever taken my side.

He rises to his feet, then pulls me up too. His hands squeeze mine for an extra second. And when he releases them and helps me put my backpack on...it seems a little lighter than it did before.

The higher we go, the quieter it seems to get. My breathing is labored, my shirt drenched in sweat, and I barely notice. My hideous brain—with its constant stream of insults and grievances—is silenced, too busy making sure I don't fall over rocks and downed tree limbs.

It's dusk when we reach our destination and I'm exhausted, but it's a good sort of exhaustion, one that makes me feel complete rather than depleted.

He puts up our tent and sends me to collect wood. Within an hour, night's fallen, but we have a fire blazing and baked potatoes are cooking in the coals . . . which he insists will work, though I have my doubts.

I skewer a hot dog on a stick and hold it over the fire while he does the same. My hands are filthy and this dinner is disgusting and yet . . . I'm still happy.

"I forgot to get mustard."

"You also didn't get ketchup," Beck adds.

"I *chose* not to get ketchup, because ketchup on a hot dog is vile and childlike."

"Your hot dog is burning."

"Fuck!" I swing the flaming skewer away from the fire and narrow my eyes at him as he laughs.

"You can make another one."

I grab the bun I'd set out and shake my head. "I'm too hungry to wait."

Shockingly, my charred hot dog on a bun, minus any condiments, is fucking delicious. I moan as I inhale it. "Oh my God, this is the best thing I've ever eaten. How is that even possible? I *hate* hot dogs."

He laughs. "I told you."

It takes a little bad to appreciate the good.

Maybe he was onto something. And maybe the bad I've gone through will make me appreciate Caleb that much more if we get back together. It wasn't perfect with him—there's a reason we were on the outs by the time I found out I was pregnant. We still won't go to concerts, we won't swim at night or ride on a motorcycle, but I'll remember the pain I went through and make it work somehow.

But there will also be no camping with Beck, no more shared looks at the bar, no more Game of Thrones. The future I killed myself to move toward suddenly doesn't appeal the way it's supposed to. I press a hand to my neck, reaching for the locket.

"What happened to it?" Beck asks, pushing our potatoes farther into the coals. "The locket."

I can't believe he remembers. I'm not sure Caleb ever noticed I had it in the first place.

I place another hot dog on my stick. "On my final night at Kent's, I had this dream," I begin slowly. "I was in the hospital with Caleb, and we'd had another baby. She looked just like Hannah."

When I woke, I could still feel her weight in my arms. I can feel it even now. God, it was so real.

He looks at me, waiting for the rest.

"From the moment I realized I could have another daughter just like her, nothing mattered more in the entire world than making it happen. I was still high, but I tried to leave and Kent ripped my locket off my neck. He said it was 'collateral' so I'd come back."

Beck rises to his feet. "Where is this guy? Is he in Elliott Springs or somewhere else?" His voice is a low hiss, tinged with violence.

"Don't," I say firmly. "He is *not* someone you fuck with."

He raises a brow. "I'm not either."

"Yeah, except he has guns, and guys who do shit for him." I

pull my hot dog off the stick and throw it inside a bun. "I'll get it eventually."

He crouches so that we are face to face. "Don't go without me, okay? Please."

"Do you promise no punches will be thrown?"

"As long as none are necessary."

I laugh. "If you're going to equivocate, then so will I. *Maybe* you can come."

"You're a pain in the ass," he says, smiling, retaking his seat beside me, his thigh brushing mine.

He really isn't judging me for what I did. He isn't judging me for losing the last memento I had of my child, her tiny little lock of red hair.

It's a gift, that lack of judgment of his.

"That's why you got clean, then? That dream about Hannah?" he asks after a moment.

I nod. I wanted a baby with eyes like hers, staring up at me again. I'd do anything, give up anything, to have that moment...

And for that, I need Caleb. Because my little girl looked just like her dad, and he's the only way I'll ever bring her back.

THE POTATOES TURN OUT PERFECTLY, just as he promised, and though I'm absolutely stuffed, we roast marshmallows as the night grows colder. I burn those too, so Beck takes over, providing me one that is perfect: crisp on the outside, dripping on the inside. "You're good at everything," I groan. "It's a little unfair."

His glance slides over to me, a hint of something dirty around his mouth. "Yeah? Tell me what else I'm good at."

"Carrying stuff."

He rises, throwing the rest of his water on the fire to put it out. "That's the most boring thing I've ever heard."

I grin. "Yes, but it's that *plus* the marshmallows. Either one on its own is kind of lame, but together they're spectacular."

"Well, since I've already wowed you with my two greatest skills, I guess we should call it a night."

He hangs all our food from a tree so bears won't get into it while I go into the tent. I remove my bra from under my T-shirt, peel off my leggings *and* my panties—ever the optimist—and climb into my sleeping bag. Under normal circumstances, I wouldn't be a fan of this sleeping situation, but I'm so exhausted from the hike and sore from exertion that simply lying down is bliss.

He crouches to enter, consuming every available inch of space.

I laugh. "I think by 'two-person tent,' they meant persons of *my* size, not yours."

"I think I'll fit just fine," he growls, and my stomach tightens. I've got no idea if he meant that to sound as filthy as it did.

I hope so.

There's a thud as his hiking boots land in the corner of the tent, the slide of his zipper. I clench around air simply at the sound, and then he slides into the sleeping bag beside mine but doesn't pull me toward him.

"Did you have fun today?" There's detached curiosity in his voice. He doesn't need me to say *yes*. It's one of the things I love about Beck...he doesn't make me pretend things are okay if they're not.

"Yeah, actually. I'm surprised."

"Flattering."

I laugh. "You know what I mean."

I picture what could happen next—how he might say, "*I know how to make it more fun,*" and roll me beneath him. His mouth on my neck, on my breasts, on my hips. His weight pinning me to the ground as he takes over.

I'm still picturing it when I hear him zip up his sleeping bag and disappointment lands deep in my gut. *I guess we're not making it more fun, then.*

The crickets' buzzing becomes a cacophony outside, but inside the tent I hear only his quiet breathing, which grows even as he falls asleep.

Meanwhile, I'm taut with yearning, nipples stiff against my T-shirt, imagining all the things he *could* have done tonight. We are like a story that was cut off just before the end, a story I was *really* invested in.

I roll his way. I never get to just gaze at him. It's a somewhat pathetic silver lining to tonight's abrupt end, but it's all I've got.

He's wide awake, facing me. "I thought you'd fallen asleep," he says.

Our eyes hold until he bridges the distance, his mouth locking with mine, making a noise that is half relief and half pain. My arms wrap around his neck, pulling him closer as he tugs my sleeping bag open and one hand slides over my hip. The kiss is soft, and his fingers are light as they brush between my legs, teasing and gentle. The world outside falls silent— there is only the sound of me growing slick at his touch, his quiet grunt against my ear when I arch into his hand.

"I've spent the whole day wanting to be inside you," he says. His voice is low and rough, a thread of an ache in it that I've never heard before. "The whole fucking day."

He reaches behind him and grabs the condom he apparently had waiting, just in case, and then he kneels between my spread thighs, rolling it on while he looks at me as if I'm the only thing he's ever wanted. He pushes inside me, and I tip from the cusp of pain to something I've never experienced with anyone else.

My skin is too tight, my blood too hot. I want every inch of him covering me and the taste of him on my tongue and yet . . . there's something sweet beneath it at the same time. Something expanding in my chest as I watch him, that happiness from earlier still echoing, demanding my attention.

He thrusts and I struggle to keep my eyes open from the pleasure. But I want to. I want to memorize the strain on his face, the focus, the way he grows heavy-lidded and dazed like a junkie as a needle hits the vein.

The tent echoes with the sounds we make—the wet slap of skin on skin, my gasps, his grunts. I cry out and he swells inside me, coming with those violent, involuntary thrusts of his.

He lets his weight collapse on top of me the way I'd hoped he would, leaving us joined and perfect.

Why is it so much better with him?

I silence the thought the second I hear it. And then another deeply disloyal thought comes unbidden, one I can't entirely silence: *How will I stand to go through my whole life without ever having this again?*

28

BECK

W e don't discuss it because that would require words she can't say.

But every minute I'm inside her is more perfect than the one before it.

It's different with us. I know she's aware of it.

In the morning, I'm up—and hard as a rock—when she finally begins to yawn and stretch. I resist the urge to pull her against me or brush her hair back from her face. I spent most of the night resisting a whole lot of urges, so I've had some practice.

She's facing away from me but turns her head up to stare at the ceiling of the tent. "It's raining?"

It is, which means the trip back to the car is gonna suck. Kate enjoyed yesterday—she's hardly the type to claim she's pleased when she's not—but hiking with a pack on in pouring rain might sour her on ever doing this again. Not that I should be *hoping* we will ever do this again. I've always thought about the future with her, though. Even when she was pregnant with someone else's kid.

"Yeah," I reply. "Yet somehow the weather said there was zero chance of rain."

She glances over her shoulder at me. "You don't really expect me to hike in this, right? Can we just stay in the tent until it passes?"

My tongue glides over my upper lip. "What would we do in here for hours though?"

She scoots against me, and I hear a muffled noise, a laugh and a groan combined, when she feels me pressed hard to her back. "I can think of a thing or two."

If she were anyone else, I'd slide against her ass, back and forth, savoring the buildup. But she's the one who *ostensibly* wants her husband back, and each time with us has had the appearance of a mistake, something that happens at night in a haze, when it doesn't seem to entirely count.

"The ball's in your court," I tell her.

"Literally," she says, and my laughter is cut short by the slide of her hand down my waistband.

She tugs my boxers down and climbs above me, sliding over my cock simply to torture me until I can't stand it anymore.

I flip her on her stomach and am pulling her up by her hips before I've even thought it through. I slide my fingers between her legs—she's so slick and tight that I want to come just at the thought of pushing inside her...until I remember we can't.

I flinch. "Fuck. We used the last condom already."

There are other things we can do, but right now I just want this—her back arching as I push inside her, those breathy, animal sounds she makes as she gets close, and the way I have to fight not to lose it when it happens.

She glances at me over her shoulder, all feline-eyed and breathless. "Are you okay? I got tested in rehab and still have my IUD."

I haven't had unprotected sex since I was a moronic high

school student, but I want it with her more than I've ever wanted anything in my whole life. "Yes."

I tug my shorts down and I'm bottoming out inside her a second later.

The heat, the wetness...my God, it's so different. She's pulsing around me like the beat of a heart, and when she starts gasping and pleading, I have to shut it out. If I don't, this will end far too soon.

She no longer supports her weight, her face pressed to the sleeping bag, flushed and dazed, lips swollen, unspeakably beautiful. This is Kate under my sway, begging for things she wants from *me*, not him. I've fantasized about this a thousand times, but the reality of it is so much better. "I don't want this to end," she whispers.

I don't want *any* of it to end, and she doesn't either. I just wish she'd fucking realize it.

29

KATE

M id-morning, he ventures into the rain to get the bear bag. We cut off wedges of pepperoni and eat it with a chaser of trail mix. And then I climb above him again, because torturing Beck until he pins me down and fucks me is my new favorite sport.

The rain has slowed but not stopped when we finally pack everything, and the slog back to the truck is straight out of a survival show—the trail slick with mud, and the extra-heavy wet backpack making every slip that much more terrifying.

We cross a stream that didn't exist the day before, and I fall flat on my back. Thanks to the backpack, I'm unable to right myself until Beck returns to help me up.

"I hate this," I tell him as he grabs my hands. "I hate this so much."

He gives me a hint of a smile. "No, you don't."

I'm caked in mud, starving, and my thighs are so sore that every step I take is agony, but even as my mouth opens to argue, I know he's right: the past twenty-four hours are the best ones I've had in years.

We reach the truck at last. I let the pack slide to the ground with a groan and massage my aching shoulders. He lowers the tailgate and I hop up, groaning again as I sit.

He pulls the dry bag out of his pack and hands me a hoody. "Put that on. Once we're in the truck, the sweaty clothes are gonna make you cold. Take off the sports bra too."

I raise a brow. "Trying to see me naked again?"

"Face it, Kate," he says with a muffled laugh, pulling on a clean shirt while I slide my sports bra out through the sleeve of my shirt. "I could tell you to get naked and on all fours right here and you'd do it."

Okay, yes, perhaps.

Once the stuff is in the truck, I climb in, marveling at how luxurious car seats are for the first time in my life. He cranks the heat—another luxury. It's too late in the day for breakfast burritos and we're too muddy to go into a restaurant anyway, but nothing has ever tasted better than the cheeseburgers and fries we get from a drive-thru on the way home. He's got some early 2000s station playing and I sing along with every song, still happy, still wanting for nothing.

The sun is out by the time we arrive. He showers while I throw our filthy clothes in the wash, humming a song we heard earlier. It's not until I'm standing in the shower myself that reality sets in. I'm still his closest friend's wife and there is no way for us to incorporate who we've been for the last day into our normal lives.

But then I emerge from the shower. My face is bare, my hair is wet, my legs are covered in bruises...yet he still watches me as if he's never seen anything as delicious, his features sharpening like an animal on the cusp of attack.

Gulp. Maybe we aren't returning to normal.

I sit on the barstool and start towel-drying my hair. "I guess it's safe for me to leave the room wearing a T-shirt now?"

"Define *safe*," he says, walking toward me. My heart is fluttering and the excitement borders on unbearable.

He pulls the towel from my hands as he moves between my legs, his tented shorts brushing my inner thighs. "It's probably time I stop pretending this isn't happening. And you're not wearing panties. So I guess you were done pretending too."

This development should terrify me. Instead, I'm simply relieved.

I'D THOUGHT it might be weird if I stayed in his room. It's something couples do, and we are not a couple.

It is not weird, given that I'm still half asleep when he's inside me the following morning, and it's pretty hard to pretend something didn't happen when it's still going on.

He goes into work, assuring me we won't have sex again for "at least seven hours," but when I walk through the bar's saloon doors, my gaze is on him like I'm the bad guy in a western, and he's the sheriff. As if he's my only reason for walking in here in the first place.

This time I don't give him my standard half-assed wave—nor do I act as if I haven't seen him. I walk straight to the bar with blinders on, drawn to that dirty thing in his eyes, that filthy half-smile on his face. "If you keep looking at me like that, we aren't going to make it seven hours."

His gaze drops to my mouth. "Hasn't it been seven hours already?"

I glance at my watch. It's been ninety minutes. "Yes, it's definitely been seven hours."

We have sex in his office. Later, it's the ladies' room at The Midnight House. In the days that follow, it's in his truck, the stairs to his front door, the stairs out the back door, and atop every piece of furniture he owns. We are like children playing obsessively with a new toy we know we can't keep.

He closes the bar a lot less than he used to. On the nights when he does come home late, I'm already in his bed or he scoops me off the couch to bring me there. In his spare time, he talks about places he'd like to see and even pulls up Shelter Cove online and plots out a weekend there for us.

It's as if we're on vacation from real life, except we're not. He's still got this bar he hates and a group of friends who'd probably never forgive him for what's going on with me. And I'm still planning to move my life forward, somehow, in ways that can't involve him.

"Anything today?" he asks when I walk into work after my standard hour of combing the Internet for jobs.

"There was one, actually. Holzig. This ski company. They're hiring a vice president of business development."

The moment I saw the job in my inbox, my blood began to flow faster. Holzig makes amazing, cutting-edge ski and resort wear. They have the potential to become a Hurley or North Face with the right guidance, and *God*, I'd love to be the one providing it.

He closes the dishwasher. "You'd want to do that?"

"It's the job of my dreams, but I'll never get it."

"You don't know that. I'd hire you if I was their CEO."

I need to change the topic because this one depresses me. I lean closer, though no one else is around to hear us anyway. "That's because I'd blow you every day after lunch."

His eyes grow hazy. *Mission accomplished.*

He lifts two clean glasses from the dishrack and slides them onto a shelf. "You know, when you say shit like that to me, it sounds like you're offering."

I grin. "I thought it went without saying that I'm offering."

He braces himself on the bar with a brow raised. "First, we need to discuss why you're so scared to apply for this job."

Dammit.

I throw out my hands. "I'm not scared. There's just no point!"

"Would you stake your life on it? Is there even a *one* percent chance that their CEO is as idiotic as me and would hire you?"

I shrug. "Fine. *Maybe* a one percent chance."

"Then you don't know for sure, and you're being a coward."

I laugh. "Calling me a coward is not the way to make this conversation lead to sex."

His tongue slides over his upper lip. "I don't need to make this conversation lead to sex. That part was already established. But now you're not getting it until you've applied for that job."

BECK READS my cover letter to Holzig over my shoulder the next morning like a helicopter parent. He hasn't laid a finger on me in a full day.

"No," he says.

I turn to look up at him. "What the hell is wrong with it?"

"You know exactly what this company needs to blow up, but that cover letter sounds like one you've sent to a hundred other places. Stop phoning this in like it's something you're certain isn't going to happen."

"Funny how the guy who faked tax returns four years in a row is suddenly a master of industry," I mutter, turning to delete the letter.

He leans down, laughing as he presses a kiss to the top of my head. "It's cute, the way you get so irritated when I'm right."

Once he leaves, I turn back to my laptop and begin again. This time, I lay out what they're doing well—*and* what they could be doing better.

It's a risky strategy, one that could easily piss off whoever's reading it, but if Holzig is actually interested in winning at this, they might be willing to hear some constructive criticism.

I'd hire the person who wrote this letter. But would I hire her after I learned she was a drug addict? Would I hire her if I discovered there'd been some financial mismanagement at her last job?

Probably not. I guess I'm really just hoping someone at Holzig has more faith in human nature than I do.

30

KATE

I'm standing at the bar with Beck, nagging him about paperwork, when Rachel bursts in, waving a file in the air. "Look what I have!" she cries. "Berkeley sent your list!"

She pulls me toward the office. "There are a lot of names," she warns, handing me the file. "It's going to take a while."

My stomach tightens. I might know who my father is today. Maybe he has no clue I exist or maybe he's an asshole who just wishes I *didn't* exist. Maybe I have brothers or sisters and will go from having no family at all to a large one in a matter of hours, or maybe he's a gross old man who preys on his students and will deny everything.

When we get into the office, I open the file—between visiting professors, research faculty, and teaching assistants, there are at least fifty names. I increasingly want to forget this whole thing. "I appreciate this, but you didn't need to drive it over. You should be resting."

She shoves my shoulder. "Are you kidding? We need to start researching!" She grabs one of the two sheets from the folder and marches toward Beck's desk. "You take half and I'll take half."

"Rachel, what the hell are we even going to do? Do we write and ask if they slept with one of their students a couple decades ago? They probably *all* did. And who's going to admit to it?"

"We can narrow it down somewhat. It had to have been a man, first of all, and he probably wasn't eighty?"

I walk with resignation to my laptop. "She was only nineteen when she had me, so I really hope not."

But I have no idea who my mother was as a person or why she was sleeping with this guy. Would a girl failing a freshman econ class be desperate enough to sleep with a man old enough to be her grandfather? I'm pretty ruthless—she may have been too.

We agree that sixty-five is a reasonable cut-off and spend the next hour in silence looking up names. Searching almost any name along with "Berkeley" and "economics" leads to a thousand worthless results. I sink a little farther into my seat with every false lead.

"So far, I have eight different guys who could potentially have fathered me. And that's assuming my mom even *slept* with the mystery professor. This is a wild goose chase."

"It's not," she says, stretching her arms overhead. Out of nowhere, exhaustion seems etched across her features.

"Are you okay?"

She smiles and yawns. "Yes. Although I think it may be nap time soon."

I hesitate. I mostly act as if I've forgotten she's going to be a parent, but I don't resent her the way I do Lucie and others. It doesn't feel as if her pregnancy has taken something away from me.

"You must have the nursery all set up by now," I venture.

"Getting there," she replies. "If you'd come to our house-warming, you'd have known that already."

"Sorry. I'd thought it might be awkward with Caleb and Lucie there."

She leans back in her seat, placing a hand over her baby bump and smiling. "I keep forgetting you were married to him. I can't see you with anyone but Beck."

"I'm not *with* Beck."

Her eyes roll and she yawns again. "Are you seriously still pretending that? The two of you were *seconds* from banging when I walked in. Probably back here." Her nose wrinkles. "God. Please tell me you don't have sex on this desk."

She doesn't really want the answer to that.

"I'm ignoring you," I reply, putting the list of names back in the folder. "But you should go home and nap. The rest of this can wait. I'm not even sure I want to know."

"Fine," she says, slowly rising, holding a hand to the small of her back, "but I'm not letting you off the hook."

I nod, though once she has the baby, she won't have time for any of this. She leaves and I promptly shove the folder in a drawer. I'm back at work and have half-forgotten the whole thing when Beck walks in.

"Any luck?" he asks.

I close the laptop again. "So far, we have a list of twenty guys who *may* have slept with my mom, in violation of university policy. In unrelated news, we also have a list of twenty guys who probably won't admit they slept with my mom."

He comes around to my side of the desk and perches on the edge before pulling me up to stand between his legs. "You're going to find him," he says, brushing a lock of hair behind my ear. "He probably has no idea and will be thrilled to discover you exist."

God, he's sweet. And biased. "I'm not sure an unemployed drug addict is really the kid anyone's thrilled to find out about."

His finger lifts my chin so I meet his eye. "Stop that. You're a gorgeous, brilliant twenty-eight-year-old who grew up in foster care and still managed to get a degree from the best business school in the country. And you're going to find a better job than this eventually."

My heart races. As much as I want him to be right, I also...don't.

The idea of not living with Beck anymore, not working for Beck, terrifies me.

It's made me soft, these months of leaning on him, and sleeping with him probably hasn't helped either, but I don't want to think about that now.

I press my mouth to his as I glide my palms up his thighs. "Did you lock that door, by chance?"

"I didn't." He releases me. "Are you asking because you want it, or because you're trying to change the subject?"

I cup him. He's hard in the time it takes me to reach his belt. "Can't it be both?"

I slide to my knees.

"Yeah," he says with a quiet smirk. "I guess it can be both."

On the Sunday before Labor Day, we take his bike to Carmel. Mostly it's an excuse to go for a ride, but it's a town I've always loved. The air is crisp and the colors around me are saturated—the September sky bluer than the deepest ocean.

The foam of the cappuccino he bought me rests on my upper lip. He swipes it off with his thumb, allowing it to slide down my lower lip as it goes. The way he looks at me as he does it makes my eyes want to shut, makes me want to open my mouth and suck hard.

He laughs. "Jesus, you've got a dirty mind."

"Right. It's just *my* mind that's dirty. That's why you knew exactly what I was thinking."

We walk and his fingers twine with mine. I allow it, even though that's not what this is. And just for now I imagine a different life, one where I can walk down the street with him just like this, in a town I love under a brilliant sky. If I were someone different than I am, a life like this would make me ridiculously, exquisitely happy.

That night, we drive out to the beach to camp. We dare each other to jump in the ocean and, as neither of us can turn down a dare, we both wind up soaking wet, shivering next to the fire.

He pulls a sweater over my head and looks at me—my hair wet, my face without a stitch of makeup—as if he's the luckiest man alive.

"How's this comparing to Shelter Cove so far?" he asks with a soft smile.

I laugh. "I wouldn't know. I'm sure it sucks, but I was a six-year-old in foster care. Those false promises people make stick with you."

The waves crash, filling the silence that stretches out. I wish I hadn't brought it up.

"Who the fuck promises a kid in foster care something like that and doesn't follow through?" he finally asks. "Is this the same woman who said she was adopting you?"

"Yeah."

Those afternoons in her house were a little like this time with Beck—all sunshine and bliss, unsustainably so. Except I was too young to realize joy like that doesn't last, which made the end hurt that much more.

"One of her kids had just died, which can lead to bad decision-making. But what really sucks is that I don't know how to turn a discussion about Mimi into sexual innuendo. I should be better at this."

He laughs. "Take off your clothes. That's all the innuendo you need."

I rise and pull my sweater over my head, followed by my T-shirt. The heat of the fire creeps along my side as I turn to face him. His eyes glitter, darker than they were a moment before. I step out of my sweatpants and panties and straddle him, relishing the press of his erection between my legs.

"Get that bra off too," he rasps.

I reach into his shorts. "Don't worry. It's all coming off."

Perhaps I haven't changed all that much since childhood. Because right now, happiness like this feels like it could almost be permanent.

31

KATE

The missed call notification from an unknown number means little to me until I play the message that was left.

"Kate, this is Adam Weintraub with Holzig," the voice begins. Weintraub is the CEO. *The fucking CEO called me himself.* And he sounds cheerful, as if he's got amazing news. "Your letter just came across my desk, and I'm really excited to talk to you a little more."

Oh my God.

Oh my fucking God.

There's a buzz of excitement in my chest, whether I should allow it to be there or not. It will probably come to nothing, but simply the fact that he's called and my letter got him interested thrills me.

I call his number with shaking hands and leave a message before racing out of the office to tell Beck. "I got an interview. With *Holzig*. I just sent them my resume on Thursday. I can't believe they've already called."

He shuts the dishwasher door, happy for me, hopeful. Except hopefulness here is ill-advised.

"I'm not going to get it, though," I add.

He scoops ice into a glass and sprays it full of soda. "You might. If you actually try."

"I always *try*."

He raises a brow. "Do you? Or do you hold back just a little each time so it doesn't hurt as much when you lose?"

I hate when he's right. I haven't prepped for a single interview since I got back, and it wouldn't have mattered in either case if I had, but I didn't know that going in. I expected to fail, and I wanted to be able to tell myself afterward that I hadn't tried my hardest.

I can't keep expecting to fail. It's going to matter eventually.

"You really do know me better than I know myself sometimes," I admit. "It's creepy."

"That's because we are so much alike."

"So what are you not putting yourself into a hundred percent?"

His eyes flicker over me and away. "Plenty."

He doesn't want to fully invest himself in something he might not get to keep.

I wish I could tell him he was wrong.

FOR THE WEEK before my interview, I study Holzig as if my life depends on it—their strengths, their weaknesses, the competition.

Just sitting down at my laptop to research has me breathing a little fast. I'm *made* for this job, and if I don't get it, my heart will break.

Which scares me. Because it's been broken once too often already.

I'm awake at dawn on the morning of the interview, too

excited and nervous to sleep. I have abundant time to get ready, but suddenly it's ten and there's no time at all.

"Where the hell are my heels?" I shout, more to myself than Beck. "How could I have lost them when I only own six fucking things?"

"They're right behind you, babe," he says, watching my meltdown with quiet amusement.

He crosses the room, towering over me as he places my phone in my hands. "Kate, *breathe*. You're going to be great."

And before I can process it, his palms cradle my face and his mouth fuses with mine, stealing my breath and running all that chaos off to far corners of my mind. When he pulls back, my brain is stunned into silence. We don't do this. We don't kiss if we aren't in the process of inserting body parts into other body parts, but he just kissed me like he actually cared.

And I liked that he did it.

It's dangerous.

"Okay, thanks," I whisper, before I turn and half stumble toward the door.

DOWNTOWN SAN FRANCISCO is nearly ninety minutes from Elliott Springs. I give myself an extra hour to allow for traffic and parking and I need every minute of it.

By the time I walk into a conference room flanked by floor-to-ceiling glass windows, I could swear this day has already been a hundred hours long.

Adam Weintraub enters right after me, alone. I sort of knew what to expect since he's been getting a lot of publicity and his brother is a pretty well-known snowboarder—dark hair and stylish glasses, trim, mid-forties—but he's much more buoyant and friendly than I'd have anticipated. He's also gay, so at least I don't have to worry that he's brought me in here to offer me a *special friendship*.

We shake hands and take our seats, and then he grins at me. "Kate, welcome! What's up with the long absence from the workforce?"

I choke on a nervous laugh to cover the way my stomach is sinking. "Wow, I thought I'd get some time to work up to that part."

He smiles again. "I like to address the elephant in the room first. Easy to do, I know, when it's not my elephant."

Fuck my life. I guess we're doing this. Will I even get a chance to show him how much I've prepared?

I swallow, pressing my palms flat to the table. "I went to rehab three times. It took me a while to make it stick, but I've been clean for nearly six months. I know that's a huge red flag for a lot of people, but I hope you'll at least hear me out. I've researched you extensively, and I have a lot of ideas about where the company could go."

"Three years?" he asks. "Then it took you half as long as it took my little brother to get through it."

What? I knew his brother had flamed out during the last Olympics, but I hadn't seen a word about substance abuse. "I had no idea. I guess he kept it out of the press."

He shrugs. "Matt still thinks it hurts his cool-guy image if people know he's clean, but anyway, your time in rehab isn't a red flag for me. So, let's hear your pitch."

Hope is an emotion that shoots you into the clouds and leaves you in free fall when it disappears, but I'm feeling it anyway. Adam's willing to give me a chance. He cares about what I can do, and I *can* do this job.

I deliver every last idea I have about the direction the company should take and the challenges that lie in taking it.

He follows up with questions, even arguing at points, but always respectfully. He'd be the perfect boss.

When I leave an hour later, I'm floating and Beck's the only person I want to tell.

"I don't hear from you when things go bad," he says when I call, quiet laughter in his voice, "which means this must have gone well."

"I don't know," I tell him, fumbling for my car keys. "I'm guessing every single interviewee walks out this guy's best friend. In other words, I may be no better off today than I was after any other interview. Maybe he was just better at hiding it."

"Or maybe you killed it, and he plans to hire you."

God, I hope so.

Except it means living pretty far from Elliott Springs, a possibility that worries me the entire trip home.

I'm nearly back to the cabin before I realize it's not the distance from *Caleb* that worried me.

32

KATE

I wake one week later with my leg thrown over Beck's, his arm beneath my head.

His face is untroubled in sleep, his wide mouth relaxed. I edge closer, wishing I could see him like this all the time. Whether or not he admits it, the bar is the problem. It's too little of what he loves and too much of what he doesn't. He needs to be outside, moving. I tug the covers over his shoulders, remembering what he said about owning a gym. It would be perfect for him, and I might be able to help him make it happen.

When I get into work, I study the bar's overall profitability. I've nearly got his financials shored up, and it's clear he could easily sell or bring in investors, which would allow him to step away and do something else.

It's just guilt holding him here—nothing more. I have no idea how to deal with that part, however.

"Please tell me you're busy hunting for your dad right now," says Rachel, stepping through the door.

"I kind of put it out of my head, to be honest."

"Come on!" she says, throwing her arms wide. "We're

solving a mystery! Like a real-life *CSI*. Well, not *CSI*, obviously, because that would mean your dad had been found in a dumpster or was some kind of child rapist, but you know what I mean."

I laugh. "Your life needs more excitement."

"Tell Gus," she groans, perching on the edge of Beck's desk. "I'm no longer allowed to ride in the Jeep because it might jostle the baby, and he's even scared to have sex—not that there's any easy way to do that when your stomach juts out a foot in front of you."

My heart squeezes—a single, sharp burst of pain. If Caleb and I had worried more, could we have changed things? It's unlikely, but as Beck said when he was urging me to apply to Holzig, a one percent chance is still a chance. "Well, there are worse things than a super-involved husband."

Her laughter comes to an abrupt stop. She places a hand on her chest. "Fuck. I'm sorry. I'm sure it sounded like a complaint. It really wasn't."

"I know."

She continues to look so horrified that—though searching for my dad is the last thing I feel like doing—I wave her toward Beck's desk. "Okay, *CSI*. Let's do this."

She sits before pulling out her laptop, and we return to our search, working in silence. After thirty minutes, I've added five more names to the list of people who won't want to admit they slept with a student.

"This is pointless." I sigh, shoving my laptop away.

I look over to where she's staring intently at her screen. "I don't think it is," she says quietly.

She turns her laptop toward me, and I jolt as if I've been shocked.

The eye shape. The cheekbones.

They're mine.

He's young and handsome, but that's not why I continue to

stare. There's something more about the picture, something I can't place. A distant bell rings in the far recesses of my brain. "I feel like I've seen him before."

Her eyes widen. "Really? You know him?"

I shake my head. "It's not exactly that. I just...There's something familiar there."

I skirt around the desk to read his name. Walker Collins.

It takes a second. It takes a second for *Collins* and *Walker* to register. For me to connect it to a photo I once saw of a happy little boy camping with his family on Shelter Cove, so cheerful on the other side of that paper. A little boy who's no longer alive.

Which means this hunt was truly for nothing. And Mimi, the woman who'd said she was going to adopt me then skipped town without saying goodbye, was my grandmother.

"He's dead," I announce quietly. "I knew his mom."

Her face falls. "Are you sure?"

"I'm pretty sure," I reply.

It took us ages to find this guy, but we manage to locate an article about his death in seconds.

The body of a man who allegedly jumped from the Golden Gate Bridge Tuesday night has been identified as that of UC-Berkeley associate professor Walker Collins. The body was recovered 10 miles from the bridge late last night. Collins, a graduate of MIT and Oxford, was well-liked, according to a campus spokesman. Errol Laudberg, Dean of Economics at MIT, said he was "devastated" by the loss. "He was a brilliant economist and a good friend. It is a loss for our entire field, and a very personal one for those of us lucky enough to have known him."

Collins is survived by his parents, Francesca and Duncan Collins, and his sister, Natalie Collins. He will be laid to rest on Saturday at St. Paul's Church in Tacoma, Washington. In

lieu of flowers, the family asks that donations be made to the National Suicide Hotline.

My throat aches, though sadness over the death of a man I never knew makes no sense. Maybe it's simply that looking at his picture is like looking at a version of myself. Maybe it's because I understand too well the kind of despair that would lead you to jump off a bridge. The hardest part of it all, though, is that my own grandmother knew me well...and decided I wasn't worth her time.

I didn't bring enough to the table for her, just like I didn't bring enough to the table for anyone else. Not my father, not my mother, and not Caleb.

I came into the world by accident and made most of my foster parents miserable. Someone married me because he thought he had to and I cheated on him and cleaned out a bank account.

And then there's Hannah—to whom I was going to give everything, all the love no one else had ever wanted from me. She stared up at me with absolute faith in those brief moments she was alive, but then I failed her too.

It's hard to fault Mimi when it's so clear she made the right choice.

33

KATE

The news about my father sits like a brick in my stomach for the next week. There's no word from Holzig, either. It was unrealistic of me to hope I'd get the job in the first place, but that doesn't make the silence hurt less.

I just wish all this news, or lack thereof, hadn't occurred *now*, just before Hannah's birthday. I have to go to her grave, which means I can finally stop lying to Ann, but I'd hoped to feel a little stronger than I do at this point.

On the eve of her birthday, before Beck gets home, I pull out the box I keep under my bed. It only brings pain, but I return to it compulsively because it's all I have left. The child I never raised is a wound inside me that just won't heal, and this box is how I scrape away the scabs to make sure of that. Because she deserves to be remembered.

It holds a few of her sweetest, tiniest clothes—all unworn. It holds every sonogram picture, her hospital bracelet. And then there are the letters. Letters I wrote her every single week, waiting for her to be born. I pull them out, knowing I shouldn't read them.

Knowing I'm going to do it anyway.

Dear Hannah,

Today I am thirty-one weeks along, and I'm already planning ten years out. When you're old enough, we're going to hike out to Shelter Cove. Someone told me about it once. We will camp on the black sand beach, and I'll teach you how to bake a cake in a fire using an empty orange peel. I bought you a dress for Christmas today and told your father he didn't want to know how much it cost. He said, "I've got another eighteen years of hearing that, don't I?"

Love,

Mommy

DEAR HANNAH,

You are due in five weeks. That means five weeks from now you'll be here, in this rocking chair with me. Five weeks from now, your tiny fist will grab my pinkie. I don't know how it's even possible to love someone as much as I love you, but it's the realest thing I've ever felt.

Love,

Mommy

I read through every last letter, full of details I'd have forgotten if they weren't written down. That Caleb had insisted he could install the car seat himself and it flipped over the first time we drove anywhere. That I'd promised to take her to Park City, where we'd learn to ski together, and that I'd teach her what every fork was for at a fancy dinner so she wouldn't get ridiculed in grad school. One letter is just a list of names Caleb liked that I'd vetoed. *"You owe me one,"* I told her. *"His top choice was Clementine."*

I don't cry, reading the letters, because I won't stop if I let myself start. But the ache in my chest as I put the box away feels like more than I can bear, the kind of ache that could send me to a dark place, though I suspect I'm already in one. I wish I could tell Beck, but it sounds too crazy.

"You're not gonna eat?" he asks over dinner, nodding at my largely untouched plate.

"I'm not all that hungry. Do you want it?" He's already had seconds, but there are no limits to how much food he can put away.

"No," he says. "I want *you* to eat it. You skipped lunch too. Are you sick?"

I shake my head. "I'm just not hungry."

I try to force down another bite, but it's stuck in my throat. Three years ago tonight, I sat with Caleb eating a Cobb salad. I'd asked for it without blue cheese—one of a thousand foods you can't eat while pregnant—but it came with it anyway. I picked most of it out, but I wondered afterward if *that* was the culprit, those traces I'd left behind.

The things I might have done differently, the things that might have saved my daughter, are endless. Maybe if I'd deserved her in the first place, I'd have done them.

Beck holds me close that night. He places his hand on my forehead to check my temperature and I insist that I'm just tired.

I'm scared that if I tell him all the things I could have done to prevent what happened, he'll agree. I couldn't survive hearing him agree.

When I wake in the morning, there's a sick thud in my stomach. He presses a hand to my forehead again, a deep groove forming between his brows. "Stay home and rest," he insists.

It's probably the last thing I should agree to, especially as I have no intention of remaining at home. The minute he leaves for work, I'm out the door too.

I reach the graveyard quickly and walk the overgrown path.

Hannah Lowell

September 28, 2020

I take a seat in the grass, remembering her first thin, reedy cry, a miracle I'd waited forty-one weeks to hear.

I held her and marveled at her perfect mouth and fingers and her wide-open eyes, so alert for a newborn. Caleb's eyes. She looked up at me in a way I'd never expected, as if she were already trying to figure things out.

"Hannah," I whispered, slipping a pinky into her tiny fist, "you're already smarter than me and your dad put together, aren't you?"

The nurse fussed over me, pitying me for my husband's absence. I'd been mad before, that Caleb had gone down to San Diego for a meeting, but it no longer mattered. I had my daughter, and I didn't need anything else.

The nurse offered to take Hannah to the nursery and give her formula so I could rest, but I insisted on keeping her with me. I marveled at her tiny hands, at her perfect toes, at the way her mouth began to root at the air, wanting to be fed.

She'd be a survivor like me—I could already tell. I dropped the shoulder of my hospital gown, and Hannah continued to stare up at me with her trusting eyes as she latched on. I smiled as her lids fell shut.

It was perfect. It was my most perfect moment.

And then everything went wrong. The room remained sunlit and still, but she was choking, and chaos ensued as I screamed for help. Suddenly my arms were empty, and the room was full of staff.

None of them could meet my eye when the doctor turned to me with a long face, moments later, no longer trying to save her.

I've held those minutes under a microscope, asking what I could have done differently. Learning the answer won't bring my daughter back. It will just tell me precisely what percentage of her death was my fault, and that's a statistic I already know: it is one hundred percent my fault, because had I done something different, *anything*, she would not have died.

Meconium aspiration is rare, but more common in certain circumstances: pregnancies that go past term, cocaine use. If only I'd agreed to be induced early. If only I'd had a C-section or hadn't done that line of cocaine with my colleagues before I knew I was pregnant. If only I'd allowed the nurse to take her to the nursery so I could rest—a place where they might have noticed the blue of her nails that hinted at oxygen deprivation before she began to gasp.

A single, small action on my part could have saved her. But I didn't take it.

At the minute of her birth, I hold my breath and wait. I'm a reasonable person, but I can't help but hope each year that something might change, be fixed somehow, if I can just find the loophole, the way back to her. But at 3:25 PM, the world remains the same. The birds chirp and the breeze makes leaves rustle along the ground like skittish ghosts. And Hannah continues to lay silent somewhere beneath me, and nothing I can do will bring her back home.

34

BECK

Kate's absence makes it obvious that the bar is no longer where I want to be.

When she's here, there's this small fire in my stomach: the anticipation of her, the hope that she'll emerge from the office to wave a form in my face that I failed to sign months ago, or casually stake her claim the way she does anytime there's a female at the bar—resting a hand over my arm or referring to 'home'—though she'll later say it was an accident.

I should probably be asking myself what the fuck I'll do when she's gone, how I'm going to weather the next five decades at a job I hate, but instead, today, I'm just worrying about her.

There was something off with her this morning. She doesn't reply when I text and I take a quick breath through my nostrils, trying to shut down the possibilities in my head: that she's hanging out with Lucie's ex...or that she's using again.

She's not. I fucking know she's not.

Except when shit fell apart with her in the past, it was at the exact moment Caleb was assuring us she was fine. "Loves the new job," he'd said that last time. "She's doing great."

He lied to himself, often, because he didn't know what else to do. When you're with a woman who insists she's fine...what then? Do you drive home to check on her or have her followed as if she can't be trusted? I hated Caleb for fucking it all up, by not being there when she needed him. Now *I* may be the one fucking it up.

When she doesn't answer my phone call, I ask Mueller to take my spot behind the bar and drive home. She isn't there. She isn't at the storage unit either.

I tell myself to stop worrying, a tactic that has never worked once in my entire life, and isn't working today either. I return to the cabin, pacing the living room, and then I finally do the thing I've avoided for weeks: I call Caleb.

Though we put the argument behind us, it hasn't been the same. We've never gone more than a day or two without a text or call. Even when he was away at school, we played fantasy football and exchanged a constant stream of shit talk. Now the texts are more restrained and less frequent—the exchange of two people who are trying to move past something but haven't entirely.

"Hey," he says, "hang on." In the background there's a wave of high-pitched giggles. A second later, a door shuts and the noise falls away. "Sorry, I'm at ballet with Sophie. It's the part of the class where parents get to come in and watch, so I've got to go in a second, but I've been meaning to call. Liam said Kate's working at the bar?"

I slam a cabinet door with more force than necessary. "At a certain point, you probably need to stop worrying about the woman you're planning to divorce."

His tongue clicks. "I'm still allowed to worry. I'd worry about you too. And this time of year is hard for her, so a bar is the last place she needs to be."

At any other point, I'd have a serious issue with the tone he's taking—*he has no fucking claim to her anymore*—but I push that aside, because something he said has triggered a new fear, one I know needs to be examined.

A little over a month ago she was crying over that sonogram, in which Hannah was pretty far along. Which means . . .

"What day was Hannah born?"

He exhales heavily. "Today."

Fuck. Today's the day it all went wrong. That she's off somewhere quietly reliving it is the *best*-case scenario here.

"I've got to go," I tell Caleb, grabbing my keys. "But keep your phone close. I might have questions."

If she's not at home and she's not at the storage area, I've got one last place to check before I start hunting down her dealer.

THE CEMETERY SITS NOT FAR from Caleb's end of the lake. Her car is the only one in the lot.

I didn't want to find her at Kent's, but...I didn't want to find her here either.

I scan the grounds until I see her bright hair in the distance. She's facing away from me, sitting cross-legged, with her head in her hands. My feet crunch the leaves underfoot and she glances back furtively, like an animal expecting a chase. Her eyes are red-rimmed and raw, and the look on her face—*Jesus*. I don't know how Caleb stood it, that kind of grief, day after day. I reach her and drop to the ground, wrapping my arms around her tight, and she folds into me as if she's suddenly boneless. She isn't crying, but her whole body shakes. It's almost as if she's beyond sadness, as if grief has bled her dry.

"Kate...you've been here all day? What are you doing?"

"She's out here every single night alone," she whispers. "I can't stand that she's out here alone."

This is why she snuck out of rehab last year.

I'd bet all I own that this is where she came. It's why she fought Caleb so hard about leaving for treatment at all, why she begged him to let her stay. And it's why, at least in part, she doesn't want to leave now either.

It isn't her addiction she can't seem to move past. It's her daughter.

We sit for long minutes until even *I'm* cold, and she was already shivering when I arrived.

"It's time to go," I finally tell her as gently as I can. She nods, leaning over to press her lips to the top of the grave, whispering something I can't hear, something I'm *glad* I can't hear. Every aspect of her pain is intolerable to me.

I take her keys and usher her into the passenger's seat of her car.

"I'll get it later," I tell her when she glances over at my bike.

I turn the heat as high as it can go and drive south to Santa Cruz. She stares out the window for a long time, saying nothing. "Why aren't we going home?" she asks at last.

"You need a change of scenery."

I park in front of a restaurant and when I climb from the car, she does too, following like a child.

She's still shivering, so I get us a table near the fireplace. She stares out at the ocean. "I had no idea this place existed."

"Maybe you need to get out more," I tell her, and she laughs at that, her voice raspy from sadness.

The waiter brings our drinks, but Kate still hasn't even looked at the menu, so I ask him to come back. We're not leaving here until I've seen her eat something.

I place one of her cold hands between mine. "You should have told me what today was. I'm sorry I didn't remember."

"I wouldn't have expected you to," she says, not meeting my eye. "Caleb was sad for about two seconds, and then his life went on."

Not exactly. Caleb just had his own especially shitty way of handling grief. If it wasn't for Lucie, he'd still be burying himself in work, pretending nothing ever went wrong.

"You can remember," I reply gently, "without choosing to let it destroy you."

Her eyes fly to mine, and she slides her hand away. "You think I'm *choosing* this? You think I *want* to feel like this all the time?"

I sigh, leaning back in my seat. "I think maybe you're choosing it without even realizing that's what you're doing." I shove my menu off to the side. "When my mom died, I thought if I wasn't still sad about it, if I moved on at all, it was like I was forgetting her. I wanted to feel that pain because I thought the only other option meant leaving her behind. I guess it's part of the reason I haven't given up the bar."

She plants her elbows on the table and buries her face in her hands. It takes her a long moment to reply. "I already left her behind," she whispers. "I let them take her."

My stomach drops. I knew she hadn't gotten over it, but this is a whole different level of mourning. This is the kind of guilt no one can live with.

"Jesus, Kate. You had to let them take her. There wasn't another option."

"I just want her back," she says into her hands. "I want a second chance."

"You can have a second chance and a third chance and a fourth if you want it. You've just got to be willing to move forward with your life."

She nods, but her face is vacant, unmoved. She doesn't want *any* baby. She wants the one she lost, and this is how Caleb wins, no matter how wrong he is for her, no matter how unhappy he makes her: because he gave her something she loved, once upon a time, and she still believes he's the only one who can give it to her again.

I'm beginning to think that will never change.

35

KATE

When we get into the house, he undresses me and I allow it, apathy making my limbs hang heavy. I assume undressing will progress the way it normally does—his mouth, his hands—but instead he pulls me into bed, cradling me against his chest, and tells me to go to sleep.

I wake still feeling as if I'm under water or coming out of a long illness. My body is heavy, my brain muddled. I'd like to just stay in bed.

I didn't wind up at Kent's yesterday. I guess it's a victory, but I'm still closer to the girl who gave up last year—the one who felt ambivalent about her outcome—than the girl I was a week ago.

I go into work, ignoring the grief and the exhaustion. My steps are leaden; my smile is forced.

Nothing changed yesterday. Hannah isn't coming back. Caleb is moving on.

I've ignored Kayleigh's texts about yoga for so long that she's stopped reaching out. Jeremy's calls go to my voicemail unanswered. I'm tired of his plots. I'm tired of hoping for anything. I was expecting Holzig would have had the decency to send me a rejection letter, but it looks like that won't be happening either.

Rachel comes in, so pregnant she's waddling and wearing sneakers for the first time. She asks how I am and I lie to her, just as I lied to Beck. He knows something's wrong. When I tell him I'm fine, his frustration is palpable.

I wake the next day and the day after that, hoping that if I just keep moving my feet forward, I'll come up with a destination for myself, a thing to want.

But I don't think it's going to work.

THE SKY IS gray on Monday morning as Beck leaves for the bar. "I'm taking the truck since they're saying it might flood. You want to ride with me?"

I shake my head. "I have some errands to run first."

His glance flickers to me before he nods. I guess he knows I've started going to the cemetery every morning. I'm glad he doesn't feel the need to stop me.

I sit at Hannah's grave, dry-eyed and empty. How do I move on from this? How do I let her go when I'm the only one who even seems to remember her, when I can see so clearly who she could have become?

The rain starts as I return to the car, and it's torrential by the time I reach the office. No one should be out in this weather, and the bar is dead, yet two hours later, Rachel enters—her cheeks pink and glowing, her hair soaking wet. She's thirty-eight weeks along, and today was probably her final checkup before delivery. Her broad smile strikes terror in my chest. She doesn't understand how wrong it can go. I can barely stand not to grab her by the shoulders and detail it for her.

"Everything's good?" I ask as we sit at a table to order lunch.

"Other than my husband's needless panic," she says with a laugh. "He suggested flipping the car to make sure the car seat would remain in place."

I glance outside. "Maybe not the craziest idea with the way Elliott Springs floods."

She glances out the window, her brows raised in surprise. "Wow, it's really coming down, isn't it? I hope Gus cancels his afternoon tour. I don't want him climbing in this."

I shove my menu away from me. "I think we should skip lunch. You should get home in case the roads are blocked off."

She laughs and shakes her head. "It's just *rain*, Kate."

I nod, but my tension remains, and by the time our food has arrived, I've lost my appetite. If I was Gus, I'd have enshrined Rachel in bubble wrap and forbidden her from leaving the house.

She starts telling me about her trip to the farmer's market last weekend, and I fret, pushing the food on my plate.

"What's wrong with you?" she demands. "Your mood has plummeted since I arrived."

My lips press together. "Look how high the water is in the parking lot while you're telling me about Gus not realizing arugula was a vegetable. Please, *please* go home."

She laughs. "Just for *you*, I'll go home. But you're being ridiculously paranoid. You're my Gus away from Gus."

"Thank you." I let out a breath as she gathers her things. "Straight home, okay? And don't come out until it's tapered off."

"Okay, Mom," she says with a laugh, and then the blood leaches from her skin. "Jesus, I'm so sorry. I was just joking and —" She covers her face with her free hand. "I'm so sorry."

"It's okay. Really. Now get the fuck out of here."

She smiles at me again, shrugging on her jacket, and heads for the door. I go back to the office every bit as tense as I was.

What if the roads are already flooded? What if her car stalls out and no one's around to get her? My throat constricts as if it's already happened, and I grab my purse.

"I've got to run an errand," I tell Beck, without slowing.

The water in the lot is up to my ankles. How much worse must it be at the low points outside of town where Rachel lives?

The logical part of me knows following her at high speed just to make sure she gets home is insane. But the logical part of me never wins, and it won't win today either.

I head down Main Street, slowed by the swell of people who've decided they better get home. I can barely see out the windows with my wipers on full blast, and just as the light turns green, a cop stops in front of me to halt traffic for a fire truck.

I scream in frustration and the second he gets out of the way, I blow through the light, then turn left onto the road that leads to Rachel and Gus's neighborhood...only to crest a hill and discover an eight-car pileup in the intersection below.

And one of those cars is Rachel's.

I pull off to the shoulder of the road and then I slip all the way down the hill, arriving just as she climbs out of her car. "Kate!" she exclaims. "What are you doing here?"

My relief is so sudden and sweet that tears sting. "I was worried you might need help." I swipe at my eyes. Jesus, I can't believe I'm *crying*. "Are you okay?"

She nods, blinking, placing a hand on the hood of her car as she stares around her. The water is up to our knees. "We need to check on everybody else."

"Fuck everybody else," I reply, marching over and linking her arm through mine. She isn't standing here in the middle of an intersection just waiting for a car to crash into her. "Let's get away from this mess and call Beck. He's got the truck today. I promise to check on everyone once you're out of here."

"It happened so fast," she says as I lead her away. "I could have made it, but the car in front of me stopped and then I got rear-ended and...how the hell did you know to come down here?"

"I didn't." I guess my paranoia was warranted, but it's still embarrassing. I reach into my pocket—the phone isn't there. I must have left it in the car. "Can you call Beck? We need to get you out of here and I don't trust my tiny car in this mess."

She hits his number on speed dial.

"Is Kate with you?" he shouts. "I can't find her and she won't answer her fucking phone!" His words are so enraged, he barely sounds rational. She raises a brow and hands the cell to me.

"Hi. What's wrong?" I demand. "I need—"

"I thought you were fucking dead! That's what's wrong!"

I hold the phone away from my ear as Rachel and I stare at each other. "Why would you think *that*?"

"Because I saw you fishtailing in the parking lot and took off after you! I drove all the way back to the house and you weren't there, and you weren't answering your phone, and I just heard about some huge pileup north of town. What the *fuck*?"

"I was checking on Rachel and—"

Rachel's face goes pale. She grips my arm and stares at the ground.

"Oh God," she says. "My water just broke."

BECK and I sit side by side in the waiting area at Labor and Delivery. Rachel's emergency focused both of us, but now that it's over—sort of—he slumps in the chair and leans his head back as if he's just finished a marathon.

"What's the matter?" I ask.

He releases a slow exhale. "Why would you follow her? What in the hell were you thinking?"

I cross my arms over my chest. "I was worried about her.

And it's a good thing I was, so why are you giving me a bunch of crap about it?"

"Because you scared the living shit out of me, Kate!" he says, climbing to his feet. "That's why!" He storms off toward the elevators.

My jaw is open wide as he stabs the button to go downstairs. "Asshole."

"Your husband loves you an awful lot," says the woman across from me. She's older, worn-looking, and *knitting*. Not someone I'm especially inclined to take advice from. "You're mad, but do you have any idea how many women just wish their man loved them that much?"

My arms remain folded. There's so much to correct in that statement I don't even know where to begin. "That wasn't love. That was blame."

She shakes her head. "I promise you, sugar," she says, going back to her work, "that was love."

I have no intention of taking the counsel of a woman who looks like a character from a Steinbeck novel. And it wasn't love. It was duty. He takes responsibility for me as if I'm a child, which is fucking ridiculous. Yeah, I did some things I shouldn't have. But does that negate every success? The near-perfect score on my ACT, the full scholarship undergrad and Wharton for grad school? Am I going to have to live down my mistakes forever?

I watch the elevators with growing impatience until he finally reemerges. The five minutes he spent somewhere pouting was five minutes too long, and now I'm as fired up as he is.

I march toward him. His arms fold, ready for battle.

"I cannot believe you're making such a big deal of this," I snap. "I'm a grown woman and just because I messed up once doesn't mean I'm some child who requires constant care—"

He steps into my space, backs me to the wall, and kisses me with his hands in my hair, my body tucked into his. "You. Scared. Me," he says. "That doesn't mean I think you're a child or incompetent. You fucking scared me because that's what happens when you care about someone and they *disappear*."

There's this sweet, aching thing in my chest, rising and rising. He's acting like this is a relationship and I like it. *Jesus.* I like it and I *can't* like it.

I've been asleep at the wheel over the past month. I've allowed our casual, no-strings relationship to turn into something else entirely, something that will really fucking hurt when it ends—and it *does* have to end.

He's waiting for a response. My mouth opens, then closes. I'm spared by the appearance of Rachel's husband, grinning broadly, still dressed in scrubs.

I met him only briefly when he ran through the lobby in a panic earlier, but he comes straight over and throws his arms around me. "It's a girl," he says with a smile that splits his face from side to side. "Jane Katherine. Jane after Rachel's aunt, and Katherine after you. God only knows what would have happened if you hadn't gone after her." His voice breaks, and Beck and I both pretend we haven't heard it.

"I didn't do anything," I reply. "I'm just glad it worked out okay."

"Congrats, man," Beck says, clapping him on the back. "When can we see her?"

Gus swallows, recovering. "They're just giving her a bath, but I'll come out in a few and grab you when they're done?"

I force myself to smile, but my knees lock. I've got no fucking intention of going back there, in the same place where they took my daughter.

When Gus walks away, I frown at Beck. "Why'd you make it sound like we'd both go? You know I can't do that."

"*What?* That's...They just named their kid after you."

"I know," I say, moving toward the elevators. "But I'm still not going. I'll see you later."

He shouts my name, but I keep walking.

Our little game of pretend has gone way too far.

36

KATE

I'm back in the hospital. The same room, the same blue curtain dividing my bed from the one beside mine, the same pretty nurse with the foreign name and cheerful demeanor. But Caleb's there. He wasn't there, the first time, but somehow he's fixed things. He's here, and I'm not alone.

The small bundle he holds is tightly wrapped and tiny, but I already know how she'll feel in my arms.

"She's alive?" I scramble upright to see her more clearly. "She's okay?"

I reach out, desperate for that solid, warm weight. Eager to see her looking up at me with Hannah's eyes.

But the bundle is cold, and the eyes that look up at me do not belong to my daughter. They are the eyes of someone else's child, with an emptiness to them that terrifies me.

I wake gasping in Beck's room, my heart exploding in my chest. Beck curves a protective arm around me, somehow knowing even when he's sound asleep that I need help. For once, though, his heat suffocates me, and I slide away from him.

That wasn't how the dream was supposed to go. It was

supposed to end with Hannah looking up at me the way she did, so alert, watching my face with absolute faith. I want to make it up to her, all my failures. I want to prove to her that I can do this, that I'm worthy of the way she trusted me.

That dream is what got me sober. It's what led me, still high, to stumble out of Kent's house and make my way back to rehab. I left everything I loved behind, all in my blind pursuit of that moment: the warmth of her in my arms, Hannah's eyes on my face.

Now it's all slipping away, and I don't know what's left without it.

BECK TRIES to get me to go to the hospital and then Rachel's house in the days that follow. His jaw grinds every time I refuse, and there's an answering tick of anger in my stomach. Expecting me to go fawn over someone's newborn daughter in the very hospital where I lost mine is unfair. Being *annoyed* about my refusal to go is absolute bullshit.

Prove you're better, Kate. That's what he's really saying. And why do I *have* to be better? Why do I have to prove anything to him?

"We're going today," he announces Saturday morning. "I'll leave the bar around four and come get you."

I picture pink walls and a white rocking chair, a room identical to the one I created for Hannah. And a baby in an identical crib who is not mine.

"No thanks."

He pushes away from the counter. "You're being fucking ridiculous. And rude. She named her kid after you. The least you could do is make an appearance."

I narrow my eyes and manage my best evil queen smile.

"Aren't you worried I'll run into Caleb? Since you're apparently so threatened by that."

Something hardens in his face. "Caleb takes Sophie to dance on Saturdays. So *no*, I'm not threatened."

It's a slap in the face, the fact that Caleb is parenting someone else's daughter. That's exactly what Beck wanted it to be. "Not pulling our punches anymore, I see."

His face holds no apology. "Maybe you need some sense knocked into you."

He walks out, and I quietly fume. I should absolutely have known a fling with him would go like this, this progression from *casual and uncomplicated* to *abandon everything you want from life to make me happy, Kate.*

"Fuck you, Beck!" I shout, knowing he won't hear me. I wouldn't care even if he did.

My phone rings, and I glare at the sight of Jeremy's name there. I'm not sure why I answer.

"How's my favorite scorned spouse?" he asks. "I thought you'd disappeared. Everything okay?"

I sigh, pushing my plate away. "Yes. Just sick of this endless well of sympathy for Caleb and Lucie when everything's come so easily to them."

He chuckles. "Preaching to the choir, babe. Meet me for lunch. We can commiserate."

Jeremy's a douche, but it actually sounds nice. Right now, I just need one person who isn't demanding I move on. I want an hour or two with someone who agrees that I don't have to move forward until I'm good and fucking ready to do so.

Two hours later, I'm at the restaurant he's chosen, one where the patrons are clad in golf attire and speak in hushed tones over their steak and hundred-year-old scotch. If this is the kind of treatment Lucie expects from Caleb, she's got some disappointment in store. Then again, Caleb seems willing to pull puppies and sunshine from his ass where she's concerned—I still can't believe the same guy who never found time to attend a single sonogram is now driving someone else's kid to ballet.

Jeremy rises as I approach, kissing me on the cheek as if we are actually friends, which we are not, or as if this is a date, which it most definitely is not. He holds me by my elbow as I pull away, casting an appraising glance over me from head to toe. "If it's any consolation, I'd hire you. I don't even know what you *do,* but I'd give you any job you want, looking like that."

"I'm pretty sure that's how sexual harassment lawsuits start," I reply, sliding into my seat.

He laughs. "You keep me on my toes, Kate, and I *love* it. I can't imagine how Caleb could have given you up."

I suppose I should reply in kind, but anyone who's seen Caleb knows why Lucie was willing to give this guy up. And he's just saying it to kiss my ass. I wish he'd tell me what he's after and drop all the compliments.

He orders a bottle of wine without asking me first. He knows I was in rehab, but maybe it's okay that someone's finally not treating me like I'm too weak and ill to relax around.

He reaches for my glass and I wave him off.

"Sorry," he says. "Is it a problem?"

"No. I just don't like wine."

"You want something else?" he asks. "Gin and tonic? Margarita?"

He's making slightly more effort than he should to get me to drink midday. There's probably a reason for that. "I'm good, thanks."

"You know your husband is picking my daughter up from dance this afternoon?" he asks, changing the subject with gritted teeth. "*My* fucking daughter, and I'm not even allowed to pick her up when her mother can't be bothered. You're lucky you guys don't have a custody battle on top of everything else."

"If we had custody of something," I reply tightly, "we wouldn't be in this position in the first place."

He offers a sympathetic wince that is clearly feigned. "Right. Sorry. It's just so hard to be away from my kids. I get them for the weekend, and it kills me the way they cry at the end. They ask me every damn time when they can move home and all I can say is '*soon*.'"

I set my menu off to the side. This conversation is killing my appetite. "You think they'd rather live with you?"

"I don't know. I'm sure it's easier to be in my position—I get to be the parent who spoils them. I'm not there day in and day out. But they want more time with me, and I could easily get fifty percent custody—I'm just not sure I could do that to Lucie. The kids are her whole life. She doesn't have anything else."

I sip my water. "Doesn't she work for Caleb?"

He throws out his hands. "How much work do you think she's actually doing? She isn't qualified for anything. She's basically just hoping to be Caleb's trophy wife. The kids are telling me Caleb stays over. I mean, what kind of example does that set?"

My stomach twists as I picture Caleb on Saturday mornings, waking up with his new family, making them pancakes. He was never around on weekends when we were together, but now, *now*, he's got time for fucking ballet lessons and sleepovers.

The waiter takes our order, and when he leaves, Jeremy picks up right where he left off.

"Caleb's distracting her. The last time I got them up, they both had fevers. She couldn't even bother taking them to the doctor. And she's routinely late for school pickup. If she keeps going the way she is, I'm going to have to try to get full custody."

Lucie sucks, but not two minutes ago, he said he wouldn't even try to get fifty percent custody because it would hurt her, and now he's considering taking *all* of it? "I thought you said you couldn't do that to her."

"I don't *want* to do it," he corrects, refilling his wine. "But I may be forced to. I have to make sure my kids are safe. I'm really hoping it won't come to that, though. If she thought I was going to get custody, she'd come running back so fast it'd blind you."

I laugh. "Why would *you* get full custody? I think the bar is set pretty high for that."

His smile sends a shiver up my spine. "My uncle's the DA. If she got caught for something, it'd be pretty easy to make her look unfit."

I stare at him. Lucie appears, on the surface at least, to be the ultimate rule-follower. "What would she get caught for, though?"

"Well," he says, leaning forward, planting his forearms on the table, ready to deliver a sales pitch, "if she got caught with drugs in her car, for instance."

"Does she *do* drugs?" The woman I see on Instagram looks like the only drug she's even heard of is aspirin.

"She's sleeping with her boss, openly. She's not taking the kids to the doctor. Who knows what she's doing?"

"Are you saying you have reason to hope she'll get caught, or are you talking about framing her?"

He shrugs. "It all works out the same, one way or the other. It helps you, too. Your divorce could be finalized really fast if you don't find a way to stop it."

Holy shit. He *is* talking about framing her. Though I might not be a model of ethical behavior, I have no intention of helping this guy commit a felony. And even if Lucie isn't the greatest mom, Jeremy is hardly parent-of-the-year material himself.

"Don't you think this whole situation sucks?" he asks. "I don't know how you stand it. Seriously. I can't even imagine what you went through with your daughter. I just wish Lucie could be in your shoes for a single hour so she'd realize how lucky she is to have the kids. Instead, she's ignoring them all day to go fuck your husband."

It's insulting that he thinks his little manipulation here will work when it's been done so clumsily. But that doesn't prevent a tiny spike of anger in my chest.

If Hannah had lived, I'd *never* have been the mother Jeremy is describing. I just don't understand how Lucie has wound up with everything—my husband, two kids, a job that's fallen into her lap—while every effort I make seems to lead nowhere. I carry a child for forty-one weeks and go home empty-handed. I spend months applying for jobs and going to interviews, and I've still got nothing.

"Look, I'm just going to level with you," he says. Jeremy is so routinely dishonest that he has to announce the moments when he's *not* dishonest. "If I could get *ahold* of something, I could fix things faster for both of us."

I blink. It's not a hypothetical plan at all. He really intends to go through with it.

Our meals arrive and we both sit back, thanking the waiter with polite smiles.

I wait until he's gone to lean in. "So you're going to plant something?"

He picks up his knife and fork. "I was hoping that's where you'd come in. I'm going to be the number-one suspect, so I need a bulletproof alibi. I have a key to her van—if you put something in there, I could call in an anonymous tip when she goes to school to pick up the kids and say I saw her doing cocaine in the parking lot. She'll get stopped, and voila . . . mission accomplished."

I poke at the salmon I ordered and force myself to take a small bite. "I'm not sure it's as easy as you think. She'll say she was set up, and they'll find nothing in her bloodstream."

He hitches a shoulder. "It doesn't matter. She'll still have to explain how she wound up with cocaine in her car. I'll get temporary custody of the kids while it's being adjudicated and she'll come running."

I laugh unhappily. "You make it sound so very easy, yet I notice you've got me handling the parts that are actually *illegal*. And I want Lucie and Caleb to split up as badly as you do, but even *I* don't want to be responsible for making someone lose her kids."

He leans forward eagerly, planting his forearms on the table. "But that's not what you're doing. She's never going to lose custody no matter what because she'll get back together with me before that happens. She loses nothing, my kids regain their family, and you regain yours."

The whole plan is awful. My brain vacillates between sudden, unfortunate sympathy for Lucie, because she is clearly married to the world's biggest jackass ever, and something steelier. Am I really going to pity her? No matter what he does, she comes out of this with two adorable little kids.

I don't want any part of his plan, but the Lucies of the world don't deserve all the fucking joy there is—I'm sort of relishing the idea of Jeremy redistributing the wealth.

"Needless to say, this whole thing has to stay between us." His hand lands atop mine, but the gesture isn't meant to be affectionate. It's a warning. "You trusted me with some sensitive information that could make you look really bad if it got out— the whole Miami thing—so I'm doing the same."

Our gazes catch as I grasp his meaning: if I breathe a word of this, he'll tell everyone what I did. Will his next step be to blackmail me? To force me to plant the drugs, or do something even worse? The strange thing is that it's not Caleb's reaction I worry about when I picture it—it's Beck's.

On the way home from lunch, I imagine coming clean. I could tell Beck about the ads, Kayleigh, Miami. Surely it would be better to confess than let Jeremy pull me into a plan that could get me thrown in jail, but God only knows how Beck will react. If he kicks me out on my ass, he'd be right to do so, because what kind of person does the shit I have?

I decide to make dinner for him, a small penance for meeting with Jeremy, for refusing to give him what he wants, for not going to meet Jane. It's probably too small a penance, but it's all I can come up with.

I drive to the store, swallowing hard when my eyes land on the guy with the vacant stare standing near the doors—the same guy who was across the street when I first returned to Elliott Springs. My mouth waters at the idea of *absence*. Of having this knot in my stomach slowly unwind until I'm floating above it all and empty.

I move past him and into the store. But even as I pick up chicken and mushrooms and potatoes like some 1950s house-wife, there's a voice in my head whispering justifications. *You just need a little bit to unwind. It's tension making things bad with Beck now, and maybe this will help.*

I pay for the groceries and practically run to my car lest that voice in my head offer an especially good argument at the wrong moment.

The cabin is dark and lonely. It's nearly six—I'm surprised he's not home yet, if he left the bar at four the way he'd said he would. I picture him telling Suzanne about my bullshit while she ties a cherry stem with her tongue. I bet *she'd* be thrilled to go to Rachel's with him if he asked.

Resentment swirls in my chest, though I've got no proof he's done anything wrong. I peel the potatoes so aggressively that it's a miracle I don't lose a finger in the process. I did what I was fucking supposed to: I fought the urge to use. I didn't agree to Jeremy's plan. I'm here making this lame dinner in Beck's empty cabin, but when is it going to actually feel *good* to do the right thing?

The food is done by seven and is cold by eight. I text him and he doesn't reply. By nine, I'm screaming at the cabin walls, and by ten, when he finally walks in, I'm ready to throw knives.

"You want to tell me why you're home this late?" I demand.

He leans against the door, folding his arms across his chest. "You want to tell me why you had lunch with Jeremy?"

I suck in a breath at the pinch of fear. We ate in another *city*, for Christ's sake. And if he knows about our lunch, what else does he know? "I wasn't on a *date*. He just wanted to commiserate."

A muscle in Beck's jaw spasms as he grinds his teeth. "That's fucking great. You're still weeping over a guy you haven't had anything to do with in over a year. Thanks for fucking explaining."

I stiffen, suddenly unsure. I wasn't really talking about Caleb at all today, was I? I don't think I ever even alluded to missing him, which is strange. It was all about Lucie. But Beck is not going to turn this around on me. I'm allowed to be upset that my husband has moved on. I'm allowed to still be bitter. "You knew the deal. This can't be news to you."

"Stupid of me," he says, grabbing the helmet and opening the door again, "to think it might have changed."

I hold a hand to my throat as he walks out, and even as I'm raging at him for expecting too much, for turning our relationship into something it's not, I'm fighting the urge to cry.

He knew I wanted Caleb back. Was I ever unclear about that? Does he really think I'd give up my plans for some amorphous thing with him we've never even discussed?

I don't *want* to discuss it. But I do want him to come back home.

I'll set things right if I can.

But I still can't promise him anything.

37

BECK

You knew the deal.

I can't believe she fucking said those words to me, but I knew the minute Mueller told me he'd seen her with Jeremy that this needed to end. That we'd reached the point where any reasonable person would just fucking give up.

I grip the handlebars of my bike and bank hard to the right, faster than I should.

Caring for someone will rip your heart out. It's what turns a normal guy like my dad into a monster who throws shit at his ex-wife and can't have a single conversation without calling her a whore.

If Kate wants Caleb after all this time, then she needs to leave, and I guess I'm free to do whatever the fuck I want. To stay out all night, to sleep with someone else. I'm just too fucking whipped to do it. And I don't want to hurt her, though she's got no compunction whatsoever about hurting me.

I ride for another hour, considering my options, before I head home.

I'm not going to be the one who destroys everything. She seems to be doing that pretty well all on her own.

She's still awake, sitting on the couch and looking just like the girl I once met, the one who hadn't been completely hardened by life. I want to shake her until she fucking sees what she's doing to both of us.

I head toward my room instead. Nothing good can come of a conversation right now.

"Beck?" she asks from behind me.

I turn, glaring at her. "What?"

She runs her index finger over her lip as she climbs from the couch, looking up under long lashes, her gaze hungry and certain, as if she intends to eat me alive. Her hips sway as she approaches and she doesn't look away as she reaches to the bottom of her shirt and pulls it over her head, letting her hands palm her breasts as she does it.

"What are you doing?" My voice is a low growl, tinged with disgust at both of us. I know exactly what she's doing. I also know it will work.

Her hand goes to the button of her jeans. She shimmies out of them and reaches back to unclasp her bra.

"Stop," I say roughly.

But she doesn't. The bra comes off and I take her in, against my will. She has the tightest, most perfect body I've ever laid eyes on, lean and muscular, her breasts just slightly larger than what could fit in my hand. She steps close enough for her breasts to brush against my shirt, and I've had enough.

I push her to the wall and she gasps.

"What the fuck are you doing, Kate?" I grab her hand and hold it against my hard cock. "Is this what you want? Are you fucking happy now?"

Her eyes grow glazed, heavy lidded, and her breathing is uneven. Our mouths are close enough to brush if either of us moved forward, and I slide my hand down into her panties, pushing my fingers between her legs to find her so wet and ready that I'm giving in to her before I've admitted I'm going to do it. I grab her arm and pull her into my room, shoving her on the bed. She watches me push my jeans down, her lips swollen though I haven't touched them. I strip her soaked little panties off and pin her wrists over her head as I thrust into her hard, without warning, wishing I could save her sharp gasp to replay later.

"Like that, Kate?" I hiss. "Is that what you wanted?"

I thrust again. "Answer me. Is that what you wanted?"

"Yes," she breathes, stretching out like a cat beneath me, wanting more. I release her wrists and grab both of her hips, pulling her onto me as I thrust. I'd like to go slowly, to torture her until she's desperate and apologetic and will say anything to get off, but I have as little control as she does. All too fast she's clenching around me, telling me she's about to come.

There's a sharp tug in my gut. I push harder, faster, filling her with a low groan.

Beneath me, her face is flushed, her mouth open. Hungry for more. So beautiful and so hard to look at right now.

"That didn't fix anything," I tell her, pulling out.

She gives me a smug little smile. "You already want to do it again though, don't you?"

I grab her thighs and tug her down the bed toward me, letting my teeth sink into her hip.

Yeah, I already want to do it again, but no matter how many times she comes tonight, no matter how many times *I* come, it's still going to hurt to look at her.

And I'll still know it needs to end.

My little striptease didn't help anything. It's as if I attempted to summon someone from the dead and got a lifeless husk in his place.

Days pass while I wait for us to recover, and we just...don't. There used to be moments of affection between us—the quick flash of his smile, the graze of his fingertips as I'd pass by—but now it's only sex. He still locks the office door in the middle of the day and bends me over the desk, or sets me on the kitchen counter at home, but it's swift and compulsive, as if he hates himself for doing it and hates me for letting him.

I miss the other side of us. Only a little over a month ago, we went camping for the first time. He'd asked me if I was happy and I was shocked to discover the answer was *yes*.

I wish it had lasted. I wish I knew how to get it back.

Jeremy calls to say Caleb has been shopping for rings, and it's strange how little I care when normally news like this would send me off to stalk Lucie on Instagram or plot with Kayleigh. *What did Caleb and I even do in the evenings?* I hunt for good memories of him but struggle to find anything that isn't related to Hannah or the pregnancy.

I barely see Beck anymore now that I've got his book-keeping squared away. He works out in the morning but rarely eats breakfast, and he's gone back to closing most nights.

Caleb's moved on, the bar has moved on, Beck has moved on. I'm the one who remains behind—waiting for a single job to appeal to me the way the job at Holzig did or for my personal life to miraculously right itself.

The only person who hasn't left me behind is Rachel. She texts to thank me for the blanket I sent, and a few nights later, she follows it up with a call.

"I'm sorry," I burst out, before she can say a single word. "I'm sorry I haven't come by."

"Oh, Kate," she whispers, and she sounds so sad for me that my own eyes sting. "I get it—believe me, I do. But you can't go through your entire life avoiding all babies. Someday, you're going to try again."

"That seems pretty unlikely, what with Caleb shopping for engagement rings."

She pauses. "I wasn't talking about you and Caleb. Beck comes by here almost every day. Sometimes he takes Jane for an hour and lets me nap. I don't think I've ever seen a guy who wants kids more than he does."

A small hole opens in my chest, something hopeful and painful all at once. Is that even something I want? And if it is, did I just ruin any chance I had of getting it? "He's never been in a relationship. There's probably a reason for that."

"Yeah, a reason like he was waiting for *you*," she says with a sigh. "I don't know what's up with you two, but he's been miserable for days. And no offense, but the only thing with the power to make him *that* unhappy is you."

Ouch. I hate that.

When I end the call, I curl up on Beck's sofa with my face pressed to my knees. How do I fix this? How do I put things back the way they were? As much as I wish I could just seduce him into complacency, that's clearly not going to work. I have to apologize, except he's never here anymore. Sure, I could wait until two AM when he's trudging up the steps, exhausted, but I'm not sure he'll hear me out.

Which means I need to go to him. I'm not sure how earnest I can be in a crowded bar, but I guess I'm about to find out.

I get dressed in the kind of outfit that will help my case—tiny skirt, leather blazer with nothing on beneath it—and drive across town.

As I walk through the parking lot to the bar, hope stirs in my chest. It's like the big scene at the end of some romcom, where the guy who's fucked up makes some grand gesture and all is right with the world.

At least I hope it is.

I take a deep breath and push through the doors, searching for his face, which is the only thing I want to see in the entire world right now. The room is crowded, but fortunately he's so big I could find him anywhere. I take in the sharp jaw and the mouth I love and the soft divot under his cheekbone—and my heart beats erratically, too hard and too fast, and not at a steady pace. I could stare at him all day.

They're busy, so it's a struggle to even get past the foyer. He's going to tell me to leave, but he'll have to carry me out of here to make it happen. I'm not going anywhere until he talks to me, and I've got no problem at all with irritating him into a conversation if I must.

I push my way to the bar, but he's now at the other end, and Suzanne—the object of his attention—has her hand trailing over those biceps I love, tracing his tattoos. Her fingers pull at his, and then, capturing his wrist in her hand, she leans forward and sucks his thumb into her mouth.

I don't think. I all but knock over the two girls in my path and reach Suzanne's side just as he's removing his hand from her grasp.

He looks at me and there is nothing, nothing at all, in his eyes. No guilt, no concern. As if I have no right to question anything he does. My stomach drops. "Why are you here?" he asks.

"Why is *she* here?"

It's not at all what I'd planned to say.

He looks bored as he grabs the rag off the counter and flips it over his shoulder. "What's the matter, Kate? I thought you, as you yourself said, 'knew the deal.' Has something changed? If so, I'm all ears."

Rage has me swaying. I grip the bar to remain upright, and possibly also to keep from grabbing Suzanne by the hair and swinging her to the floor.

This is my chance to set things right from the other day, to tell him that yes, things have changed and that he means something to me, but he just stood there letting this bitch suck his thumb, and it's not as if he's ever put anything on the line himself, so why the *fuck* should I?

"Are you serious right now?" I demand. "You expect me to make some heartfelt speech while she sucks your thumb?"

"No," he says, turning away. "I don't expect you to say a goddamn thing. You never do."

There's a hundred-pound weight in my chest as I turn, numb, to walk back to the car, blind with shock. I can't believe I came in here to make things right, and he basically told me to fuck off. I expect that kind of treatment from everyone else in my life, but not him. I tell myself not to allow this to hurt, not to give him that kind of power.

It hurts anyway.

39

BECK

K ate walks out, and I'm torn between wishing I'd
hurt her more and wanting to run after her.
Though, why the fuck do I believe I could actually
hurt her in the first place?

Suzanne laughs. "What a bitch."

"Don't call her that," I warn.

She rolls her eyes. "Please tell me you're not sleeping with
her."

I was. And then she walked in and saw some other girl
fellating my thumb, so I guess I won't be again. *Fuck*.

I no longer want to be here. But I don't want to be at my
own home either. Kate has ruined everything for me by making
my life so much better for a while that I've realized how shitty it
was before. I manage to do my job for another hour, until the
crowd clears a little, and then I tell Mueller I'm heading out.

Liam's in the corner, talking to some girl he used to sleep
with. I walk over, my head too full of chaos to mind the fact that
I'm intruding. "Let's get out of here."

The girl's jaw drops. I guess it was rude of me. Don't give a fuck. Liam takes one look at my face and nods. "Sorry," he tells the girl. "Bros before...never mind. Sorry. I gotta go."

"I'm driving," he announces, "because you look inclined to run into a tree on purpose, and I'm too handsome to risk that."

He heads to the outskirts of town to a dive bar that didn't card us when we were sixteen and appears to still have the same high standards today.

"You just cockblocked me with Arielle Dawes," he says while the bartender pours me a double bourbon on the rocks. "So this had better be good."

I slam the bourbon, relishing the burn in my throat, and hold my hand up for two more. "She's still not over Caleb. After all this fucking time."

He groans, running both hands through his hair in frustration. "Look, I like Kate, and I *do* think she's cleaned up her shit, but that doesn't mean she's good for anyone right now. And you've got to be realistic: she and Caleb aren't even divorced yet, a divorce she didn't want. What made you think that was going to change?"

I ignore him. He doesn't know how she is with me, how *content* she is when she forgets for one goddamned second about the ex she never should have been with in the first place.

The bartender slides another double my way. "He always wanted her to be someone she wasn't. She wanted novelty and excitement, and he acted like there was something wrong with her for wanting it."

I wait for him to remind me that there *was* something wrong with it, given where it led, but he simply shrugs. "I remember. What's your point?"

"My point," I say, pulling the second double shot toward me, "is that it's good with us. Really good. And she's a thousand times happier with me than she ever was with him, but she's incapable of admitting it." I push a hand through my hair, try to find the words. My head is foggy. "I love her, but I can't deal with this anymore."

He sighs. "Does *she* know you love her?"

"She must. It couldn't be more obvious."

He shakes his head. "Sure, but have you conveyed this with *words*? Kate's a smart girl, but she's fucked up enough to be stupid about a lot of things too, and this is probably one of them."

"She's had a thousand openings to tell me she's not after Caleb. I'm not saying shit until she can at least do that much."

"You may be nearly as stupid as she is then," he concludes.

I WAKE on his couch with the sun high and alcohol pounding in my head like an alarm that can't be turned off.

I groan into my hands as I sit up. "Fuck."

"You hit it pretty hard," Liam says from the kitchen. "I haven't seen you like that since college."

"What time is it?"

We both glance at the clock behind him. It's nearly ten.

Fuck, fuck, fuck. Even if things need to end with Kate, I don't want to end them like this—with her thinking I cheated.

I rise. Jesus, my whole body hurts. "Thanks for letting me stay."

"I figured if I didn't, I'd be helping you dispose of Kate's body all morning. This seemed easier."

I lean against his kitchen counter while my head swims. "Man, if she was pissed before, she's on fire right now and Kate doesn't do shit halfway. She saw me with Suzanne, and I didn't come home. I'll be lucky if my house is still standing."

"Yeah?" asks Liam, raising a brow as he sips his coffee. "Gee, she kind of sounds like she might care about you, albeit in a completely fucked up, *Kate* sort of way. So maybe you should talk to her."

Maybe I should.

Liam drops me off at the bar to get my bike. I don't even go inside but simply fly out of the parking lot, heading for the cabin.

Her car isn't there. My heart beats faster, and I take the steps two at a time to make sure she hasn't moved out—I wouldn't blame her if she had.

Her belongings are scattered across her room, but the bed is still made. It never occurred to me until this moment that she might have slept somewhere else last night too.

I storm out of the house and get back on my bike, looking for her car as I ride through town, though I don't know why. Do I actually *want* a public fight with her about where we both spent the night? I guess even that would be better than discovering she went to see her dealer.

I spy her car beside the diner on Main Street, but my relief is short-lived. *Since when does she eat breakfast out?* She doesn't even like breakfast.

If she's in here with a guy, wearing last night's clothes, our public fight is gonna be a lot worse than I'd thought it would be. I take two steps off my bike, then do a double take at her car and the one beside it: a brand-new Audi A5 convertible.

The exact car Jeremy bought himself while refusing to pay a dime of child support to Lucie.

I can't fucking believe she's out with him again.

40

KATE

J eremy is waiting in the corner booth where he has a view of the entire restaurant, so he'll know if anyone is listening to us.

I've let his calls go to voicemail ever since lunch last week. When my phone rang this morning, there was a pathetic part of me—the same pathetic part that once prayed I'd hear from Caleb—that wanted it to be Beck, as if there's anything he could say at this point to fix things. He slept with Suzanne, which is a step lower than even *I've* gone during our brief fling.

But it was Jeremy and that it *wasn't* Beck felt like the final nail in the coffin, somehow.

The only reason *not* to hear Jeremy out was basic human decency, something no one seems to have a surplus of at the moment, and I never pretended to have it in the first place. I needed to hold this meeting no matter what, to protect myself. And if means I also get to spend a few minutes believing in a world where Lucie loses instead of me, that's okay too.

The waitress delivers my coffee and his eggs. I wait until she's out of hearing distance before I speak. "Okay, so tell me the plan again," I say, my voice distant, empty.

"It's pretty fucking simple," he says. "Are you sure you made it through Wharton?"

"Are you sure you need me to get you cocaine?" I retort.

"Fine," he says with a beleaguered sigh. "You get ahold of the cocaine, and make sure it's not some trivial amount either. I'm talking like at least a gram."

"I'm going to need money for that."

"Don't you have a job?"

No, actually, I don't. "Doesn't mean I'm funding your plan."

"It's not *my* plan, it's *our* plan, but fine." He opens his wallet and pulls out five hundred. "That enough?"

I could buy five grams for that much. But I'm happy to part an asshole from his money. I slide the bills across the table and tuck them into my purse. "So I buy the cocaine, and then what?"

"Then you plant it in her car while she's doing this kid shit at someone's house for Halloween. It's pretty secluded, so no one will see you."

"How do you even know where she'll be?"

"I have a bunch of her passwords," he says, untroubled by how invasive this is. Of course, he's framing her for drug possession, so I can see where Internet surveillance might seem like an easy day on the job by contrast.

"So I plant the cocaine, and then what?"

"Then you tell me you've done it, and I place a call and report her as soon as she's picked the twins up from school. The rest should take care of itself."

I finish my coffee and leave him at the table, only halfway through his meal. By the time I reach the door, I've put the conversation out of my head.

But I remember it pretty fast when I see Beck standing beside my car.

"Were you with Jeremy?" he asks, but his voice is flat and certain, as if he already knows.

I've been caught doing a lot of shit in my life, but it's been a long time since I've felt this guilty about any of it. My stomach falls so hard that I have to fight the urge to hold it in place.

As they say, though—offense is the best defense.

"Did you *follow* me here?" I demand, mastering the tremble in my lips as it comes out. *And why the fuck am I trembling? He slept with Suzanne, for God's sake.* "I have the right to go to breakfast with a friend if I want."

"As I've told you before, there are only two reasons you'd be talking to Jeremy, and they both suck." His eyes are empty as he speaks. That he isn't even reacting frightens me—he's not mad. He's *done*. Done with me, done with my bullshit, and I guess I should have figured that out last night, but my stomach drops anyway. I want to scramble, beg, do or say whatever I can to change his mind. It's that same embarrassing weakness I allowed myself to show as a kid, and it never paid off once.

"You seriously think I'd date Jeremy? Unlike you, I don't fuck any human garbage I find in my path."

"So you and Jeremy are trying to break Lucie and Caleb up."

I might as well come clean—*nothing* I've done to Lucie is as bad as him sleeping with Suzanne last night, and I'm not giving him another chance. "Have we tried to make Lucie think Caleb was cheating in a variety of ways? Sure. I went to crazy lengths to make her think that. But that's not what was happening today, and just because you and I have been fucking around doesn't mean you get to dictate how I spend my time. Especially after you spent the night with Suzanne."

His eyes turn black, utterly cold. "I was with Liam, not Suzanne, but it doesn't matter at this point."

He didn't cheat.

God. Of course he didn't.

I'm not even *surprised*. I ruined it...because I wanted to ruin it, didn't I? Because the mere possibility of him cheating took my breath away.

I didn't want to be hurt again, but I wound up hurting us both.

He climbs on his bike and doesn't even turn to face me as he speaks. "I've been in love with you since the day we met. From that first night I saw you standing outside The Midnight House. So, I waited, because I knew you and Caleb wouldn't last." He puts on his helmet and flips up the visor as he starts the bike. "But who you are right now? That's not the girl I met that night. And that's not the girl I waited for. Hannah's gone, Kate. So is Caleb. And one of these days you'll need to move on, but I'm done waiting for it to happen. I'll give you a few hours to get your stuff out of my place. Be gone by the time I get home."

He backs out and drives away, and I grip the door of my car, swaying on my feet. Tears stream down my face, and I can't summon the effort to wipe them away.

Why am I here, outside this restaurant? Why did I ever agree to meet Jeremy in the first place? It's not Caleb I want now, and I'm not sure it ever was.

He loved me.

I think I knew this. All those nights he spent helping me get the nursery ready because Caleb was at work, all the times I heard him argue with Caleb on my behalf. And I loved him too. I told myself I just wished my husband were more *like* him, but there was a part of me that wished I were with him instead. Only I didn't want to admit it, I couldn't admit it, because it would have meant losing what I had.

My phone begins ringing in my purse just as I've climbed in the car and I dive at it, praying that it's Beck calling to give me one last chance, telling me how to fix this. When I see Caleb's name instead, the disappointment is overwhelming. I laugh and sob simultaneously at the irony as I let the call go to voicemail. It doesn't really matter what he has to say. There's a hole in me Caleb can never fill—he never did in the first place. It was only Beck, the one person who saw anything good in me.

And even he can't find it anymore.

41

KATE

K ent's house is at the end of a long private gravel road, hidden from view. The driveway is full of cars, as if there's a party going on...but there's always a party going on here at any hour of the day.

I park and walk to the door, already envisioning the way I'll later tell this story in rehab. I won't get halfway through before people are shaking their heads, thinking *of course it went bad, you fucking idiot*.

I knock and a blonde girl I vaguely recognize answers, staring at me through dreamy, drugged eyes. She's high as fuck.

"Katie," she says with a lazy smile, wrapping her arms around me, not entirely supporting her own weight. It doesn't make me think *oh, gosh, drugs are bad*.

It makes me think *I wish I was her right now*.

I imagine giving in—the bliss, the nothingness. It would feel so fucking good to let go just one more time, and all the reasons for denying myself this are moot. I'm not getting back together with Caleb. I'm not replacing Hannah. I don't have Beck waiting to provide things I didn't even know I loved until they were gone. New Kate, the better one who doesn't do drugs and doesn't frame people for shit—couldn't I just be her tomorrow instead of today?

And if she never rises again...well, I'm kind of ambivalent about that too.

There are people everywhere, and music is booming through the speakers. Kent spies me from across the room, and his face breaks into a wide, jubilant smile while my stomach turns with the same disgust I felt every time I woke up with him.

He comes around the big marble island in the kitchen and wraps his arms around me. "I've missed you, babe. Welcome home."

I step back, my mouth a firm line. "I'm not back. I'm just here to get my locket."

He grins, placing his hands on my shoulders to turn me toward the counter, where lines of coke are laid out on a mirror with machine precision.

My mouth waters at the sight. I want it so bad that I'm already sweating, already desperate.

I want to not hurt. I want to no longer give a fuck about Beck and the thing I saw in his face today, something broken I never, ever wanted to be responsible for. And I don't *have* to feel any of it.

"Dig in, honey," says Kent in my ear. "You know you want to."

I squeeze my eyes shut and try to channel the thing that kept me strong in rehab. Except it was Caleb, and that no longer works. The flavor has been bled from that dream like a piece of gum that's been chewed too long. His is no longer the face I care about, the one I don't want to disappoint.

My jaw grinds as I force my reply. "I'm good. I just want my locket. We had a deal."

"Come on, babe," he says, rubbing my arms. "Stay and hang out with us. We haven't seen you in forever."

"I don't do that anymore." My voice is frosty. "I've been clean for months."

"Fuck. You know how good that first line will be after that long without it? I want to be clean for months just so I can see what that's like."

He's right. It'll feel like heaven. And there's no reason not to anymore. I've got no job to lose, no parents to disappoint, no husband or daughter waiting at home.

No Beck.

"I just want my locket," I tell him, my voice edgy with craving. He hears the way I'm weakening.

"Okay, babe," he says, placing his hand on my hip. "Come on. It's in my room."

I follow him upstairs, my heart drumming faster than it was. He's never forced me to do anything, but he never *had* to force me either. Until now, there was always something I wanted badly enough.

He shuts the door behind us when we enter and backs me to the wall.

"I missed you, sweetheart," he says, tucking my hair behind my ear.

I place my hands against his chest, futilely attempting to push him away. "I'm not here for that. Where's my locket?"

"What are you going to give me for it?"

I cringe at his nearness. Dear God, in a lifetime full of bad ideas, coming in here with him may have been my worst. "It's not worth anything. It's just sentimental. I'll give you two hundred bucks for it."

"Two hundred?" He laughs, waving his hands around the room—at the massive television and ridiculous custom bed. "You think I care about two hundred bucks?"

"Five hundred. Please, Kent. This is all I've got left of my daughter. It doesn't mean anything to you."

"The fact that it means something to *you*," he says, wrapping his hand around my hip, "means it's also valuable to *me*. I don't want money, babe. Tell you what: do one line, just *one*, and I'll give you the necklace."

My mouth waters at the idea, a deep, ugly anticipation cresting in my chest.

I could do one. It's just to get the locket back. I could do one line, just one, and prove to myself and to him that it's behind me. "I don't even know that you still have it."

He reaches into his nightstand and pulls it out, swinging it to and fro. "Of course I have it. I knew you'd come back for it eventually. It was the only thing you ever loved."

"That's not true," I whisper.

He laughs, tossing it from one hand to the other. "Sure it is. Think about the shit you did to get coke. You were willing to steal, you were willing to cheat on your husband, you were willing to give up every fucking thing, but you never, ever agreed to give up this gold-plated piece of shit. It was a game to me. I'd always ask you to give up the locket first, remember? And when you wouldn't, we'd move on to option two."

I stare at him, at it. That can't be true. I couldn't have loved a *thing* more than my husband. I couldn't have loved a *thing* so much that I'd sleep with someone I hated instead of giving it up. Except...it wasn't just a necklace to me. It was Hannah. It was a way to hold onto her, to pretend she wasn't gone. And getting back together with Caleb, having another child just like her...it was a ridiculous, comforting fantasy, one I chose over the real, beautiful, terrifying thing I had with Beck.

I hurt him, which is why I have to stop choosing her. It's time to let go of the fantasy and enter the real, beautiful, and terrifying world again.

"Forget it," I say, heading for the door.

"You'll be back," he warns, tossing the locket in a drawer and perhaps he's right, but I continue down the stairs, through all the people in the living room, ignoring every greeting, and get outside to my car.

I'm still sitting in his driveway when I call Ann for the first time in weeks and finally admit what I've really known all along:

I'm still not well, and I have no idea what the fuck to do about it.

42

KATE

A few hours later, I'm at my first NA meeting in four months. It's as *un*thrilling as the ones I remember. Same shitty tile floor in a church rec room, same folding card table with coffee, same fluorescent light and stench of desperation.

The stories I hear are, arguably, worse than my own. The guy beside me has only been clean for about ten hours, and at one point stole his parents' life savings. There's another woman whose kid got into her stash and overdosed. But my errors feel no more minor because I didn't expect anything of these people, while once upon a time, I expected a lot of shit of myself, and I failed at all of it. Mostly, I failed Beck. I shudder, recalling that broken look in his eyes before he drove away.

I did that to him. To big, unbreakable Beck. Of all the unforgivable things I've ever done, that was the worst. The one that made him finally give up.

They go around the room. I am reluctant to speak when they get to me, but Lynn, Ann's psychotherapist friend in San Francisco—isn't about to let me off the hook.

"I'm Kate," I tell them.

"Hi, Kate," they say in unison. That greeting has always annoyed me. There's nothing genuine about the rote welcome they offer every person. But I digress.

"I've been clean for a few months, but just last night I was at my dealer's only half sure I wasn't going to do anything."

There are nods, which I expected. I'm not the only one who's gone right to the line before backing away.

I tell them that I got clean for the wrong reasons, and that I now want to stay clean for the right ones. That I want to become some semblance of the person I was before my daughter died, and that I suspect it's going to be a lot harder the second time around because I no longer have a reason to bother.

I'm no better when it's all out—I'm just empty. I want to sleep for a hundred years, but perhaps that's because I drove straight to San Francisco from Kent's house last night and haven't seen a bed in far too long.

When the meeting concludes, Lynn and I walk to the back table where a pot of coffee and a plate of store-bought cookies awaits, like anyone wants cookies at six in the morning.

"Would it kill them to provide real milk with the coffee?" I ask Lynn. "Haven't we all suffered enough without enduring powdered creamer?" I do not especially care about anything I'm saying. I just want to keep the focus off myself.

She bites into one of the gross cookies. "Come on. Let's get some decent coffee and have a chat."

Apparently, we're going to be putting the focus on me anyway.

Outside, the morning sunlight is too bright, and nothing feels real. She directs me up a long hill. I don't actually want coffee, and I sure as hell don't want to climb this big-ass hill for it.

"What did you mean in the meeting?" she asks. "When you said you got clean for the wrong reasons?"

I reluctantly start climbing the hill, letting the story of Beck and Caleb and some of the shit I did wrong unravel. I'd probably lie to her about the details if I wasn't so tired. Laid out in all their glory, the facts make me sound evil, and not an evil *queen*, as Beck would once have said. I'm too filthy and exhausted right now for anyone to see me as powerful.

She opens the door to the coffee shop. "It sounds like you have some amends to make."

My teeth grind as we get in the very long morning line. I can't believe I'm standing in line for coffee I don't want only to have to listen to this crap. I still don't entirely buy all the NA garbage about amends, and I can't make up for it anyway. "Beck doesn't want my amends. He wants nothing to do with me. He's seen too much of my bullshit for too long to believe anything I say now."

"I wasn't talking about Beck," she says. "I was talking about Lucie."

I blink, awakened by rage. "*Lucie?* Why the hell should I make amends to *her*?"

"You're telling me that you've spent months trying to make her think her boyfriend is cheating on her, and you met with her ex-husband to discuss framing her for drug possession." Her hand rests on her hip. "Is it really not clear to you why amends might be called for?"

I sigh. "I didn't go through with it. I just heard him out. And why the hell should I apologize? That bitch has two healthy kids *and* she has my husband. It seems like she's got enough without amends from me."

She gives me a gentle smile. "Less than an hour ago you said you wanted to be the old Kate, the one who wasn't bitter and full of rage. So tell me something—would the old Kate be enraged by a single mom with kids? Would she take the side of a guy who's trying to *trap* her into remaining married to him?"

Ugh. "No."

We've reached the register. I order a latte and Lynn laughs. "Make hers a decaf. She's about to go to bed. And I'll take a large tea, thank you."

I want to resent the way she just changed my order, as if I'm a child, but instead my eyes sting. It was sort of maternal of her. It reminded me of Mimi.

We move to the end of the counter to wait for our drinks. "Lucie represents all the things you want," she continues. "Children, stability. So maybe the first step toward becoming that person is to stop hating someone who is. She doesn't have your daughter. She doesn't have the man you're in love with. Stop blaming her for living her life and start figuring out how you can live yours."

I suck in a cheek, fighting my desire to argue with her though she's right.

At what point did all of this become less about Caleb and more about punishing Lucie for having the life I wanted? Because that's what it's been, for weeks if not months. From the moment Beck first kissed me, I haven't missed my life with Caleb once.

"Maybe," I finally reply. My voice is barely audible.

She grabs our drinks and hands me mine. "Come on. You can stay in my guestroom. Things always look better after a few hours of sleep."

I swallow hard and nod.

Mimi used to say that too.

LYNN and her husband Jamie live in a surprisingly nice two-story walk-up in North Beach, and are far better to me than I deserve. They insist I stay with them until I get back on my feet, which is good since I've got no clue where I'd stay otherwise. I haven't heard a single word from Beck since I left.

Every afternoon, I help Lynn make a nice dinner and try to pretend that I'm happy, that I'm not waiting to feel my phone vibrate with a text that says I'm forgiven. It's not the box of Hannah's things that has a siren's call for me these days—it's Beck. It's his photo I want to see. It's the memories of us together I want to sift through my fingers like sand. It's him I want to tell about my day.

EACH MORNING, Lynn and I get up at the crack of dawn to attend that same NA meeting I went to on my first morning here.

Today, the woman whose son overdosed when he got into her stash wept as she told us that her husband had forgiven her.

"I don't understand why he would," I tell Lynn as we walk up the hill for coffee. "I wouldn't forgive her."

"It seems to me that's kind of your problem," she says. "You don't expect anyone to forgive you because you don't forgive anyone yourself, *including* yourself."

I frown. "Who haven't I forgiven?"

She laughs. "Who do you have to forgive?"

I shrug. "That douchebag who tried to get me to sleep with him in exchange for a reference?"

Her nose crinkles. "No, definitely don't forgive him. How about your grandmother and aunt?"

I stop in place. "I don't have any family."

"Mimi and her daughter...Natalie? Wasn't that her name?"

I start walking again. "Mimi died a few years after she ditched me, apparently—I looked her up—and Natalie can go fuck herself. She's had two decades to reach out, and she chose not to."

"You can't truly choose *not* to forgive her until you know what happened," Lynn says.

I disagree. I can choose not to forgive whoever I want. But

when we get back to Lynn's place, after an hour of internal debate, I pull out my laptop and search for Natalie's name. The fact that she's a doctor makes her relatively easy to find.

Natalie Collins, molecular oncologist, National Institutes of Health.

"Nice of you to look for a cure for cancer but leave me in foster care," I mutter at her perky staff photo.

Lynn, puttering around the kitchen, simply laughs. "Try not to say that right away."

I tap on her email address and stare at the blank screen as I channel a professionalism I don't feel. This woman and her mother left me to languish, but my purpose here isn't really to rage at her *or* to forgive her. I just want to know who my father was. I want to understand what happened...and if I'm the reason he did it.

Hi Natalie,

This is Kate Bennett. I assume you know who I am. I'm doing some family research and had a few questions when you have a minute.

Best,

Kate

I expect nothing to come from this exercise, aside from shutting Lynn up, but within minutes, Natalie's response has landed in my inbox.

Kate,

I honestly don't know how to begin this, so let me start by telling you I'm sorry. I've spent twenty years feeling guilty about how I handled things, knowing you were somewhere out in the world, and you probably wonder why I never reached out. I don't have a good answer. Just a couple of bad ones.

My mom (she had you call her "Mimi" but her actual name was Francesca) had a stroke in the process of adopting you and needed full-time care for the rest of her life, but you

were pretty young then, and I wasn't sure I should tell you all that. It seemed like it would upset you less to simply think she'd moved, so I sent you a letter implying she'd changed her mind.

She didn't change her mind, I promise. I'm not sure how much she understood during those last few years, but she adored you and my greatest regret is that I didn't find a way to let her see you again.

My second greatest regret is that I didn't do more to help you. I blamed your mom—and by extension, you—for his death because we'd found letters from her threatening to tell the university about their affair. I know that wasn't your fault, and maybe it wasn't entirely your mom's fault—my brother was someone who could never stand to fail in any way, and that's on him.

I'd love to talk if you're open to it, and perhaps one day, you might even want to meet your cousins. In the meantime, I'm happy to answer any questions you might have.

Best,

Natalie

My throat is tight as I hand the laptop to Lynn so she can read it too. It shouldn't matter after all this time that Mimi didn't abandon me, didn't just decide I wasn't worth her effort, but it does.

"Do you forgive her now?" Lynn asks when she's done.

I hitch a shoulder. "Yeah. I'd probably have done the same thing in her shoes. I don't love the fact that I'm the product of a sketchy professor and a blackmailer, however."

She smiles. "Or maybe you're the product of a brilliant man who made a mistake and a resourceful nineteen-year-old whose back was against a wall. You get to choose which parts of your DNA you hold dear."

If I could forgive myself for what I did to Beck, I might even believe her.

43

KATE

I'm walking into an afternoon NA meeting two weeks later when my phone rings. At this hour, it's typically Rachel, calling after she's gotten Jane down for a nap. Occasionally, it's Natalie, whose only free minutes come in the afternoon when she's driving from NIH to her sons' school in DC.

This time, though, it's Jeremy.

I've been ignoring his calls since our breakfast meeting, and I'm tempted to ignore him now, too, because I just want to forget it all, but it's probably time to get this over with.

"Where the fuck have you been?" he snarls.

I tuck into the ladies' room of the church's basement, bending low to make sure all the stalls are empty. "I've been out of town."

"Whatever. This still needs to happen tomorrow because I've got no idea how long I have before she changes the password. She's helping set up some haunted house. I'll text you the address—just get out by two and let me know when it's done."

He hangs up. I put my phone away and enter the meeting, taking the seat Lynn's saved for me so I can tell an entire room full of people how much I've changed.

"I feel like a different person," I say, and they all fucking believe me.

THE PLACE where Lucie's setting up a haunted house isn't actually in Elliott Springs but just to its north. It's one of those glass and cement monstrosities that dwarfs every other home on the street, and the one thing about it that isn't shiny and new is Lucie's beat-up Toyota Sienna.

My shoulders sag. Her minivan with the small dent on the left side and an elementary school bumper sticker on the rear window doesn't exactly scream *archnemesis*.

It's also not the ride of a woman who theoretically doesn't give a shit about her kids.

My stomach tightens as I climb from my car. I'm nearly to her van when the door opens and she walks out in a pink peacoat and ballet flats, all wide-eyed innocence.

Jeremy was full of shit. This girl isn't a neglectful parent doing drugs with her kids asleep in the next room. She's the exact kind of girl Caleb *should* have wound up with in the first place.

She freezes when she sees me and I take a deep breath as the truth of the situation finally hits home: this woman has two young kids and a psychotic ex-husband, and all I've done is give her something more to fear. *Jesus, Kate.*

I approach slowly, as if she's a rabbit who'll hop away at my first errant move. "Don't worry. I'm only here to help you."

She remains frozen. I suppose that *did* sound like something I'd say if I was here to kill her.

"I'd have called, but Jeremy might be tracking your phone. He seems to have a bunch of your passwords."

Her eyes glisten with frustrated tears. "I can't believe this is still happening. I've switched phones twice."

Jesus. What else has he been doing all along? Why did I believe a word out of his mouth? I knew he was untrustworthy the same way I knew Kayleigh was untrustworthy, but I let myself buy into their bullshit because I wanted allies.

I pull the flash drive out of my pocket and hand it to her. "He's calling in a tip to the police in about forty-five minutes, when you're on your way home with your kids, because he believes I'm here planting drugs in your car. He thinks if you lose the kids, you'll come back to him. I recorded him laying out the plan."

"Oh my God," she whispers. "I can't believe you did this for me."

I don't correct her, even though helping her was never at the top of my priorities list. I mostly just thought I might need a recording to blackmail him with if he tried to threaten me into helping him. But even then, I half expected I'd wind up exactly where I am now.

"If I were you, I'd contact the police before the call comes in, so it's documented and they're looking for it. He can be arrested immediately for making a false statement, if nothing else." I reach into my pocket. "And here's his key to your van."

She stares at the key in her palm. "I'm speechless. Why are you helping me?"

It's a question I never even asked myself.

It isn't because I care about her. It's not even because I care about her kids or Caleb. It's simply that it's the right thing to do. "I guess I'm not quite as evil as Caleb's implied."

She shakes her head. "Caleb's never once said a word against you. Sometimes I wish he would." She gives me a tentative smile. "You're a hard act to follow."

Joy and sadness twine together at once. I never made Caleb happy the way she does, and he never made me happy the way Beck does. But I can still picture a world in which our daughter didn't die, in which we figured it all out. "Good luck with everything."

I'm walking back to my car when she finally speaks. "I hope things work out for you and Beck."

I turn toward her, blowing out a breath to deal with the wound she just re-opened. "There's nothing going on with me and Beck."

"Maybe there should be, then," she says. "He's been in love with you for a long, long time. Way before you came back."

I laugh, but it gets caught in my throat, like a sob. "Beck doesn't even *like* me, much less love me."

"Yeah, he does," she says softly. "And with the way he wears his heart on his sleeve, a part of you must already know that."

I suppose she's right. I did know that. But I can't imagine it's still true.

I climb in my car and head toward Elliott Springs because I have one more stop to make. And coming face-to-face with Lucie like I just did seems like a walk in the park by contrast.

Gus answers the door, looking tired and happy and in need of a shave. He grins, those laugh lines around his eyes seeming more deeply etched than they were a few weeks ago. "And Beck said you weren't coming."

Just the sound of Beck's name makes my heart beat harder. I want to ask what else he said, as if I'm a thirteen-year-old with a crush. "He doesn't know everything."

Gus smiles. "He doesn't know *anything*. He's just so besotted with the baby he can't imagine how everyone else isn't here on a daily basis."

My chest floods with something that is half sweet and half sharp. Beck has always been so closed off and alone that I never imagined him even wanting kids, though I'd seen firsthand how excited he was about Hannah. I was an idiot. About so many things.

Gus leads me upstairs to where Rachel sits in a rocking chair, holding her daughter. I freeze, certain that I cannot walk a step farther into this room. I've imagined all of this so many times for myself. But before I can think of an excuse to leave, Rachel gives me a gentle smile and crosses the room to deposit Jane in my arms.

The baby probably weighs ten pounds more than Hannah did, yet she's still so very tiny in my arms. She has wisps of blonde hair like Gus's, her mouth pursed in sleep, her chest rising and falling rapidly, the way a baby's does.

I adored Hannah from the moment she was born, *before* she was born, even. But I could love this little girl, too, if she were mine. I could love this little girl who looks nothing like Hannah or Caleb so hard my heart would break.

Maybe I could have had this, instead, with Beck—the person it should have been with all along. I can't believe I threw what we had away.

I take a seat in the rocker with Jane in my arms and Rachel sits on the footstool, smiling at both her daughter and me, as if she knew we'd get here one day.

"Doing okay?" she asks.

I nod, blinking back tears. "Yeah." My voice is hoarse. "It's weirdly...fine."

"I figured it would be," she says, giving my knee a quick squeeze.

We discuss how the past few weeks have gone, and when she asks what I've been up to, I tell her all about Natalie and Mimi.

"It's sort of like the story had a happy ending after all," she says when I conclude. "A bittersweet one, sure, but you're talking to Natalie, and you know you were loved. And you're starting over in San Francisco."

My laugh is more miserable than joyful. "I wouldn't say it's a happy ending just yet."

She hitches a shoulder. "So you're bickering with Beck, and you still don't have a job. You can fix those things easily."

I shake my head. "I don't think I can."

But when I go to my car an hour later and pull out my phone, there's a voicemail from Adam Weintraub at Holzig.

He's offering me the job.

I cry the whole way back to San Francisco, and my tears are happy and sad at once. I wound up with almost everything, but I'm not sure it's going to be enough.

44

BECK

Last week was terrible. This one is shaping up to be about the same. To be honest, I'm kind of surprised, given how I've been driving, that I'm still around to suffer through it.

I got an email from Kate last night, which I haven't opened. I'm not sure why I'm not opening it—probably because if it's an apology, it'll be insufficient, and if it's not an apology, that's even worse.

The sight of Caleb walking into the bar is like salt in the wound. Things are fine between us, but he's the one she wants, the one she chose. That isn't his fault, but it's always going to hurt.

He takes a seat in front of me. I breathe deep, willing a calmness I'm nowhere near feeling.

"What's up?" I ask, in a voice that suggests he should make this fast and be on his way. I can't help it.

"Just checking in," he says. "You've been quiet."

"I've been here." The way I always fucking am. Day in and day out. Except now it's with the admission that I'm not needed. This bar runs itself. I'd already largely outsourced the management to Mueller over the past two months anyway. Unlike me, he actually enjoys it.

Caleb's fingers are tapping on the bar. I come out of my self-indulgent funk long enough to notice that his eyes are light. He's excited in the way he used to be when he was a kid.

"Something's up with you," I say.

A sheepish smile crosses his face. I never thought I'd see the day when Caleb in his thousand-dollar suit would look *goofy*, but he looks goofy as fuck right now. "Well, I'm getting married. So there's that."

That frozen thing in my chest takes its first fledgling beat. "Don't you need to be divorced for that to happen?"

He shrugs. "My divorce will be finalized in February, but it's just a formality, and Lucie's got a court date in April."

I swallow. My heart takes another tentative beat. "Kate signed the papers?"

He straightens as his smile fades. "Thought you'd already know. She signed them last week. And the stuff she gave Lucie is giving us all the leverage over Jeremy we needed."

Another beat. Another tiny, hopeful impulse I need to fucking crush before it takes over. "I don't know what you think Kate did for her, but I'm telling you right now that anything she gave Lucie was probably laced with anthrax, or it's a trap."

His eyes narrow. He's never allowed anyone to badmouth Kate. I normally wouldn't either.

"What did you do?" he demands. "If you hurt her after everything else she's been through, you and I will have a serious problem."

I glare at him. "Why the hell are you assuming that *I* did anything?"

"I'm not. But you're in here now, sour as fuck, and from what I hear, driving like a fucking maniac when you're not here. So one of you did something, and all I'm saying is it better not have been you."

My mood is bad enough that I'd welcome a fight right now, too, and—unfair or not—Caleb's high on the list of people I'd like to punch.

I close my eyes, breathing through my nose. *He's just defending Kate.* I guess it's good there are still people looking out for her.

"Believe me, I did nothing wrong. So how did she purportedly *assist* Lucie?"

"She met Jeremy for coffee or something and recorded this crazy plan he had to get the kids. He wanted Kate to plant something in Lucie's car. He'll probably just get his hand slapped, but he's never getting custody now."

Maybe I was unfair to her that morning she met with Jeremy. Maybe...

No. No, it's still not enough. It doesn't change what she said outside—*"Just because we've been fucking around doesn't mean you get to dictate how I spend my time"*—as if everything we had was meaningless.

Caleb and I shoot the shit for a few minutes, trying to leave things on even ground. But he's long gone before I finally ask Mueller to take over so I can go to the back and read her email at last.

Beck,

I set up all your financials on the computer at work (beckfinances.xls) so that if you decide to sell, it's all ready to go. There's also a PowerPoint to present to investors in case you don't want to sell but would like to share the burden (beckstopbeingapussy.ppt).

You said I needed to move on and maybe you were right, but I'm not the only one.

K

It's not an apology. It's not a change of heart. I suppose I expected that but *fuck*. It still hurts.

I review the spreadsheet and presentation she created. The

research and level of detail must have taken her weeks, and she did it without ever saying a word. There are notes everywhere that make me smile against my will. "*Please start saving some money,*" she's written in the assets column. "*This is ridiculous.*" In the debts column, which is empty, there's a note that says, "*You have the financial profile of a human trafficker.*"

My smile flickers, and then fades. She made me so fucking happy until she didn't. I've got questions, but I remain certain about the most important thing—if I was what she wanted, she'd have fucking tried to fix it.

45

KATE

When my flight lands in Frankfurt on the way home, my first call is to Adam.

Working at Holzig is everything I'd hoped it might be, and working for Adam is even *better* than I'd hoped. For the past three months, he's not just my boss, but my friend, and he's been in my corner since day one. It's the board that held up hiring me in the first place, conceding to Adam only if he agreed it would be probational. They haven't even given me the job title yet. But as of today, I've cut the company's costs by six percent. They owe me.

I already emailed him the renegotiated contract with our down supplier just before my flight boarded, too excited to keep the news to myself. This gamble, and all the other ones I'm taking on behalf of Holzig, are panning out just as I'd promised. Not since I was in New York, in those halcyon days straight out of grad school, have I felt this sure of myself and this committed.

"If you were any more perfect," Adam says when he picks up, "I'd probably have to leave my boyfriend for you."

"I'd still have a vagina."

"I didn't say I wouldn't be *disappointed* eventually," he replies.

I laugh as I enter the terminal. "And? Have you told the board?"

"They want to see you when you get back," Adam says. There's a smile in his voice. "I'll make sure I'm filming as they eat crow. And don't kill me, but I already called Lynn. I was too excited not to tell someone, and your flight hadn't landed."

He and Lynn are now thick as thieves, having met at my birthday party, which is a blessing and a curse. I'm too old to have people fretting over me, and I definitely don't need *two* people fretting over me.

I smile. "I assume she reacted with her customary restraint?"

"I'm pretty sure she's trying to hire a skywriter to announce your new job title to the city as we speak."

It's everything I wanted, yet when I hang up, the moment is a little empty as well. Emptier than I'd thought it would be. Maybe it's just that there's no one else to tell.

I wander through the airport, stretching my legs before the eleven-hour flight home. I buy a pastry I'm not interested in eating and wander through shops I'm not interested in purchasing from until I wind up looking at men's watches in the Omega store. I can't begin to count the number of times I've found myself somewhere like this, thinking of Beck. I am still searching, in every store, in every spot of color, for the thing that will make him forgive me. But not even the De Ville Tourbillon in front of me, worth well over a hundred thousand euros, could accomplish that.

Nothing can. But I can't stop hoping I'll find it anyway.

The salesman approaches—I suppose I now appear to be the kind of woman who could afford an insanely expensive watch.

"For your husband?" the salesman asks in German.

I know just enough German to tell him I'm not married, which is untrue, but a mere technicality. My divorce will be finalized next week, but even that isn't particularly significant. I've been alone for a long time now. It's not like anything's changed.

I give him a polite smile and turn from the store. Beck wouldn't want a watch anyway. A Ducati, perhaps. But no, even that would not be enough. I'm not sure anything is.

Twelve hours later I walk off the plane, exhausted though I slept for a good bit of the flight. There's something about arriving after a long trip that always depletes me. I suppose it's the realization that there's no one waiting for me at home.

I pull my carry-on through the crowd, forcing down a spike of irritation as a woman stops in front of me to hug someone she's picking up. I can't imagine caring about anyone enough to drive to the fucking airport on their behalf anyway. Parking here is a nightmare.

"Kate!" a voice shouts. It's a common name, but my head turns on reflex to discover Lynn pushing her way through the crowd. She wraps her arms around me. She knows how I feel about hugs but persists in doing it anyway.

"What's up?" I ask. "Are you and Jamie finally taking a vacation?"

She grins. "Nope. I just thought I'd give my favorite vice president a ride home from the airport."

My head tilts. "I travel for work constantly, Lynn. You've never shown up at the airport before."

She leads me toward the parking garage. "I wanted to celebrate. And Adam and I were worried about you."

I release a heavy sigh. I should be grateful that these people care enough to discuss me behind my back, but it's also a little tedious that I'm twenty-eight and still have the grown-ups acting like I'm a wild card who can't be trusted. "I just learned they're making me vice president. Why would you worry?"

"Sometimes the good news is harder to take than the bad," she says. "And sometimes getting the thing you want makes you realize you wanted other things."

The words sit like lead in my stomach. She's right. Discovering that I've finally got exactly what I was working toward has not felt like a victory at all. It's felt like a beautifully wrapped gift that contains only air.

She pops the trunk, and I throw my bag inside. "Yeah, I guess. I suppose you're going to tell me to go to a meeting."

"Actually," she says, "I was going to suggest that you figure out what you want."

I climb into the passenger seat and swallow hard as I turn my face to the window. "I already know what I want. It just doesn't want me back."

She throws the car into reverse and begins carefully backing out. "Did he love you?"

The lump in my throat is getting harder to form words around. "Yeah."

"And you really think that just stops? Did it stop for you?"

"No, but he never did anything wrong."

She reaches the exit and fumbles, scanning her ticket and inserting her credit card. It was so nice of her to come all the way here for me. She really shouldn't have. "Did I ever tell you what I did to Jamie while we were engaged?"

I raise a brow. Lynn is a therapist—she wears sensible shoes and drives a Prius. "I'm guessing it didn't involve trying to frame someone for drug possession so you could steal her boyfriend?"

"No, it's worse," she says as she pulls out. "I slept with his brother."

I suck in a breath. Lynn and Jamie are the living definition of relationship goals. It's just not possible. "You're making that up."

"It's true. We weren't even married yet, and I was drunk and high at this party, and Jamie and I had just fought about it. I stormed out and his brother followed me..." She stops for a moment, her voice catching. She's been married for twenty years and it's clearly still painful. "But he forgave me. And that's what did it. I wanted him back so much that I'd have given up anything, and I just didn't want to be that person anymore. I never used again."

I sit with that. Could Beck forgive me? Is it possible?

"If Beck is what you want," she says, "then don't you owe it to yourself to try?"

My voice is a whisper. "What if he says no?"

"Then you wind up exactly where you are right now," she says. "And we go from there."

46

KATE

On the first Friday in February, I return to Elliott Springs to finalize the divorce. I stop on the way to see Rachel—though I'm really here to see Jane. I've come by a few times. It used to hurt a bit, but it no longer does. She's her own little person. I can look at her without seeing Hannah.

"She's gotten so big in the past month," I say, taking Jane in my arms. "Aunt Kate is going to give you so much ski gear once you're older."

Jane clasps my index finger and gives me a toothless smile.

"Oh Lord," sighs Rachel. "Don't even start with that. Gus already bought her skis, for God's sake. He's convinced she's the next Lindsay Vonn and she can't even *walk*."

I sit and bounce Jane on my knee. "I'm gonna have to leave in a minute, unfortunately. I hit more traffic than I expected on the way here."

"I assume you'll be okay today," she begins, "but I'm happy to be there for moral support if you need me."

I give her a small, grateful smile. "I'll be fine." Honestly, the only part of this that's even sad is that after the papers are finalized—aside from visiting Rachel and Jane—I have no reason to come back.

She kicks my foot. "You should go by the bar."

My eyes widen. "It's almost creepy the way you knew I was thinking about him."

Her smile is sad. "That's because I suspect you think about little else. Neither does he. He's been miserable since you left."

Except, if he's so miserable, why did he never reach out? He must be aware by now that I wasn't meeting with Jeremy that day for nefarious reasons. Maybe he just can't look past all the half-truths I told or the fact that it took me so long to figure out that he's what I want, and I can hardly blame him. I jerked him around for too long.

I could grovel, but I doubt it would help. And I'd rather not know how he feels than know for certain he feels nothing at all. The bleak, empty thing in his eyes when he said he was done with me? I don't ever want to see that look again.

CALEB IS WAITING outside the courtroom when I arrive, handsome as ever in an Armani suit. It was thoughtful of him not to bring Lucie, though unnecessary. I just want him to be happy, and if she's capable of giving him that, she has my blessing.

The small talk we make as we wait for our case to be called is the sort you'd exchange with a former colleague. Our jobs, cities we've flown to lately, our shared love of British Airways. I'm not sure he was ever much more to me than that. We were two people who liked sex and were too busy for a real relationship, then two people preparing to raise a kid together.

There wasn't much more to us than that.

The divorce, once our case is called before the judge, takes five minutes at most. I'd expected to feel sad as Caleb and I walk out of the courthouse together, but I don't feel much of anything.

"I never got the chance to say it before," he says, "but thanks for what you did for Lucie."

I stop in place. "Well, I never got the chance to thank you, either, for the grant. But it really helped. I couldn't have gotten back on my feet without it."

Of course it's also part of the reason I clung to him for so much longer than I should have, thinking he must still care. But he couldn't have realized that at the time.

His brow furrows. "Grant? What do you mean?"

"That postpartum loss thing. I know it was supposed to be anonymous, but it was clearly you. The paperwork was registered here."

He continues to stare at me blankly and I laugh in exasperation. "If you're making so much money that you just forget about donating all of that in my name, maybe I *should* have asked for alimony after all."

"I have no idea what you're talking about. I paid for a lawyer to get the possession charges dropped, but there was no *grant*." He frowns. "So who would have done it?"

We look at each other, and it seems to hit us both at the same time. There's one person, aside from Caleb, who would have cared enough to do it and had that kind of expendable income. A person who claimed he had "no idea" where all his profits had gone.

Caleb shakes his head and pushes a hand through his hair. "I probably shouldn't tell you this, but he was outside the courthouse this morning. I saw him across the street in his truck."

"Outside *here*? Why?"

He gives me a small smile. "Come on, Kate. You're a smart girl. Think about it."

I swallow. "Maybe he just happened to be passing by."

He shoves his hands in his pockets and stares at the ground

between us. "Look, this whole situation is uncomfortable for a lot of reasons. I'm not sure he's the best guy for you, and I'm not sure you're the best person for him either. But he—" Caleb bites his lip. "He wasn't himself for a long time. And I didn't see it until you came home. It's like you brought him back to life. So pull your head out of your ass, Bennett. Of course he was here to see you."

He wraps his arms around me for only a second, tight, then heads down the street. I've never felt closer to him than I do as he walks away. Because we weren't meant to be, but he loves the person I love, and he loves him enough to put him first.

Maybe I should do the same.

I walk to my car, my hands shaking as I fumble with the keys and I drive to the bar, though I'm still not convinced I'll go inside.

I *want* to go in. I also want to drive home to the comfort of my job and an NA meeting. I can already imagine the conversation I'll have with Lynn later on about this. *I just decided it wasn't the right time*, I'll tell her. *And I didn't know what to say*.

That much would be true, certainly. In the entire English language, are there words that will make him forgive me for abusing his trust, for hurting him and taking way, way too long to figure out what I wanted? I'm not sure, but I'm positive that even if there are, they are not currently in my possession.

I glance at the clock. *If I don't get out of here soon, I'll hit rush hour traffic. Maybe I should come back another time*.

I start the engine and put the car in reverse. And then I think of Beck. Beck who, according to two people I trust, is miserable. Beck, who potentially sat outside the courthouse this morning simply to see my face.

I put the car in park again, turn off the engine, and climb out before I can change my mind. I march toward the bar with my fists clenched, as if I'm going into battle, and push through the double doors.

It's relatively empty inside, just a couple at one of the high-tops and a lone drinker sitting at the end watching sports. I don't care about them, though. I only care about Beck, currently sitting behind the bar, reading a book.

When he looks up, I freeze.

I knew I missed him, but I had no idea just how much until this moment. His is the face I've had in my head as I fall asleep every night for three months. Seeing him now is like seeing a ghost brought to life.

He doesn't smile. He just stares, his jaw shifting as if he's trying to keep himself from saying words I won't want to hear.

I need to get mine out first.

I cross the room to him. God, everything about this sucks. The couple having lunch at the end of the bar is watching; employees' heads are turning. I can't believe I thought this was a good idea, coming here to let him reject me out in the open.

"I'm sorry." My voice cracks. "I know I should have said it a long time ago, but I needed to get my life together."

He's silent, regarding me with that face of his, the one that gives nothing away. I saw through it once, could read him like no one else, but it's closed to me now.

I swallow, trying to hold my shit together through the next bit—to say words that will clearly prove futile but that need to be said anyway. "And Caleb was never the person I was in love with. It just took you leaving for me to see it."

"Okay," he says, setting his book down on the counter.

I wait for there to be more, but no words come. He's looking at me blankly, as if the conversation is over.

Of all the responses I expected to get, *okay* was not one of them. The pain is so sharp and sudden I can't breathe.

I pivot on my heel and walk back out the doors, tears already streaming down my face. I'm not going to Kent's. I'm not going to use. But it really fucking hurts, and it's going to take a long time to recover.

Somehow, I get to my car. I'm opening the door when I hear my name shouted, and then Beck is marching toward me, the same way I marched toward him a few minutes ago, with nothing conciliatory on his face whatsoever.

I sling my purse in the car and turn back toward him, bracing myself for pain. For him to put the final nail in the casket.

"Jesus, Kate," he says. "Why'd it take you so long?"

His palms slide past my jaw and into my hair, and then his mouth is on mine—hard and insistent, as if this is something it pained him to wait for.

When he finally releases me, I take a weak swing at his shoulder. "Why the fuck did you let me walk out?"

His laughter is sheepish. His hand cradles my face, his long fingers brushing my temples, my chin at the base of his palm. "I have no fucking clue. I've been watching that door every day for three months, hoping you were going to be the next person to walk in. And then you did and it just...took me a minute. I was waiting for you to say it was me you wanted, and you didn't."

"I thought it was obvious."

"Yeah, Mueller thought it was obvious too. If he hadn't been eavesdropping, I'd still probably be standing behind the bar waiting. But Kate—"

No good sentence ever began with the words "*But Kate.*" My stomach ties itself in knots.

"I need all of you this time. I don't want you here because Caleb isn't an option. I want you to be here because I'm the option you want."

I press my face to his chest, reveling in the warmth of him, in his smell and his size and all the other things I've missed. "You are. You always were. I want everything now. And I only want it with you."

His smile is like the sun breaking through clouds. "Then let's go home," he says, "and get started."

47

KATE

I normally drive to Elliott Springs on Friday nights and stay for the weekend, but my flight from Tokyo got in late, so I told Beck I'd come out in the morning.

It is, therefore, a little surprising to wake with a man's limbs wrapped around me, though not especially worrisome. Very few men have arms that size. It's either Beck or Jason Momoa, and Momoa doesn't seem like the breaking-and-entering type.

I snuggle closer. Certain parts of his anatomy make it clear that he's most likely awake. "I don't know who you are or why you've broken into my apartment," I announce, "but it would be a shame to let an erection of that size go to waste."

His sleepy laugh gusts over my hair. "I missed you. We aren't usually apart this long."

Normally, he comes to San Francisco mid-week and I go to Elliott Springs on the bar's busier nights, but my travel schedule threw us off. I wrap my hands around his forearms. "I missed you too. What time do you need to get back to the bar?"

"I don't. I figured they'd survive without me. Especially since it's about to be someone else's problem."

The sale of the bar goes through in two weeks. He could

have just hired people to manage it but decided it was best to make a clean break.

He moves here to start construction on his outdoor gym at the end of the month. I've found investors, and the financials look really good at this point. Whether it works out or not, I'm just glad he's getting to take his shot, to make his own choices.

And I'm glad he wants to make them with me.

"An entire weekend where neither of us is working?" I yawn and press my ass toward him. "I can't imagine how we'll spend the time. Actually, yes, I can."

"I've got a better idea," he says against my ear, his voice low and rough.

"Anal?"

He laughs. "No. But *like* anal, it's something people are scared to try, but like once they give it a chance."

I roll toward him, biting down on a smile. "Bondage?"

"Jesus." He huffs a silent laugh. "I thought *I* had the one-track mind."

I groan. "Okay, what's this completely-not-related-to-sex thing you think we should try? It already sounds boring, by the way."

"Marriage."

The room is suddenly silent. I swear to God, even the traffic outside must have come to a halt and the birds have stopped singing. Because we've talked about the topics *I've* suggested plenty, but this one is entirely new.

It's not that I don't want it, but it was only months ago that I was the girl at Kent's house wondering whether she could still do a line of coke, months since I was having lunch with Lucie's ex-husband simply out of bitterness.

I sort of thought he'd want more proof that I was okay before he brought this up.

"Marriage. You mean . . . between the two of *us*?"

"No, Kate. Between you and the guy in 21B with the oxygen

tank. Because you're so nurturing, and he looks like he's got money."

I elbow him. "But, I mean, *today*?"

He frowns. "I didn't peg you for the type who'd want a bunch of showers and eighteen bridesmaids. We could be in Vegas by this afternoon."

I stare at his chest. "I just...are you sure?"

His hand moves to my chin, tipping it up so I have to meet his gaze. "Are you asking if *I'm* sure or are you asking if *you're* sure?"

I run my index finger down his nose. God, I love his perfect nose. His dark eyes. That lopsided grin. I want to marry him so much it hurts. "You. I guess I just thought you'd want to wait a while."

He presses his lips to the top of my head. "I've wanted to marry you since I first saw you years ago. Why the fuck would I want to wait?"

I hesitate. I don't want to accidentally remind him of the reasons he should be cautious, but I also need to know that he's really thought it through.

"To make sure I'm okay. To make sure I'm really...the girl you fell in love with the first time."

His smile is wistful. "You're never going to be that girl again. You're never going to be the person who thought nothing could beat her and nothing could go wrong, but that's okay. It's better that you're not. We were kids then, and we aren't now. When you realize you can actually lose the things you love, you treasure them a little more."

Which reminds me, of course, of the only thing I've ever loved aside from him.

I can't meet his gaze. "We've never talked about children."

He pulls me closer, pressing my head to his bare chest. "I know you're scared, after what happened. I hope you'll consider trying again, but if you can't, that's okay too."

"Of course I want children. I just didn't know if you'd want them...with me." I raise my chin, scared that I'll see some part of him that isn't sure.

"I don't want them with anyone but you," he says against my mouth. "When you're ready, I am too."

I swallow hard at that telltale pinch behind my eyes. Jesus, I've turned into such a fucking crybaby of late, but a child...It's what I've quietly longed for, no matter how perfect things are with Beck.

I hadn't even allowed myself to hope we'd get here so soon.

I spread my hands over his chest. "If we're going to Vegas, can you dress like Elvis?"

"I'd rather not."

"Can we be married by Elvis?"

He runs a hand over my back. "Real Elvis or an impersonator?"

"Real Elvis."

He laughs. "Only *you* would ask me to bring someone back from the dead to perform our wedding."

"Fine," I reply. "You don't have to bring anyone back from the dead. I guess I'd better pack."

He climbs from the bed and places my suitcase before me. "I already packed for us both while you were asleep."

"I don't trust you," I say, unzipping it. "You probably packed six kinds of lingerie and no pants."

Inside, there is indeed a staggering amount of lingerie for a two- or three-day trip, along with a white sundress he must have bought for me, and a small velvet bag off to the side. "What's this?"

He shrugs. "Something of yours I thought you should have back."

I open the pouch and my locket slides out. Goose bumps climb my arms as I press it to my chest and close my stinging eyes. I'd mostly given up the idea of getting it back. "How . . .?"

"I paid Kent a visit," he says. "He let me take it."

I raise a brow. That sounds unusually *cooperative* of Kent. "Just like that?"

"Well, I wound up knocking him unconscious, so it's hard to say for sure, but yeah, I felt like he and I would be on the same page once he came to."

The locket rests in the center of my palm. My hand curves tight around it as I hold back tears.

Beck comes to my side of the bed and wraps his arms around me. "I know it's something Caleb gave you, but if this is going to work, I have to accept that he was a part of your life and in some ways, he always will be."

I turn. "You thought the locket was about *Caleb*? Did you *look* in it?"

His brow furrows. "No. It seemed too personal. If it's not about Caleb . . ."

I click it open and allow my index finger to slide, briefly, on that single lock of her hair. "It was about Hannah, not Caleb. *Everything* was about Hannah." I click the locket shut and set it on my dresser. "But I also don't need it the way I used to."

If she hadn't died, I wouldn't be here right now. I am never going to say that it was for the best, or that it was meant to be. But I *can* say that sometimes from darkness a beautiful thing emerges, something you'll call your own. And the man in front of me, and the future we share, is mine.

EPILOGUE

BECK
1 Year Later

It's just after sunset when Grace Bennett Beck enters the world.

She has a head full of dark hair, which she got from me.

She screams when unhappy...she got *that* from her mom.

When I hold her for the first time, I'm stunned by how small she is. Somehow, I never expected her to feel so terrifyingly small and fragile. I place her in Kate's arms as if she's made of blown glass.

Tears run down Kate's face. "She's so perfect."

We marvel at her tiny fingers, watching each tiny breath. I'm wondering how this much good fortune could have been bestowed upon people who never had an ounce of good fortune between them.

"You ready to try feeding her, Mom?" asks the nurse.

Kate tenses, shooting me a panicked glance.

"It's going to be fine," I tell her.

She lowers the side of her hospital gown as if she's got to force herself to do it. After a few uncertain seconds, Grace latches on. We watch, and wait, but this time the world doesn't fall apart. Our daughter nurses for no more than a minute, then falls into a sated sleep, safe in her mother's arms.

Kate's blinking back tears as she glances at me again. "Thank you," she whispers. "For her. I have a family for the first time in my life."

"I think you already had a family," I tell her. And as all the people from the waiting room begin to file in, group by group, she sees it too. Lynn and Jamie, Adam and his husband, Kate's aunt Natalie. Rachel and Gus, along with Liam, Harrison and Caleb. They're here for me and they're here for Grace, but they're here most of all for Kate. They're the family who chose her, who saw some good in her when she couldn't see it herself.

When the last of our visitors has been ushered out, joy and exhaustion are etched in Kate's face—sixteen hours of labor will do that to you.

"Go to sleep," I say, scooping up Grace. "We'll be here waiting when you wake."

Kate smiles at us as she drifts off, and I look down at the little girl in my arms.

I already see hints of her mother in her tiny face, in the rosebud mouth and the slant of her cheekbones.

I'm already thinking about teaching her to surf and ski, about taking that camping trip Kate claims she doesn't care about anymore.

I already love her so much that it would destroy me to lose her.

It hits me like a freight train, suddenly, this thing Kate already knew: Life is fragile and there are no guarantees. Everyone you allow yourself to love is someone you might one day lose.

And that I get to take this risk with Kate and Grace makes me the luckiest man alive.

ACKNOWLEDGMENTS

Thanks so much to Katie Meyer who loved this book from the start, and my beta readers—Samantha Brentmoor, Maren Channer and Jodi Martin—plus Laura Pavlov for coming up with the title!

Thanks so much to my editing dream team: Sali Benbow-Powers and Lauren McKellar (if I ever fly to Australia, it's solely to meet you) and Christine Estevez—proofreader, PA and friend.

Thanks as always to the amazing team at Valentine PR (Nina, Meagan, Kim, Sarah and Christine...I love you all), Lori Jackson for another glorious cover, Kimberly Brower and Piatkus for making sure it gets read outside the US.